Iggy & Jake
Jake England Thriller Book One

Thomas M. Jardine

ISBN: 978-1-62420-801-0

Credits
Cover Artist: Design by Ms G
Editor: Amanda Armstrong

Dedication
To my sons, Colin and Craig.

PART I

Chapter One

Early 1968-February 1970

JACOB ENGLAND was in a hurry to get to his hometown of Chatham, New Brunswick. It was six pm on a Friday night in May 1968. He had left Moncton a half hour earlier after spending the week at his current employment with The Bank of Nova Scotia as a Loans Officer. At the rate he was driving he'd be home by 6:45 at the latest...time to drop in to say "Hi" to his folks, grab a quick bite and shower, then head over to the Wing and meet up with the Wee Three, a popular folk trio in the area. Pat Jenkins, one of the members had asked him last night if he might be interested in playing bass guitar in their group, to which Jake had agreed. Pat was a good friend and besides, Jake was looking forward to having some fun after the past week working behind a desk.

The Wee Three consisted of two former High School classmates, Pat Jenkins and Jane Reynolds, plus a third performer whose name was Ignatius (Iggy) Myles. Jake had been introduced to Iggy in February 1968 by Pat, when he was on another one of his frequent weekend visits home. It was then that Jake had first heard the trio and he was impressed with their harmonies. As well, they had a certain rapport with their audience that Jake envied. But it was Iggy's attitude that he really liked. The guy was cool, and he could capture a crowd with his humor and his musical ability.

Jake's experience with performing to that point had been limited to playing in a rock band; five guys who put out a good sound, but all they did was play music. There was really not much connection happening with the crowds they entertained, at least not like The Wee Three. So, he was anxious to see how they would sound tonight and frankly, he was looking forward to being part of a group that actually *entertained* an audience. He was there on the proviso that he could leave the trio at any time if he didn't see it

2

working out.

They were playing at The RCAFA Wing or simply "The Wing" as it was known to the locals in Chatham. The Wing was a source of entertainment for the serious drinking, youngish well-to-do on "The River." At least that was how it had evolved from being a watering hole for DND employees at CFB Chatham along with the officers of the Air Force Reserve Cadets after the war. Since then, it had gone downhill due to a lack of funding and now there were only the sons of the officers and various merchants in town who preferred to sit at this bar and expound on their philosophies rather than at more refined centers such as the Miramichi Golf and Country Club or the Officer's Mess on the Base.

The town of Chatham itself was a relatively small community situated in the northeast section of New Brunswick on the south side of the Miramichi River. It had a population of around 3000 plus the air base personnel. The community would eventually merge in later years with the neighboring town of Newcastle to form Miramichi City. In 1968, however, the area was small, and most people were simple, hardworking, non-sophisticated folk. Not unlike most small towns in Eastern Canada, Chatham exhibited a domination of *waspish* type people who bored Jake. He thought he was going to be able to leave the small town with its narrow-minded people behind when he was transferred with the bank to Moncton, but he found the same attitudes prevailed in the larger center.

Jacob England had graduated from Chatham High School in the spring of 1964. He was "recruited" that fall by the Bank of Nova Scotia by the accountant at the local branch of the bank who was a son of his father's friend. This led to Jake's getting hired into his first real job. While the bank provided Jake with a secure, steady income, he found it to be a boring career. At the time, he was pursuing his main passion in life since his early teens, which was playing bass guitar in a popular local rock group called The Esquires. The fact was, he was making as much, if not more, in the band as he was with the bank. Consequently, he had yet to really take the bank work that serious, giving more of his time and energy to The Esquires. Then, soon after he started working at the bank, Jake was transferred to Moncton, some ninety miles away, and it was necessary for him to exit The Esquires for practical reasons and much to the delight of his parents.

The Wee Three performed folk tunes; stuff by Joni Mitchell, Joan Baez, The Kingston Trio, Burl Ives. They were good at what they did but Jake sensed the guys in the trio, particularly Iggy, who he didn't even know much about, would rather be doing something a bit raunchier. Maybe more along the lines of Donovan or Dylan. Or Arlo Guthry, or even Neil Young. There were some new artists who were playing tunes that were excitingly different. Popular songs were more and more reflecting the attitudes of the youth of the day with lyrics that were sexually suggestive and frequently protested either the war in Vietnam or simply the *Establishment*. The new wave was finally becoming popular in Canada, and it was leaning more towards Rock, the "Devil's Music." Not the 50s style Rock n' Roll by artists like Chuck Berry and Little Richard, but Rock that was angry, loud, and kicked ass. And Jake couldn't get enough of it.

Chapter Two

THE GROUP finished their last set and moved to a table for a couple of "freebies." Free drinks and thirty bucks for a long night. *Wow! They were really getting ripped off here!* thought Jake. Oh well, there wasn't much else going on in town and Jake was currently without a girlfriend. So, he had agreed to the gig and, if not challenging, it was fun.

Jake had graduated with Pat, along with Jane, who was a real beauty. Iggy met Patty and Jane while they were at teacher's college in Fredericton. He was a pretty cool guy with attitude, who had a nice way with his D28 Martin acoustic, the audience, and the ladies. Patty, at the time, while being a pretty solid drummer, handled harmony vocals for the group and restricted his rhythm talents to a tambourine or maracas, befitting the small folk combo. And Jane was... well, she was hot! Sure, she had fairly good vocals, but then, she didn't really need to do anything on stage other than smile.

The Wee Three liked the addition of an electric bass guitar to their sound and Iggy was able to add a few new tunes to the group's repertoire to include cover work on artists such as Gordon Lightfoot, Simon & Garfunkel, and Tom Jones. They wanted Jake to play with them when gigs came up, but that was actually not that often.

At least now Jake had something to look forward to when he visited the Miramichi once a month or so. He *did* like the sound they were creating and from the rounds of applause he heard that first gig, it was apparent the group was appreciated by the locals. But most important to Jake, he was learning something new. Iggy was able to connect with his audience in a way Jake hadn't experienced before with The Esquires.

Whenever he could, Iggy would change the lyrics of popular tunes to reflect the times or the environment of the day. Tom Jones' *It's good to touch, the green, green grass of home* became *It's good to smoke the green, green grass of home!* He'd continue with '*Down the lane I'd walk with my sweet Mary, one leg shaved, the other one hairy.'* You get the picture. It was hokey, but the crowd loved him! And rather than suck up to the audience like most front men in music groups, Iggy would berate the crowd or make fun of the institution they represented, whether it was a school, a business, or a particular part of the country. Still, they ate it up and kept coming back for more. And Jake grew to enjoy sharing the stage.

Unfortunately, a year later, Jake was again transferred by his employer, this time to Canada's oldest and New Brunswick's largest city, Saint John. His visits home were now not as often and his ties to Iggy and Pat became tenuous.

While getting settled in Saint John, and in order to break up the boredom of working with the bank, Jake played with a rock group in the area called The Frank Donnelly Band. They weren't totally bad, but the singer Frank Donnelly was a far too serious dude, and they were not having much fun. In fact, most of their time was spent in practice sessions at their singer's house in West Saint John. They were gaining their chops, but nobody was getting rich or famous.

Then one day at work in early 1970, Jake met Bruce White, who came into the bank to open a commercial account for The Trade Winds Bar & Grill, a new restaurant that had just opened in East Saint John.

Jake discovered he and Bruce had a lot in common and a solid friendship was instantly formed. Bruce was the business manager for the club and several months later, when he found himself in need of a band for the establishment, he instantly thought of his banker friend. By that time, Jake was looking for a new group but was sticking it out with Frank Donnelly. So, when he got the call from Bruce, he was ecstatic and immediately got in touch with Iggy in Chatham. The next weekend, Iggy and Patty drove to Saint John for a meeting with Jake.

As it turned out, both Iggy and Pat were not at all satisfied with what their four years in university had given them: teaching positions at Chatham Elementary, grades six and seven. They both hated the bureaucracy of the school system and the fact that they had to follow a specific curriculum. They were not allowed to espouse nor utilize their own ideas. And it was driving them both over the edge. Jake was not surprised to hear from Iggy that they had both left their teaching positions in the summer of 1969. In addition, The Wee Three folk group had disbanded. Jane had married a pilot and their enthusiasm had left them.

It was a big step they had taken, but they were both risk takers and they were confident that life held something better in store for them.

Similarly, Jake was having problems with the bureaucracy of the Canadian Banking industry and what he saw as a hypocritical way of earning a living. He often recalled his first real position as an assistant loans officer after his training period when he first started with the bank in Chatham.

The branch manager had taken him along one day on a 'field call,' which turned out to be a collection visit to a young widow in the country. She had recently lost her job as a waitress at a local restaurant and was behind on her loan payments.

It was during the Christmas season, and when they arrived at her place around supper time, they saw a young girl of four or five sitting under a scraggy fir tree, eating a plate of fried eggs with toast. There was nothing else under the tree. Without asking, the manager sat down on a beat-up sofa which immediately sank to the floor with his weight. His legs shot out from under him and took the top off a cheap coffee table sitting in front of him. The poor woman apologized to the manager, for Christ's sake!

The manager then had the ultimate audacity to take fifty dollars from her as payment toward the arrears on her loan, along with a stern lecture on how the bank may be forced to repossess her furniture if she did not bring her account current by the following month. Jake was mortified and left the bereft widow feeling totally embarrassed. Merry Christmas!

Ever since the incident with his 'field call,' Jake's view was that things had not improved at all in the way banks in Canada were treating the general public. It seemed to him that in order to obtain a loan, a person or small business had to prove they didn't really need it.

Service charges being collected from regular customers were really outrageous. Yet, if you were able to carry large balances in your account, there were no fees. The banks were catering to the rich and disregarding the needy. They no longer relied on revenues from regular loan consumers. They were now able to meet the earnings per share ratios demanded by their board of directors through the sale of mutual funds, derivatives, self-directed plans and other bank products typically utilized by the rich. Also, Visa cards and bank access cards were allowing the banks to make large cutbacks to their personnel through the onset of automated banking. Jake did not feel comfortable working in this environment.

So, the three young musicians were looking for something more exciting and even rebellious in their lives. They decided to form a band, using the talents they had developed from earlier years. They needed a name to represent the union of the three separate soul mates. "Why not Fusion?" suggested Jake one day, and so it was agreed. The role of band leader was never really established formally, but it simply had fallen naturally on Iggy's shoulders since he was the lead singer of the group, certainly the most dynamic, and they were good to go. For their brand, they decided to focus on a mix of easy listening and light rock, and stay with commercial radio play such as The Beatles, The Hollies, Neil Diamond, the Beach Boys, and others.

Notwithstanding their mainstay as a cover band, Iggy had some good ideas of his own and in due time he wanted to write some original tunes. Jake simply wanted to play music and he didn't get hung up on what style it had to be, as long as he had a crowd in front of him. Although Pat did not have the passion for music that possessed Jake and Iggy, he had a great sense of rhythm and provided excellent vocal harmonies while maintaining the beat.

In their own way, they were taking part in a movement which was grabbing the youth of the country at the time. To the south, the U.S. was engaged in a very unpopular war in Vietnam, racism was alive and well, and The Establishment was taboo. Attitudes of Canada's youth reflected much of the tension, frustration, and anger held by their southern brothers. And grass had hit the streets of The Maritimes.

Chapter Three

February 14th, 1970

JAKE HAD enough room at his apartment to put Iggy and Pat up temporarily. In mid-February 1970, Iggy and Pat landed at Jake's and they began practicing in preparation for their first real gig at The Trade Winds the following month. For the next five weeks, Iggy, Jake, and Pat lived on beer and pizza. Jake's living room was converted to a sound studio. It was set up with his amp and Iggy brought along a small Trainor practice amp that he could use which allowed him to be heard over Jake's bass. Pat called a buddy of his from the Miramichi the first weekend there and talked him into bringing his drum kit down.

Ever thoughtful and a real charmer, Iggy asked to be introduced by Jake to his landlady. He explained to her that they were working on a new album for a certain record label and if she could be so kind as to put up with their racket for a few weeks, he would ensure she received credit on the album cover.

Folks in the neighborhood flocked to hear them practice and they met many interesting people during these sessions. It was also during this time that Iggy took a liking to the group Led Zeppelin. Iggy had a natural raw, high-pitched voice that sounded very close to that of Robert Plant and, although he had nowhere near the talent of guitarist Jimmy Page, he could get by. In any case, it was a definite shift for Iggy's musical preference which Jake could really get into. Over the remaining practice sessions, they were finally able to nail down several hits by Zeppelin, and Deep Purple. For only three guys, they were able to put out some heavy rock. Deep down, they knew they were definitely not head bangers, but they thought, correctly so, that they could gain a bigger following by now adding some bite to their show.

When Thursday, March 19th finally arrived, they rented a van and brought all their gear that afternoon to the Trade Winds Bar & Grill for a sound check prior to their gig. Both owners of the bar were there enjoying a couple of drinks and Jake recognized them from having seen them previously in the bank. After hearing the boys play only one tune, the owners called Bruce to their table, spoke quickly to him, and then left. Jake was feeling a bit insecure until Bruce came over smiling and asked them what they wanted to drink.

"Drinks are on the owner's boys. You made a hit," he said. Jake, Iggy, and Pat clinked their beers together in a toast to Fusion.

Chapter Four

March 1970-December 1970

ANOTHER THURSDAY night and the locals were starting to arrive at the Trade Winds Bar & Grill on Rothesay Avenue in Saint John, New Brunswick. As pubs go, it wasn't a bad watering hole. It had a typical ground floor layout with an L-shaped-shaped bar near the back right side of the room, an office adjacent at the top of the L, a small stage to the left of the entranceway, and room enough to seat one hundred and fifty of the Loyalist City's young party goers. There were a couple of washrooms at the left rear of the building where one could usually find someone to sell them a joint or maybe share a toke or two before the first set.

For the next three nights, Fusion played. They were being paid Union scale. Not great but, hey, it kept them in beer and pot. Jake had struck the deal with Bruce and found that it was necessary for them to join the Musician's Union Local 815. Saint John, a seaport, was big on unions and while Jake had mixed feelings regarding their purpose and ultimate benefits to the economy, he felt now was not the time to ponder such weighty thoughts.

The other two band members seemed to be okay with the arrangement, so they agreed to share the cost of Jake's three-bedroom apartment on the East Side. He had kept the lease after he and his girlfriend decided to break up a year ago.

In a few minutes Fusion would very soon be playing their first real gig and as he watched the crowd coming in, Jake wondered where the owners had come up with the name Trade Winds for the pub. Certainly, the drab interior of the place had no motif leaning towards a nautical theme. Strangely though, there was an artificial 'moat' surrounding the building over which it was necessary to cross by way of a wooden span that had fancy ropes on either side attached to chrome pipes affixed to the walkway. From what Jake had seen so far, that could prove to be an interesting challenge to some of the patrons as they pounded down their early drinks tonight.

He had finished setting up his gear, a Fender Jazz bass guitar and a Fender Bassman 'piggyback' amp with twin twelve-inch Jansen chrome speakers. While he sat nursing a beer, he saw Iggy tuning his Martin acoustic while Pat adjusted his Ludwig drum kit. They had already set up three mics earlier that afternoon. So, all told, they had pro gear, and they were satisfied with the sound system the pub had installed. Jake was looking forward to getting it on. They were ready and there was even a small 'light show' to complete the stage.

Just then, Billy Thompson, the club bouncer, came over to sit with him. Billy was a close friend of Bruce's who enjoyed working with his buddy. Jake studied Billy and thought *Here is a dude I would not want to tangle with.*

Billy played for the local Senior A hockey team, the Saint John Mooseheads. Actually 'played' was not the correct word. More like 'fought' was the better descriptor. Billy was a policeman for the Mooseheads. He was not a great skater, but he loved to fight. He had good hands for the task. They were the size of hams and as quick as the flash strobes he operated for Fusion now and then.

Yet Billy had a very deceiving manner. Six one and very handsome, he reminded Jake of a rugged Glen Campbell. Perfect blond hair covered his ears and fell down over the collar of the pale blue blazer he was wearing tonight. He was soft spoken, very polite, and a real gentleman. Until, that is, you crossed him or said the wrong thing, whatever.

"Hey Billy Boy," said Jake. "How's it goin'?"

"Not bad, Jacob. Looks like a good crowd tonight." Then his attention was drawn to a group of young rowdies making their way across the moat to the front door. "Excuse me, here comes a party of six that I gotta get seated. Have a good show, Jacob."

Jake got on the stage with Pat and Iggy. Iggy did their introduction, and they were ready to go. "How's everyone doing tonight?" he shouted. The audience was deathly quiet, and Jake was wondering what the hell they could do to loosen them up. Iggy then pulled his mic closer and said "All right, assholes, we know you're out there. LET'S HEAR YOU!!!" Then, working off their charts, they dove into a cover of "Born to Be Wild" by Steppenwolf.

The crowd erupted with applause, laughter and whistles, then settled down to hear them. Just as they got into the second verse, Jake noticed Billy was seating his party of three guys and three girls in a table directly in front of the small stage. The group was already shit-faced, and one of the guys, a particularly belligerent individual in a brown and white checked polyester suit, made a wisecrack, a little too loud, about Billy's hair style to his buddy. Billy returned to the table and smiling at the jerk, said," Excuse me?"

The guy, not wanting to lose face in front of everyone, simply waved him off. But as Billy was leaving, the idiot gave him the old 'wolf's whistle,' as if he were hustling a young chick going through some construction site. So, Billy turned around again with that huge smile and came back to the table.

Without saying another word, he reached over the table, quickly grabbed hold of the loud mouth's suit jacket by the lapels, and literally dragged him across the table, all the way back to the front entrance where Bruce, ever mindful of destruction to the building, was waiting with the door open, like this was a regular, boring occurrence. This allowed Billy to throw the guy cleanly out of the club where he landed hard on the moat 'bridge' and rolled off into the stagnant water.

Billy had returned to the table and asked the remaining party if perhaps they would like to replace the drinks that were spilled during their friend's 'unfortunate incident.' The crowd, which had fallen silent up to this point, broke out with a huge round of applause for Billy, just as Fusion ended the first song of the first set at their first gig at The Trade Winds Bar & Grill in Saint John.

"Whoa Iggy," said Jake. "This is gonna be cool!"

Chapter Five

January 1971-July 1971

SINCE GETTING the Trade Winds gig, the band decided to obtain the services of a booking agent in Moncton. Surprisingly, just one week ago the small agency was successful in getting spots for them starting Thursday to Saturday in Moncton at the Highfield Strand, then the week after that in Fredericton at The River Room, once again Thursday to Saturday. And Bruce at the Trade Winds was anxious to take them on every third weekend, so things were starting to look up.

And so, their rotating weekend tour commenced. Thursday through Saturday in Saint John, on to similar stays in Moncton, followed by Fredericton, and back to Saint John. And on it continued. It was cool. It was a steady thing that allowed Fusion to get their name out there and, although they were a cover band, they were certainly developing their own recognizable sound along with a group of regular followers.

But the circuit required a lot of driving, and after paying union dues, agent fees, travel expenses, motel and food costs, etc, the only one making any money was their agent.

Consequently, what initially was a pretty good thing for Fusion gradually turned into a drag. They were getting tired of the same old group of heads turning out to their shows. Nothing was happening with the early drafts of their original tunes, and Jake had mentioned to Iggy on occasion that maybe they should head west to Calgary.

Jake had read that the western city was hopping with opportunities. Many Maritimers were going there and doing well. They had an old buddy who had already made the move, Doug the 'Bug' Canning, who could even put them up for a while. They didn't say anything to Pat about this though, as he had recently taken up with an old flame and he was showing more interest in her than with the band. In mid-December, Pat left the apartment and moved in with his old flame.

As it turned out, they were playing at a New Year's party on December 31st, 1970 when Pat informed Iggy and Jake that he was going to be leaving the group the following June to go on a tour overseas with another buddy. He said they were looking forward to adapting a quasi-hippy lifestyle and planned to first travel to Katmandu, then go to Israel and work on a kibbutz. In only six months Fusion was going to be without a drummer, and that was their catalyst. Monday, July 5th, would be their departure date. Jake gave due notice to his landlord and informed Bruce at the Trade Winds as well as the appropriate people at the Strand in Moncton and The River Room in Fredericton.

Goodbye Saint John. Hello Calgary.

For the next six months, Jake and Iggy struggled to maintain some form of civility while playing with Pat until the assigned date for the break-up came about. Yet their desire to start something new and get out of the rat race they were in was first and foremost on their minds. It was also reflected in their lack-luster sound. Even Bruce and Billy, while knowing they were about to lose some real talent, were glad to see them on their way. Up until things started going south for Fusion, the Trade Winds was a popular bar. So, both Jake and Iggy knew that Bruce wouldn't have any problems finding a group to replace them, particularly with such a good lead time.

As the weeks went by, the notion of making a trip and maybe a temporary move to Calgary was becoming a reality. But it was going to take some cash to get there. In his previous life as a banker, Jake had been paying into a pension which at the moment was sitting in a mutual funds registered retirement savings plan, not doing anything for him.

So, he decided to take the plunge and he resigned from the bank. He cashed out his pension plan which, after tax, netted him roughly seven thousand dollars. He had spent seven years in a career that he did not enjoy, but at least it was paying something back to him now. Iggy, for his part, sold his Honda Gold Wing motorcycle and was able to come up with a similar amount. They put their cash, along with a couple of ounces of weed they had purchased for the trip, in an empty Cashman's ice cream tub which Jake then hid under the console between the front bucket seats of his vehicle.

Jake thought the trade name for their stash was cool.

On the night before their departure, Iggy and Jake were discussing the upcoming trip and expressing their thoughts about everything while they shared a joint and had a couple beers. The two had now and then smoked marijuana. Yeah, it was illegal, but the way they saw it, there was as much harm to your health, not to mention a danger to others, in using cigarettes and alcohol as there was in smoking a bit of pot now and then. In fact, some countries considered it legal, albeit you would have to travel to a place like Nepal to experience it.

All said though, they both agreed to be wary about who they hung out with. Also, they had to be careful how they handled their finances. They had a lot riding on what they were trying to achieve, and the last thing they wanted was to fall into the problems presented by drug abuse that had beset too many of their friends.

Jake was happy to hear this coming from Iggy. Fact was, Jake knew too well that he, himself, could be easily led astray by others and he had to constantly be aware of boundaries, both legal and moral, that were imposed by society. Maybe it was the ruthless way his former employer had ripped off good, hard-working people that led him into an attitude that usually ended up making him want to resist any form of authority. The so-called Hippy Movement was appealing in the sense that it seemed to allow more freedom of expression and simply made a lot of sense. With these heady thoughts spinning in their minds, they said goodnight and went to bed.

The following morning the two Fusion remnants loaded up their gear in Jake's '68 Pontiac Beaumont. The vehicle had a large trunk which was able to accommodate Jake's bass gear plus Iggy's Martin and their mics with stands. What few changes of clothing they needed were thrown into a couple of backpacks and they were good to go.

Chapter Six

Monday, July 5

JAKE'S BEAUMONT was purchased four years ago while he was working at his former bank job. It had a 396 cubic inch motor that generated 325 HP and was a real pig on gas, but at 35 cents a gallon, what the hell. It was a navy blue, two door hardtop with white rally stripes on the side and a cream vinyl top. Jake loved the deep chugging sound of the twin Thrush mufflers as they left the city and headed northeast for Fredericton. From there they would drive north up the Saint John River following the Trans-Canada Highway to Rimouski, Quebec.

They decided to travel through Montreal and Ottawa then up over the lakes. They could have saved time by going through Maine or New York State then up to Michigan, but there was no way they were going to cross into the states. Not even with the limited score they had on board. They had heard horror stories of Canadian citizens ending up in small town jails in the U.S. as the result of overzealous border inspections.

And Toronto was not to be a part of their itinerary. Too big, too many distractions to take them away from their goal. "Stick to the Plan," Iggy kept saying. The Plan was simple:

1. Take a long Canadian road trip
2. Enjoy the ride
3. Reach Calgary and get into some serious music.

It was 1971, they had transportation, roughly fourteen grand, and not a care in the world.

When they hit the outskirts of Montreal, Jake began to hear a knocking sound coming from his vehicle. Iggy knew a bit about car engines, having helped his father one summer around the garage his parents owned in Fredericton. "Sounds like one of your valves is sticking," he said to Jake.

"Better get off the highway and go into a shop."

They avoided going into the downtown area and ended up trying to explain what was happening to an old mechanic at a garage they spotted in Laval. But neither of the boys knew any French, and the old guy didn't know any English. So, they had to settle for a can of STP which they hoped would correct the situation, and on they went. The knocking had quieted down to an ominous tick. Iggy told Jake he better get the valves checked the next chance they got.

They drove as far as Ottawa and decided to call it a night. As they nursed a couple of beers at the lounge in a Holiday Inn Express outside the nation's capital, they were in good spirits. It was their plan to drive the next day as far west as Thunder Bay; by Wednesday, make it to Regina, and they could probably reach Calgary by Thursday. The weather was excellent, and they could take turns driving.

"I wonder how the Bug is making out," mused Jake. Iggy took to laughing.

"Man, what a character! Remember when we were at the place we had on Kent Street back home? The night Bug had his 'date' in the bedroom while the rest of us were partying in the living room? Christ, you could hear them a mile away! Then the Bug comes panting into the living room, bare naked, and says in his best pirate voice, "Aaargh boys, anyone got a boner I can borrow?"

"Yeah, the guy was irreverent!" said Jake. "Hope he's got his shit together out there. What's he doing, anyway?"

"Last I heard he was working at a bar called The Urban Tomato in Northeast Calgary. Dangerous combination dude. We'll give him a call Wednesday when we get to Regina."

For the rest of the evening, they had a few more beers at the bar and recalled various stories about the Bug. At one time he had supposedly "out skied a fucking avalanche in Banff." Another time he got caught making out with a guy's girlfriend. Apparently, the guy was a semi pro boxer in Fredericton. Bug said "He beat the clothes off me. Hit me with so many rights, I was beggin' for a fuckin' left." On and on the stories rolled.

The Bug was a legend. In his own mind.

Chapter Seven

Thursday, July 8, 2:15 pm

DOUG "BUG" Canning was in bad shape. His thin frame lay sprawled naked over an old rundown futon that smelled of beer and sour sweat. Somebody flushed a toilet and he slowly awoke with a terrible pain in his head and a queasy feeling in his stomach.

He had no clue where he was, how long he had been there, nor how he had gotten to the place. As he struggled to lift his 120 pounds off the bed, a young girl came out of the bathroom adjacent to him. She had greasy brown hair, tats over seventy percent of her body, which he noticed with a grimace was sadly obese, dimpled with cellulose fat, and very pale. She also had a very sharp nail driven through her left nostril and something equally lethal protruding from her right eyebrow. She was a very scary sight.

"Hey Dougie," she said. "Hope you're not gonna puke." That of course was not what he needed to hear. He rolled across the futon and started hurling halfway to the bathroom, where he ended up kneeling in front of the bowl and retched until he could bring up no more.

After throwing water on his face and rinsing his mouth out, Bug examined himself in a dirty cracked mirror above the sink. *What the hell did I manage to get myself into now*. Then ironically, he regretted his choice of words and looked apprehensively at his crotch area. Another quick look at the mirror revealed a tanned face that was once handsome but was now ravaged by too much alcohol and too many cigarettes. A mass of long blond curls fell down to his shoulders. He now looked more like Keith Richards of The Stones. The Bug was a hurting puppy.

He returned to the living room. "Jesus," he groaned, climbing into a pair of jeans. "And you would be...?"

"Betty," the girl said. "Don't tell me you've forgotten my name already? Especially, like, after last night!" she could have been twenty or forty and she was almost crying.

"Look, ah, Betty? I don't want to be mean here, but if you could tell me where I am, what day it is, and give me some idea where I left my car, I'll be on my way," he said, as he finished putting on a Tee shirt and sneakers.

Just then, a giant came in through a door which led into a kitchen. He was easily the largest human Bug had ever seen and he was extremely ugly. The guy had that typical biker look; a bald-shaven head, a scruffy goatee, prison tats galore and a stained denim vest covering a black tee that strained against his huge biceps.

"Is this little prick givin' you a hard time, Betts?" asked the biker, as he gave Bug a long scowl. "What're ya doin' here anyway, dipshit?" the biker asked.

"Dougie, this is my friend Choker," said Betty.

The Bug slowly backed his way out of the kitchen back door where he could see his brown and yellow 1963 Ambassador Rambler station wagon illegally parked by a hydrant on the street. Choker was approaching him in a threatening manner when with relief, Bug found his keys and ran to his car. "Well, big guy" he yelled back at Choker, "Everybody's gotta be somewhere, sometime." And he tore away as fast as the old Rambler would go just before the biker was able to reach him.

Bug soon realized he was driving in the northeast sector of the city up around Mayland Heights, which was close to the airport and surrounding industrial parks. He recognized his turf and with the familiar buildings, his memory of last night came back to him in bits and pieces.

He could remember leaving work. Bug was a bartender at a hipster's joint off 16th Ave NW called The Urban Tomato that catered to a lot of the preppy senior students from the University of Calgary. He was very much into the off-hours scene as were many of his bar working friends, and he now recalled going to Joey's Body Shop for a party that was pretty wild. Driving along 32nd Ave NE toward his flat, his mind took him back to his relationship with Joey, the owner of the bar/body shop.

Joey Delano owned a large warehouse that had also contained an auto body repair business in Horizon Industrial Park near Airways Properties. He had purchased it in 1966 with an inheritance when his old man passed away and the business had been struggling ever since. The Bug had run into Joey one night last year at another bar, and after a few hits of some terrific weed, Joey suggested that maybe Bug could persuade his off-hour friends and colleagues to check out his warehouse. He was thinking of setting up a bar and dance area in the warehouse section of the building.

But Joey also had other plans in mind. He knew if he could bring in the workers from The Tomato and surrounding bars, it would be easy to unload a shipment of cocaine that was recently sent his way on a 'trial consignment' basis from some associates in Vancouver.

The Bug was the perfect fall guy for Joey's scheme. Bug Canning was a wannabe player. He longed for the admiration and respect of his bar buds, but he mistakenly thought it was necessary that he was seen as some kind of cool hipster with contacts to the drug scene in Calgary. And so, he was easily introduced to cocaine. Unfortunately, he was now in Joey's back pocket.

Notwithstanding his weaknesses, Bug was generous to a fault, and in spite of his continuous bragging and bullshit, he was still a likable guy, and he had a large sphere of friends. So, over the last eight or nine months, the Bug was able to spread the word through The Tomato about a new after-hours hangout near their area. Before too long business at Joey's Body Shop warehouse was booming, and not with auto body work. Seven days a week, the doors opened at 12:00 am and the place rocked until 4:00 am.

And the Bug was developing quite a nasty little habit from frequent visits to Joey's and the back room where he and his new close "friends" consumed a steady flow of coke from Vancouver.

During the first few gatherings, Joey treated them all to some free samples. But lately, as he explained to the Bug and his buddies, his business associates in Vancouver were getting on his back about margins. Joey said they were suspicious he was skimming off the top and some not-too-subtle threats had already been made. Unfortunately, he was going to have to start charging them. That was last month, and now The Bug was having trouble making ends meet in order to feed his habit.

When he got home, the message light on his answering machine was blinking. He picked up and heard Iggy's familiar voice saying "Yo Bug, it's Iggy. It's ah, Wednesday night. Jake and I are in Moosejaw, ah,

Saskatchewan's Fourth Largest City. Can't wait to see some mountains, dude. The prairies are a real drag. Listen, we had car trouble but should roll into Calgary some time tomorrow night. See ya soon."

Not only was his financial health quite sketchy, but Bug also knew he was in trouble physically. He would never admit it to his friends, but he was definitely hooked on the shit he got from Joey, and he had to get clean before Jake and Iggy landed.

Damn. He hated what he was about to do, but he didn't have the will to resist making a call that could help him get over the edge and get into a little better state of mind before the boys landed. After he got off the phone, he quickly scratched out a note for Jake and Iggy and left it jammed in his front door in case they landed here before he got home.

Then he was off again to Joey's warehouse.

When he arrived at The Body Shop, it was mid-afternoon and there were not many people around. He checked with Sarah at the bar upon entering and was told Joey was expecting him in his office out back. The Bug walked down a short hallway until he reached the first door on his right. He rapped lightly on the door to Joey's office, and he walked into the familiar room.

Joey was sitting behind his desk acting the role of the big businessman with his feet up on the desktop. He was holding a glass of amber liquid, probably Scotch.

"Well, Doug Bug, what's up?" he asked with a sneer. He noted the Bug had his aviator glasses on, his grin was oversized, and he was grinding his teeth while he sniffed frequently. *The jerks totally hooked!* thought Joey.

"Hey, Joey, I'm kinda in rough shape and was hoping you might be able to fix me up with a few lines to hold me over until payday, later tomorrow, right? You know I'm good for it man and..." Before he could say any more, Joey threw a small soft package that hit the Bug full in the face.

"Bug, shut the fuck up. I don't want to hear any more of your shit. But listen up. I was just talking with one of my associates from Vancouver and they need a favor. Are you up for helping me out with something here?"

"Yeah, sure man. You name it." he said as he groveled on the floor and picked up the glassine pack.

"I need you to make a pickup for me tonight. It's over in

Marlborough behind the Casino. Here," and he gave Bug a sheet of paper with the address written on it. Bug folded the paper and put it in his pocket.

"Listen, all you have to do is meet a guy in the back alley at 7:00 pm and give him this package." He threw a square paper-wrapped bundle about the size of a shoe box which felt soft, and the Bug assumed it was cash. "The guy is expecting you and he has your description. He'll give you a package in return, which you will immediately return to me. Hey, Bug, you got all this?"

"No problem, Joey." The Bug started to say more but Joey cut him off abruptly. "I'd go myself but I gotta meet a dude from L.A. later tonight. So don't fuck up here. Handle it right and maybe I can throw a bit of work your way, know what I mean? Now get your ass outta here, I'm busy." And with that he got up and led the Bug out of his office.

When the Bug was out of earshot, Joey picked up the phone and punched the intercom for the bar. "Sarah, the Bug's on his way out. Tell Frank to get his ass in here."

A few seconds later a tall, Metis native with a long braid of black hair and wearing a black ten-gallon Stetson entered Joey's office.

"Okay, Frank," Joey said. "The fix is on. Dino thinks you're making the cash delivery and picking up our coke. Follow the Bug and make sure he goes to the back of the Casino on 21st NE. If I'm right about what we discussed earlier today, we should soon know where we stand with our guys from Vancouver. And be careful, don't be seen by anyone, right? You know the deal here, just stay in the shadows and report back to me."

~ * ~

As the Bug was driving toward the Casino, he checked his watch. It was only 4:30 pm so he had lots of time. He decided to first go into work and tell his boss he was going to need the night off. Shouldn't be a problem, he thought. After all, he was on good terms with John, the bar manager, plus hadn't he obtained a dime pack for him the other night?

He had managed to sneak a couple of bumps outside Joey's before getting in his car to go to the Casino and he now headed west toward The Tomato. He had no idea Frank was behind him in a new black Ford half ton pickup.

It should be a good night. He had lots of time to knock back a couple of beers and see what was happening at work, look after the delivery for Joey, then get back to his apartment and hang with the boys, assuming they'd be in town by then. Bug was aware that what he was doing was illegal. But in his hyped-up state, he was not assessing the risk of his actions very well. As well, he needed to keep on the good side of Joey, at least until he got clean.

Chapter Eight

Thursday, 4:30 pm

TRAFFIC WAS crazy, what with all the Stampede crowds filling the streets of Calgary for the first night of the Big Show. And with it, Frank was getting pissed off trying to figure out where the Bug was headed until he followed him off 16th Ave NW then onto 1st St. NW. He watched him pull up to The Urban Tomato.

Now it was getting close to 7:00 pm and Frank was still waiting for the idiot to come out. *Finally, here he comes!* He put the Ford in gear and again tailed the Bug through the heavy traffic to their destination at the Casino Calgary.

When the Bug parked his Rambler close to the entranceway of the alley off 21st NE, Frank drove by him and parked half a block further up the street. He watched in his rear-view mirror as he saw Bug get out of his car and go into the alley. Frank stayed out of sight and followed him. The back lane was cluttered with empty cigarette packs, broken beer bottles and general detritus. It was oddly quiet and hardly anything could be heard from the party crowds on 21st St NE and beyond.

Frank ducked behind a large garbage collection bin and watched as Bug waited beside a back door to the Calgary Casino marked, Service Entrance Only, No Parking. Just as Bug was checking his watch, the door opened and a lone figure appeared, carrying a large shopping bag from Sears. The guy was about thirty years of age, the size of a mountain, and white with a black goatee. He had dulled, colorless eyes which were half-lidded and looked somewhat reptilian. *Overall, a very creepy guy,* thought Frank.

"You'd be Mr. Frank, I expect, and I believe you have something for me," Frank heard him say in what seemed to be a Russian accent to the Bug. Then the Bug replied, "Right on, dude," as he pulled the paper wrapped package from under his shirt and approached the large figure. As Frank listened to this exchange, he expected Bug was too wired to catch onto the Russian unknowingly addressing him as Frank. It was a fatal mistake.

Frank then saw the Russian pass the shopping bag with his left hand to the Bug. Then Frank also saw a glint of metal coming from the man's right hand. As the Bug handed his parcel to the guy, Frank heard him mutter something like, "What the..." and suddenly the Bug was on the alley pavement, moaning loudly while the Russian deftly picked up the bag beside him and walked back into the Casino through the service door.

The whole episode only lasted about two minutes. With horror, Frank looked behind him and when he saw nobody was around, he approached Bug. There was already a huge volume of blood pooling on the ground from Bug's stomach which he was futilely clutching with both hands. He looked up at Frank and said in a whispered tone, "Oh, thank God it's you, Frank. Help me, man. Some guy just stabbed me. I think I'm in trouble. Please, Frank..." as his voice faded.

"You're not in trouble, Bug. You're dead." said Frank. Then he left the dying Bug in a mess in a back alley in Northeast Calgary while the Stampede crowd grew louder and rowdier by the hour.

~ * ~

Inside the casino, the Russian stepped into an elevator and pushed the button designated Penthouse Suites 21st Floor. He then got off the elevator and strolled down an expansive hall to the entrance of his employer's suite.

Responding to the soft knock on his door, Giovanni "Dino" Martini invited his Russian aide into his foyer. The Russian passed both the Sears bag and the brown paper-wrapped parcel to his boss. Martini opened the shoe-box-sized parcel and as he suspected, the parcel simply contained a plastic wrapped stack of paper cut to resemble the size of bills. So, his suspicions were right; Joey, the little fool, was going for a final large rip off and was probably planning on leaving town as they spoke.

"Everything go okay, Grigori?" Dino asked the Russian.

"A piece of pie," replied the aide in his broken English. "Mr. Frank is no more," he said.

Dino had met Grigori Ivanov three years ago in Palermo, Sicily where he had been visiting relatives. One afternoon, an associate of his had introduced the Russian while he was playing bocce. A "business" relationship had been established and since then, the Russian had proven his worth on a number of occasions, doing *wet work* for the Mafioso.

"We'll fly back to Vancouver tomorrow and arrange a meeting with Al and Vinnie when we're there. I think we should get any further action against Frank's employer, Joey Delano, sanctioned before making a move."

While Dino and Grigori were discussing what had just happened, Frank had hurried back *to* The Body Shop *and* reported everything he had seen to Joey. The Metis native was visibly shaken as he spoke with his boss.

"Christ, Joey, what are we gonna do?" asked Frank.

"Nuthin.' They don't know you from Adam, so stay outta sight." said Joey. "Dino's man thinks he killed *you* and he'll report that to his boss. You'll have to lay low though until we can get in touch with the folks in Los Angeles. This is heavy shit, man, and you know we're now gonna have to get out of town. Maybe the guys we know in LA will be easier to work for, since they're anxious to take over this territory from Dino."

Chapter Nine

2 Days ago, Tuesday, July 6th

WHEN JAKE and Iggy left Ottawa, it was 6:00 am Tuesday. They were on their way northwest on the TCH heading for Thunder Bay. They had been on the road for nearly eight hours now and they were halfway between "The Soo" and their destination.

"Nice country," Jake mused as they sped along at approximately seventy miles an hour. Every now and then they could spot the vast expanse of Lake Superior to their left, while on their right there was nothing but forest and the odd small town or village. There appeared to be many good-looking lakes and streams that probably held trout or perch, and they regretted not having packed some fishing gear for the trip.

Iggy, in particular, was an avid outdoorsman. Every early summer, at least since Jake had known him, Iggy spent a lot of time on the Northwest branch of the Miramichi River fly fishing. The river was renowned worldwide for the salmon that spawned there, and Iggy usually caught his annual quota. He loved the outdoors. Lately, though, there were many poachers and bad characters where he fished, and it was becoming dangerous to go out on your own. But here, Iggy thought, at least it looked wide open for some nice lake trout or browns.

Earlier they had stopped in Wawa, Ontario, Canada's prime haven for hitchhikers, and they had picked up a sorry looking kid who was heading to Vancouver. The guy was in bad shape, so they decided to buy him lunch at a small shop beside a gigantic statue of a Canada Goose. When they were driving for a couple of hours after lunch, the hippy, named Murray, from Trois Riviere, Quebec began farting in the back seat. "Christ, this is not bearable," Jake signaled with his eyes to Iggy. So, Iggy made up a story about having to visit a relative not far from Marathon Lake, the next town on their route. And so it was that Murray had to depart at a truck stop as they reached the small town five minutes later.

"Uncle Ralph? Good one there, Igster," said Jake. "Roll down your window for a while, would ya. Murray the Hippy has left an impression on us for sure."

Before reaching Thunder Bay, Jake put in an eight-track tape of Led Zeppelin's unplugged version of "Going to California" and he turned his custom speakers to full volume. LZ was one of their favorite groups and this particular tune was giving Jake an idea. The song was a definite departure from that band's usual heavy rock genre, but the sweet sound of Jimmy Page's acoustic guitar coupled with the unbelievable voice range of Robert Plant worked perfectly together for them.

Jake had to yell over the volume, but said to Iggy, "We should do this tune, man. Good to have a few unplugged numbers in our repertoire. It may take a while to hook up with a decent drummer." He was confident Iggy could cover Plant pretty good and the acoustic sound was being used lately by other artists they were already covering such as America, Stephen Stills, Lightfoot, and Joni Mitchell. It could be suitable for some lounge work down the road. Who knew? The thing was, they were now free to take on anything that came to mind, and they were eager to get at it. The two musicians worked well together, and they shared similar goals.

Just then Iggy told Jake to slow down a bit as he noticed a police car about a hundred yards behind them. They were nearing Thunder Bay and they were looking forward to calling it a day. Then the inevitable happened and the red and blue flashers of the RCMP cruiser came on behind them. Immediately, Jake and Iggy could only think about the pot they had in the car with them as they pulled over for the cop.

The big police officer studied Jake's license carefully then, in a very serious tone said to him, "So, Jacob, a long way from home, eh? 34 Prince Street, what part of Saint John is that?"

Jake was puzzled, but he was thinking this was some kind of test, so he played along with the cop. "Ah sir, that's in the North End of the City."

"Anywhere near Milledgeville?"

"Hey, you got it! You from the area?"

"Not really. Lived in Fredericton but I have a cousin that lives there.

I left New Brunswick a few years back. Saw the NB plates on your vehicle and just thought I'd have a chat with another herring-choker! It's been a while since I've seen anyone from down East."

Jake gestured to Iggy beside him. "This is my good buddy, Iggy and, hey, he's from Fredericton!"

"Yup," said Iggy, not too enthusiastically and thereby letting the cop know he wasn't anxious to take the conversation further. The officer looked at him suspiciously, then after several beats gave Jake his license back and bid them on their way.

"Shit man, you could have been a bit more friendly," Jake said.

"Come on Jake, that was a cop. Are you fucking mental? For a bit there, I was wondering if you were going to ask him if he wanted to share a joint with us." They were in the municipality of Thunder Bay and Jake was suddenly beat.

"Okay Iggy, I get it, 'kay? Let's get a motel here and relax."

They checked into a nondescript, six-unit motel outside of town and registered at the seedy looking front reception area. They were too preoccupied with the short rendezvous with the cop to take notice of the increased knocking noise that was now coming from under the hood of the Beaumont.

Before crashing, Jake suggested they light up a doobie. Iggy was reluctant, but after some teasing from Jake, he gave in and they were soon replaying the incident with the cop, getting a great laugh recalling the experience. Both Jake and Iggy liked to live a bit on the liberal edge of society but neither wanted to be labeled as druggies. In fact, they didn't want to be typecast as anything. Live and let live, enjoy the ride. So, they finished the joint along with a box of Ritz crackers Jake had bought earlier and they hit the hay.

The next morning, Wednesday, they were on their way toward Regina, and this time Iggy drove. Again, Jake had inserted another eight track, this one a new hit by The Stampeders, Sweet City Woman. "Say Iggy, maybe we can get to open for these guys some day," yelled Jake over the blaring speakers. Iggy just winked at his buddy, and they enjoyed the tune, the drive and each other's company.

Mile after mile they crossed a land so flat you could see thunder heads building fifty miles distant. Hectares of wheat or rye covered the landscape and except for the odd grain elevator, there was seldom anything to break the monotony of the drive.

When they reached Winnipeg, it was only noontime and after a quick bite at a gas stop, they decided to continue on to Moosejaw, about seven hours away, rather than stay in Regina. Anyway, Iggy wanted to spend more time in the smaller towns and villages rather than the larger cities in order to get a better feel for the country and the different places they were passing through.

"You never know Jake," said Iggy. "One day I might write some tunes about these places or the people we meet. Besides, the more distance we keep between ourselves and big city authorities on this run, the better I like it." Again, Jake was impressed with Iggy's foresight.

Taking turns driving, stopping for a leak here and there, they gradually made their way across the great Canadian Prairie. It was a long bleak drive, but the boys marveled at the immensity of the wheat fields they passed, and the huge pieces of equipment required to plant and harvest such vast tracts of farmlands. Finally, they saw a sign on the highway that stated:

Entering Moosejaw, Saskatchewan's 4th Largest City
and
Home of Canada's Snowbirds

A hill with an elevation of approximately thirty degrees stretched ahead of them for about three miles. The only thing separating the highway and the sky on the horizon was an ominous bank of blue-black clouds that promised some kind of bad weather approaching.

Chapter Ten

Wednesday, July 7 to Friday, July 9

IT FELT like they were taking a slow ride to the top of a roller coaster, but on a less steep grade, and the vehicle had actually slowed to around thirty miles per hour. Iggy rolled his window down and was alarmed to hear the loud knocking that was now coming from the vehicle. At the same time, he noticed the red engine light appear on the car's dashboard.

"Shit." said Jake. "This can't be good. See if we can make it to the crest of this hill." They were just able to do this when they found they were now on a down slope which was taking them directly into the city of Moosejaw. Lucky for them, they were in a commercial/industrial area where automobile dealerships prevailed. Their luck held when less than a hundred yards ahead they saw such a building proclaiming the business to be *Moosejaw Pontiac Buick* where Iggy carefully coaxed the wounded Beaumont to rest in a vacant parking spot just outside the service section of the dealership.

An hour later, they were waiting in the dealer's service room, hoping for the best but expecting the worst. The diagnosis was split. It turned out that a valve had stuck, resulting in a broken piston rod. It would have to be replaced. The good news, according to the service repairman, was that it could have been worse. He told them the engine was okay and would live to see further "abuse," as he looked derisively at Jake.

Furthermore, since Jake had purchased extended warranty when he bought the Beaumont, both labor and parts were covered. The serviceman eyed Jake admonishingly as he told him this. It would however take some time to repair, plus they had to order a part from Regina which wouldn't arrive until tomorrow.

"Welcome to Moosejaw. Saskatchewan's fourth largest city,

boasting some twenty-odd thousand folks" said the service guy. Later, Jake would say the guy should have said the city boasted "some twenty thousand odd folks."

After getting this news, they cautiously retrieved the Cashman tub of goodies and their backpacks from the car, then got a cab to the Drake Hotel, which according to the service manager was a cheap but clean place to hang their hat for a bit.

"Why does every city have a Drake Hotel?" asked Jake, as they sat in the back seat of the taxi. They were at their destination in a couple of minutes.

"Better yet," replied Iggy, as he viewed a decrepit looking structure from the city's Main Street. The red neon sign flashed a sorrowful *Drak Hot l* just as it started to rain. "Why does every Drake Hotel have to look like it just came out of some Rod Sterling time warp?"

They got settled in their room which was as drab as expected, and they decided to check out the bar downstairs. It was seven o'clock on a Wednesday evening in Moosejaw and two locals were shooting a game of eight ball on one of the two pool tables next to the men's room. Jake ordered a couple of beers and burgers while Iggy racked up the balls on the available table.

When Jake came over with their food, he gave a sly wink to Iggy. After he broke, he stumbled around the table and pretended to be half in the bag, cursing loudly when he missed a given shot on the five ball straight into a corner pocket. Iggy clued in and did the same when he 'scratched' on his first shot at the ten by miscuing (on purpose) and sending the cue ball into the side pocket. They were aware the couple next to them were keenly watching and were not surprised when one of them asked them if they wanted to play partners for beers.

"Hell yeah," said Jake. "We just blew in from back East and plan to see the Calgary Stampede on the weekend if we can get our vehicle fixed in time." He made sure to slur his words just right.

The fact was, both Jake and Iggy had spent much of their youth in many of New Brunswick's pool halls. They knew the sport inside out and were quite adept at it. Over the years they had both lost and won fairly large sums of cash while honing these skills. The last time they scammed someone was when they took a couple of airmen from CFB Chatham for a ride. Today, they had two indigenous guys.

After three games, the Metis decided they had enough. They couldn't believe the 'good luck' displayed by the two drunks from New Brunswick. Nevertheless, the four of them were enjoying the evening. Indeed, they were all hammered when it was time as Jake would say, to "hit the wooden hill." Before crashing, Iggy called the Bug in Calgary and, not getting an answer, had to leave him a message.

Thursday morning came too soon and with it, they saw the rain had abated to a thin drizzle as they made their way to the dining hall. Iggy remembered he had called the Bug the previous night and decided to try him again. Once more the Bug's answering machine came on. This puzzled Iggy. He knew the Bug worked late hours at the *Urban Tomato*, but he thought he'd be up and around by now. He left another message.

They called the same cab to take them to the car dealership, only to be informed by the Service Manager that the part on order from Regina was not going to be delivered until tomorrow. They were stuck for another day and night in wonderful Moosejaw, Canada's Home of the Snowbirds. Shit.

After a long day at the bar, they once again ran into the two Metis natives while they were sucking on their fifth beer. They could hardly turn down a request for a rematch from the two guys, only this time the natives insisted on playing for fifty dollars cash per player per game. Unfortunately, there was no need for the Easterners to 'act' drunk. After losing three straight games and down three hundred bucks between them, Jake and Iggy wearily staggered up the stairs to their room and passed out on their beds.

The next day, Friday, Jake and Iggy went again to the Pontiac dealership and were met with a big smile by their friendly serviceman. They determined the vehicle was all fixed and "running like a top!" Unfortunately, after reading the fine print in the Extended Warranty contract from the glove compartment, they were told it was necessary for the owner to pay the first forty percent of the claim, in this case $1450. Jake was livid, vowing to take the matter up with his dealer back home. "Good luck, sir" said the serviceman with a big smile and bid them a safe trip to Calgary.

With the motor fixed and a "I told ya so" from Iggy, they were on their way for the six-hour drive to Calgary. Jake figured they could take their time and still get to the Bug's address by seven or so this evening. The weather had cleared as they left the city and Iggy remarked about how smart Jake was to get extended warranty on the Beaumont, even though it was still costing them a good chunk of their money.

"Smart?" Jake said. "I didn't even know I had that warranty until the service dude mentioned it. I guess they tacked that on at the dealership in Chatham when I bought the car."

"How is our cash holding out?" asked Iggy.

"We were doing pretty good until coming to this shit-ass town, Ig. As of Tuesday night, we had only spent nine hundred dollars, most of that for gas. Since then, we've gone through another two grand. So, we're left with about eleven thousand."

"I'm anxious to get to Calgary," said Iggy. "We'll have to take in the Stampede. I think the Bug said it was supposed to start this weekend. There should be some good groups playing at the bars and maybe we can line up some contacts. And no more agents. Plus, I'm not planning on joining the Union out here. Just so you know, okay?"

"Fine with me, Iggy." Jake knew these were sore points for Iggy. Problem was that most bars here were probably forced to hire only unionized groups. They'd have to wait until they arrived to learn the ground rules.

The highway sign said: Calgary 350 KM.

Chapter Eleven

Friday, July 9th

THEY FOLLOWED the TCH right into Calgary which took them west across the city until they reached the Deerfoot Trail which they took north until 32nd Ave NE. They continued north and then turned right on the corner of 32nd St NE and Mallard Drive. Iggy consulted the city map he had picked up just as they had entered town.

"The Bug's flat should be a couple of blocks ahead on the right," said Iggy, as they made their way along a busy industrial part of the City. It was 7:15 pm and they were hoping the Bug had not yet left for work. By now, he would surely have received Iggy's two messages. He was looking forward to sharing a beer or two with his long-time buddy and having a few chuckles.

When they found Bug's place and rapped on the door there was no response. Then Jake saw a piece of paper on the inside of the screen door with their names on it. Pulling it out, they read the note Bug had left for them:

Sorry I'm not here for you guys. The key is over the top door mantel, help yourselves to a beer from the fridge. I should be back soon. Stampede starts tonight! Yee haw!

Bug

They found the key and entered Bug's flat. A stale smell permeated the area, a heavy cigarette odor thought Iggy, knowing Bug to be a heavy user. They went into the kitchen and pulled a couple of pilsner beers from the fridge. Besides the beer, there wasn't much in there. A bowl of cheese and macaroni with a green mold on the top, a half-liter of sour milk, two dried up pieces of chicken from KFC, and a carton containing two eggs.

"I see the Bug's nutritional habits haven't changed," said Jake, taking a sip of his beer.

"Check out his voice mail," said Iggy. "He won't mind, it never bothered him in the past." Then they heard the two messages that Iggy had left earlier. The first one had been heard but the second one was new.

Puzzled, Iggy grabbed a flyer off the kitchen table. It was a notice about the upcoming Calgary Stampede. The poster read: *The Greatest Outdoor Show on Earth - July 8th to 17th.*

"Check this, Jake," said Iggy.

"Yeah, so?"

"Now look at this note from the Bug...he mentions 'the Stampede starts tonight'."

"I still don't get it, Ig. What's the problem?"

"Well, today's Friday, the 9th. He obviously wrote this yesterday. And my message of Wednesday night was heard but not the one of yesterday. So, he's been away a couple of days. But where?"

"Okay, let's check out The Tomato and see if he's there or maybe they know where he is," Jake ventured. They left Bug's flat and headed for The Urban Tomato with a sense of foreboding on their minds.

The Tomato was packed. Kids barely over the legal age (if at all) were slamming down shots as fast as they could be poured. A very loud rock band was playing "Brown Sugar" by the Stones and were it not for the troubled feelings Iggy harbored about the Bug, he would have liked to have taken in the rest of the evening listening to them.

Shouting over the band, Iggy asked the bartender "Hey man, is the Bug on duty tonight?"

"Bug hasn't been around for a few days. The bar manager, John, told me the Bug was in yesterday and arranged for the night off. You guys know him?"

"Yeah, we're good friends from back East. Just landed in town and in fact we just came from his apartment. No sign of him, but he left a note for us that appears to have been written yesterday."

"That's weird, man. But you know the Bug. He could be anywhere, right? A couple of months ago he called me at home one Thursday night when he was scheduled to work that Friday. When he told me he was calling from Hawaii, I couldn't believe it. He and Reggie simply decided to take off one day and they caught a flight down there. Awesome. Like the Bug said, 'Here today, gone to Maui'." The barkeep chuckled at the Bug's humor.

"Yeah, that's our boy all right," said Jake. "But can you give us some idea where he might be now? Like, does he have a girlfriend we're not aware of maybe?"

"The Bug is still solo as far as I know, man. But, hey, come to think of it, he's been spending a lot of time lately with some cokeheads at an after-hours joint over in an industrial park in Horizon. I think it's called The Body Shop. Just a sec, maybe I have the address." He went into a side office. When he came back, he handed the information on a note paper to Iggy. "Be careful man, that's a rough area." Then he took the boys aside and was serious. "Guys, my name is Jimmie. Look, I like Bug. I know he has his ways and everything, but I think he's getting into something that's way over his head. If you guys are close to him, you should sit him down for a heart-to-heart regarding his habit, okay?"

This was not good news for the boys. Iggy and Jake were not against having the odd doobie, but that's where they drew the line when it came to drugs. Yet it didn't surprise them. Okay, so they'd take a hike to this Joey dude's place and see what they could find out. It was now just about nine pm and it was the start of the second night of the 1971 Calgary Stampede, *The Biggest Outside Show on Earth!*

They drove north through heavy traffic on Centre Street to McKnight Blvd., then east to 19th St NE. It didn't take them long to find Joey's place. For two blocks ahead of them, the street was filled with a throng of young partygoers. The building they were looking for appeared on their right and it was huge. In keeping with the trendy grunge look, it was very drab in the front, and it carried an all-black metal fascia with a huge red neon sign simply saying Joey's.

Jake and Iggy wound their way through the crowd toward the front entrance. Halfway there they came across a small group of three guys who were separated from the larger horde and were converged over the hood of a new GTO Ford. Jake couldn't believe what he was witnessing. There in front of them, the guys had laid out six or more lines of cocaine on the right side of the car's pristine black hood. One of the young men was bent over the car with a rolled up twenty-dollar bill, and a uniformed Calgary police officer approached the small group from the rear, not seeing what was going on. The cop tapped the back of the young man who was about to snort a line off the vehicle. He turned around and seeing the cop he immediately brought his arm across the hood of the car spilling the coke over the front of the cop's jacket while he let the twenty fall to the ground where he covered it with his foot. In the meantime, the police officer simply wiped the residue of the drug off his jacket and asked the guys what was happening inside the building.

Jake and Iggy just looked at the cop in wonder as the guys replied that there was an off-hours party going on. And that was that. No mention was made by the cop about what was clearly a drug felony that had just happened! The cop thanked them and walked away, presumably back to his own vehicle.

Jake and Iggy just shook their heads and entered the building where they each paid a ten-dollar cover charge. The constant bass WHUMP! WHUMP! tones of the music hit them as they made their way toward the bar. They could actually feel the air waves from some gigantic speakers pushing against their breast bones and eardrums.

The inside of the building was huge, about a quarter the size of a football field. You could tell that it was once a valid, working body shop but had now been converted into a dance hall of sorts. All around the perimeter of the two side walls there were tables laid out to handle individual groups of eight people. Besides the main bar where the boys now stood, there were two other smaller "shooter" bars, one on each side of the room. A cement floor that was once no doubt heavily stained with grease and spilled cleansing agents, was now covered with sawdust. At the far end of the building, they could see and hear a band playing heavy metal rock on a small, elevated stage.

Once at the bar they asked the guy at the taps if he knew of the Bug. He did a slight take at the name which Iggy picked up on, but then said he didn't know anyone by that name. Iggy was certain the guy was lying, so he insisted on seeing the owner. The bartender got on the phone and the next thing they knew, a tall Metis Indian wearing a black Stetson cowboy hat was coming their way. He had cold black eyes, pock-marked skin and a large bulbous nose. Clearly a no-nonsense guy who was now glaring down at them.

"Follow me," the Metis signaled, and he led them to a door designated EMPLOYEES ONLY which took them past several rooms to the end of the building. On the walls along the hall there were sporadic photos of muscle cars, hot rods, and monster trucks. At the end of the hallway, they stopped and faced an expensive, solid oak door with brass hardware. The Metis native ushered them through the door ahead of him into a richly designed room that would have put Jake's former bank manager's office to shame.

The slight man behind a very large desk slowly got up and offered his hand. He was dark complexioned and had slick black hair that was combed straight back from his forehead. He wore silver-framed, bronze tinted glasses, and enough gold around his neck and wrists to open a jeweler shop.

"My name is Joey Delano," he said. "I hear you've been asking about the Bug?"

Iggy shook the proffered limp hand and said with his trademark grin "I'm Iggy, and this is my buddy, Jake. Yeah, we just came to town from back East and we were supposed to meet up with Bug, actually yesterday, but he seems to be in the wind. We were told we might find him at your fine establishment here."

"You've met my guy here, Frank Trueblood, I see," said Joey. "Frank, c'mere. Tell these yahoos what you know about the Bug." Already Jake and Iggy were beginning to get pissed off with the attitude from these guys.

"What kinda name is Iggy?" said the big Metis, casually approaching with a smile that didn't reach his eyes.

"It's a *nickname*," said Iggy, returning the icy smile and speaking deliberately slow and loud like he was talking to some deaf foreigner. "You know, like if your mother called you 'penis face' because your nose looked like one, then as you grew up everyone called you 'dickhead'? See, that would be *your* nickname."

By this time, Jake had suspected Joey was going to be getting a weapon from his desk, so he had casually walked his way behind him. As the Metis rushed Iggy and was starting to swing, Iggy knew it was coming and was ready for him. With a quick duck, he landed a solid right to his opponent's nose and hit him a hard left in his kidney. As the native fell to the floor, Joey had turned toward his desk. But before he could reach it, Jake grabbed the smaller man. He twisted his arm behind his back and threw him on the sofa in front of the native.

"I think we should talk," Jake said to Joey as he pulled a .38 revolver from the desk. "Tell us what you know about the Bug, and we won't cause any more problems here. My good friend Iggy would like nothing better than to take this office apart, but that shouldn't be necessary, right?"

"Be careful where you point that loaded gun, asshole!" shouted Joey. "You guys don't know who you're playing with here. If I were you, I'd put down the gun and go back to Shitsville, or wherever you came from. The only thing I can tell you about the Bug is that he owes me big time. Now get the fuck lost."

Jake emptied the gun of bullets which he put in his pants pocket, then looped it high in the air. The pistol fell heavily on Joey's desk with a loud *thud*, taking a gouge out of the beautiful piece of furniture in the process. Iggy and Jake did not think any more information concerning their friend's disappearance would be forthcoming, so they decided to leave the two hoods for now. When they were leaving, Frank said to Iggy, "Keep in touch, white man. I'd really like to meet up with you again. Are you afraid?" He was holding his bleeding nose very carefully and because of this his voice had a heavy nasal accent. He was smiling in spite of the obvious pain. Jake was having a hard time controlling himself, the way it all came out.

"Not hardly, Pilgrim," drawled Iggy in his best John Wayne impression from the new movie that was just out called *Big Jake*.

When they were back in the Beaumont, Jake looked at him with raised eyebrows. "What?" said Iggy in response to the look. "I've been wanting to say that since we saw the movie last month." They were not much further ahead in their search for the Bug, but Iggy sensed there was something being hidden by Joey and his sidekick.

By the time the boys got back to the Bug's apartment, it was almost ten-thirty, too late to continue their hunt for Bug or any other acquaintances of his at this time.

"Say, Jake, do you keep in touch with any of your bank buds?" Iggy asked.

"Yeah, a few of them. Why?" said Jake.

"I have an idea. Did you see the calendar on the wall behind the bar at Joey's earlier tonight? It was one of those cheap giveaways the banks hand out to clients. It was from Scotiabank on 6th Ave SW."

"So?"

"Follow me here. I'd say there's a good chance his bar is actually owned by someone higher up that Joey is connected with. Not Joey himself. Someone with the kind of cash that can be generated to buy what was once a rundown body shop and convert it to a fancy bar.

"The bar would then be operated by Joey, he'd be paid a handsome salary, and proceeds from it would be deposited to his bank to make it look like a viable business. But all the while, cash from the sale of drugs to bar clients could be laundered with the same bank, deposited with regular bar sales. A nice scam."

"Wow," said Jake. "That makes sense. So, your reference to the Scotiabank calendar suggests that..."

"That their branch on 6th Ave SW is Joey's banker. Can you find out for sure from one of your friends?" asked Iggy. "If we can confirm that and find out whose names are on the account, maybe we can go to the authorities with our suspicions regarding drug money laundering and seek their help in this, you know, linking it to the Bug's disappearance."

"Sounds like a good plan, Iggy. We're on a three-hour time variance with back East, so it's too late to call anyone there tonight. How about waiting until the am and then get after it. Dunno about you, but with the long drive all day and that episode earlier tonight, I'm ready to crash, man."

Chapter Twelve

AT NINE in the morning, noon in New Brunswick, Jake called a lady in his hometown, Saint John. Her name was Sharon Donovan and once she heard Jake's proposal, and why he needed the information, she agreed to call the Scotiabank branch on 6th Ave SW in Calgary first thing on Monday. She reminded Jake that confidentiality rules were in play, so she'd have to pretend she was confirming this info for a client who wanted to transfer some money there.

"Whatever," Jake said. "I owe you, Sharon. Say hi to the gang for me on Monday and we'll talk then, okay?"

There was nothing more that could be done, short of confronting Joey with their suspicions of his actions. But they were not ready to do that at this time.

So, they decided to take in some of the Stampede action downtown and they headed for the Stampede Corral which they were able to access off MacLeod Trail SE. Earlier, they had picked up a map of the city and quickly determined how easy it was to get around the metropolis of some eight hundred thousand people.

Calgary was very well planned out. It was divided into quarters by Centre Street which ran north/south and by the Bow River which meandered through the city in an east/west direction, at least in the downtown core. The ever-present Calgary Tower sat in the middle of the city and served as a great point from which you could easily get your bearings. Additionally, all avenues ran east/west, while streets were all set in a north/south direction. Both avenues and streets alternated from one-way directions, then every third route was two-way traffic. Very cool and so much easier to navigate compared to Montreal or even Saint John.

And to top it off, they found that in each community in the suburbs, the roads or streets were theme-based; or at least they started with the same first letter of the community. And these were usually in alpha order. *Difficult to get lost here,* thought Iggy as they drove around the city after grabbing brunch in one of the many fast-food outlets in Stampede Park.

There was a lot to see. Jake and Iggy were amazed by the size of the crowds drawn to the Stampede. They saw the great hockey star Bobby Orr officially open this year's Stampede; they went to the world-famous chuck wagon races, then they attended the Stampede Parade on 9th Ave SW, which this year featured Canada's Prime Minister, Pierre Elliott Trudeau, as the grand marshal on his horse Liberal. They even took in the very exciting bronco and bull riding events, and finally they ended their evening by going to a concert at the Corral which headlined Ian and Sylvia Tyson. All told, they had a fantastic day and night. But as they drove home, the two young musicians shared guilty looks with each other as they realized that their good buddy, Bug, was not there to enjoy it with them.

The next day was Sunday, and they went down to the southeast sector again, this time to take in more of the Stampede and simply spend the day walking around the busy area. It seemed that most of the vehicles there were half ton trucks with rifle racks on their rear cab windows. Many of them had license plates from New Brunswick and Nova Scotia.

While they ate supper in the Palliser Hotel on 9th Ave SW, a drunken cowboy actually rode a horse into the ballroom of the establishment across from them. They watched with amusement as the animal proceeded to defecate in a huge pile on an ornate rug directly in front of the revelers.

In another idiotic stunt, a drunken transit civil service employee had driven his city bus into a parkade. Somehow, he had managed to get the vehicle up to the third level before it became permanently stuck in the narrow ramp ways. Jake read where it took three city engineers to have the vehicle towed back down.

Before deciding to leave the Palliser, Jake read a notice from the local newspaper, *The Calgary Herald,* advertising a show at a bar called the Maritime Pub.

"Happy Hour All Day on Sundays, Iggy," read Jake from the paper. "Live band playing until 11:00 pm called High Tide from Halifax. Hey, I think I know a couple of these guys. Let's check it out." They simply had to drive south on MacLeod Trail to Heritage Drive and they were there in fifteen minutes.

The pub reminded Iggy of the Strand in Moncton where they played for a while last year. It turned out they were able to chat between sets with the guys Jake knew and they were happy to gain a contact which they could put to good use.

Chapter Thirteen

Monday, July 12th

ON MONDAY morning, slightly hung over, Jake and Iggy drove over to 6th Ave SW to hang around the bank in the slim hopes that they might see someone from *Joey's* making a deposit. While they drank coffee at a deli across the avenue from the bank, Iggy noticed a tall familiar looking guy getting out of a black Ford 150. He was sporting a bandage over his nose. "There's our boy, Jake. We may be in luck."

Sure enough, it was Frank, and he carried a briefcase with him into the bank. While he was gone, Jake took note of the plate number on the Ford. Then they followed Frank back to Joey's, after which they went back to the Bug's and waited for the call from Sharon Donovan back in Saint John. It wasn't until noon Calgary time that Jake's friend got back to him.

According to Sharon, the account at Scotiabank was opened in early 1969 under a numbered company, *5000710 Alberta Ltd.* Joey Delano was listed as an authorized signing officer but for making deposits only.

"Okay . . ." mused Jake. This wasn't much information, but he felt it was enough to take to the cops.

Calgary Police Headquarters was located on 47 St NE, and it was a maze of activity. All manners of society could be observed here. Young kids strung out from excessive use of drugs and/or alcohol on the weekend as they conferred with their parents or lawyers; sorry looking men near the divorce courts huddled on benches, also with lawyers or girlfriends; arrogant looking judges or prosecutors strolling the halls; and above all cops, many cops. A sea of blue.

Jake and Iggy went to an information centre and told the desk officer that they were there to speak to someone about the disappearance of their friend and the possible relationship with this to a drug money laundering scheme. Only fifteen minutes had passed when two detectives came to the bench where they were waiting and brought them to an office down a long hallway. After introductions, the larger of the two officers, Detective Don Hansen, went out and came back with two coffees. The four sat around a small circular table where two other coffees and an ashtray were sitting. Gerry Riley, the smaller detective, asked them how they could be of service. Iggy took the lead and told them their story and suppositions. Jake handed them the note paper with Frank's plate info on it.

"So, your friend has been gone now for what, three and a half days?" said Detective Riley, the smaller of the two.

"At least," said Jake. "Doug knew we were scheduled to meet him on Thursday evening. We've been staying at his place since then and there has been nobody around, nobody has called or left any phone messages, other than us."

"We've paid a visit to Joey and his helper, Frank somebody, and I can tell you these are *not* good people, detective." said Iggy. "A co-worker and good friend of Doug's at The Urban Tomato bar in the city has told us he thinks Doug ran into some trouble with Joey."

"There's more," said Jake. "I know you guys can get this info yourselves, but to save you some time, I was able to get it from a friend and former colleague back home," he continued and passed the note paper with the relative account information for 5000710 Alberta Ltd to the detective.

"Have you checked with his parents back East?"

"They are both deceased, officer. There are no other known relatives."

"What does your friend look like and what was he driving for a vehicle?" said Riley.

With a description of the Bug and the info on his car (Jake assumed he still had the Rambler), Hansen then left the three to finish their coffees. When he returned about ten minutes later, he brought with him a document that looked like a printout from a telex machine that Jake had seen last year at the regional office of his former employer. Now Hansen held it at arm's length as he read it.

Jake sensed that Hansen was the senior of the two officers. He had that worn out, pessimistic look about him, no doubt the result of many years of exposure to the worst side of humanity, the too-often encounters of bureaucracy within his own environment, and the knowledge that apathy was winning too many battles on his turf. He reminded Jake of the TV character Detective Columbo. In his sad, weary voice, he told them he was able to determine a 1963 Rambler was being held in one of the city's pounds in the northeast. It had been towed away from the casino area on late Thursday night or early Friday morning. There were no records of any admissions at the local hospitals for one Doug Canning. After sharing this info with Iggy and Jake, Hansen then looked seriously at Riley, then at the two boys.

"I think we better take a ride, guys. Jake, you leave your vehicle where it's parked and both of you come with us."

When they were in the detectives' cruiser and were under way back down 47th St, Hansen checked the boys in his rear-view mirror and spoke to them.

"This is not going to be easy for you guys. We understand a body was found in an alleyway behind the Casino Calgary last Friday morning around 5:00 am by one of the city's garbage trucks while making their weekly rounds. From the description provided it could be your friend. We're going to the city morgue now, and maybe you can identify the body."

Neither Iggy nor Jake had ever experienced anything like this. Okay, they had viewed deceased people before at funerals, but never in a morgue. This was different. Over the top different.

The body of the Bug lay on a steel table that had been wheeled into a room separated from them by a plate glass window. To both the stricken boys, there was no doubt it was Bug. But his face was ashen and in death they realized they would never see that crazy smile again, nor hear any further outrageous remarks about his latest capers or episodes. The Bug was gone.

When they were able to get control of their feelings, Iggy asked Hansen "How did it happen?"

"According to the medical examiner, he was stabbed once in the abdomen. He literally bled out. Death occurred sometime between six and ten pm on Thursday. As I said, he was found by the garbage guys very early the next morning. There were no witnesses.

"We'll have a look at the crime scene today. Before that though, maybe we can check out his apartment with you on the way back to your car. Have you guys told us absolutely everything we should know about Joey and this Frank character?"

"Absolutely, detective. Doug was our good friend. We want to find out who did this and why. If there's anything more we can do we're game. I mean anything." Jake pleaded. He thought he had read Hansen's feelings about the futility of his office correctly, so he decided to take it a step further. "Detective Hansen, you should also know that the joint owned by Joey is a favorite for cokeheads. When we were there the other night, we witnessed one of your own officers coming across several young guys doing some lines of coke in the parking lot of the club. Incredibly, the officer did nothing. Sir, with all respect, you have a problem here." finished Jake.

"Your point is taken. Since last year we have been seeing the cocaine problem increase rapidly. Unfortunately, we are under strict budget restraints and I'm afraid many of our younger members lack the necessary knowledge and exposure to this problem to properly confront it." Both Jake and Iggy read the implicit message from Hansen...my hands are tied.

The drive back to the Bug's apartment off 41st Ave NE was somber, and nobody talked. Iggy made coffee for the detectives while Jake showed them around the apartment. There wasn't really much to see. The Bug had a two-bedroom pad with a single bathroom, a small living room, and a kitchen. When they finished going through various drawers and cupboards plus one closet, they had found nothing of interest and the officers told them they were finished with this part of their investigation. It was sad to see what was left of the friend they once knew who was so gregarious and "out there."

They then drove with the officers back to CPD headquarters to get Jake's Beaumont. Since it was six pm, they decided to head back to the Maritime Pub and chat with the High Tide members, maybe lift their own spirits, have a bowl of fish chowder or some fried clams and chips, Iggy's favorite.

When they got to the pub, the boys were running through a couple of numbers. When they recognized Iggy and Jake, the two front men in the group came over to their table. "Hey boys, you're looking pretty serious tonight, what's happening?" Greg, the bass player said.

"Oh man, this was definitely a bad day. We've just been with two Calgary police detectives at the morgue where we had to identify an old friend of ours from back East. We were supposed to meet him last Thursday and it turns out, he was murdered the night before we arrived," said Jake. "Poor Bug," he continued, "couldn't hurt a soul and he'd give you the shirt off his back."

Greg gave his friend Danny, the lead guitarist for High Tide, a surprised look. He looked back to Jake.

"Dude, you're not referring to Doug "the Bug" Canning, are you?"

"Absolutely, man. You've met the Bug?"

"Yeah, we go back a couple of years since we came west. It's a small world. Many of the boys from back home end up at the pub here sooner or later. Familiar turf, I guess. The Bug showed up one night full of piss and vinegar and made a hit with one of the bar girls in no time flat.

"Truth be told, he could get on your nerves after a bit, but you're right, he was a funny dude and spread his cash around while he had it."

Jake and Iggy were able to receive solace from the two other musicians as the four told stories about the Bug over the next hour and it was a bittersweet ending to a terrible day.

Chapter Fourteen

Thursday, July 15th -Saturday, July 17th

GIVEN THE fact that Doug Canning had no surviving family and that he had never prepared a will, his remains were released to Jake and Iggy. As well, the Calgary Police had Bug's Rambler towed to his apartment where it was placed in the building's parking lot.

The two boys had decided to arrange for his funeral and the necessarily small service to be held Wednesday, July 14th. Surprisingly, his co-workers from the bar had managed to collect donations from fellow bar workers in the neighborhood totaling over five thousand dollars. It was more than enough to cover the costs of the funeral and the boys were even able to spring for drinks after the service, in memory of the Bug.

Now it was Thursday and Iggy and Jake listened to Detective Hansen as he described the latest news on their investigation from the results of the info he had been given by the guys. They were back at the apartment, and it was another hot afternoon in the middle of the Calgary Stampede.

"Looks like your hunches were right," said Hansen. "We were able to determine that the numbered company account at Scotiabank belongs to another organization in Vancouver. That company is called West Coast Imports Ltd. It, in turn, however, is owned by yet another numbered company in that city. We have investigated the lawyer whose name appears on all of these businesses, and he is definitely connected with them all. We have further information to believe they all have a tie-in to an L.A. mobster, a Mr. Giovanni "Dino" Martini, one real bad actor, who has recently set up his residency in Vancouver."

"So where do you go from here?" asked Jake.

"That's where you boys come to the party," said Riley. "That is, if you're willing to help us out?"

Iggy knew this was unusual. The authorities would not normally risk using citizens to help them conduct their investigations. He figured the two cops had their own agenda in play here and he was correct. He looked directly at the senior officer.

"Come on detectives," pressed Iggy. "Since when did big city police organizations start enlisting the direct help of their citizenry?"

Hansen looked long and hard at his partner. Iggy could see that Hansen was about to arrive at a decision that he had been pondering. Then, giving a shrug, he rose from his chair, went to the open office door and closed it and returned to the table. Then he sat down and explained their situation.

"You're correct. I wouldn't normally get into this with the public, but I have a feeling you guys can help us out with bringing your friend's killer to justice, which I think is what you both want, first and foremost.

"The fact is, we need to regain some credibility in the department. During the recent arrest of a small-time pusher, a bag of cocaine had been expertly placed in my jacket pocket. After the young creep had been brought into custody, he immediately started yelling about how he had been framed. Then, in front of four or five other officers, he demanded that I be searched for drugs. To humor the guy, I foolishly emptied the front pockets of my sports jacket, only to have a five-gram bag of coke fall on the precinct floor. Both Riley, by association, and I are now being investigated by our internal affairs department.

"It was a stupid mistake on my part to allow a small-time hood to slam me like that, and while I'm confident we will eventually be cleared, you can see why we need to score a big bust to regain our creds." Hansen finished his story with a sheepish look on his face.

"I told you earlier we would do anything to find out who did this to the Bug," said Iggy. "We're in. How can we help?"

"Well, the first thing you guys should know is that our colleagues in the Vancouver PD have had their eyes on this Giovanni gangster for a while now. They have "sources" informing them on a regular basis of his whereabouts, what he's up to in the drug world, you know? We are aware that Giovanni suspects Joey, or at least somebody in his shop, is skimming off the top of his supply of product and ripping him off."

"So," said Jake, 'how does that play with us and Doug Canning's death?"

"Dino has "on demand" access to a penthouse suite at the Casino Calgary," Riley now stated. "He and his assistant were there the night Bug was murdered."

Iggy and Jake looked at each other as things started falling in place.

"Look, there's nothing we can prove at this time, but there are just too many tie-ins to disregard," Hansen now quickly added, getting back into the conversation. He started ticking his fingers in a demonstration of the number of related matters. "Giovanni is legally connected to the ownership of the bar that is operated by Joey Delano. Delano gets his coke from Giovanni. Your friend Doug is known to have recently started a serious cocaine habit through Joey and you have indicated to us that he is, sorry, *was,* a follower, a wannabe, easily manipulated. His body is found in the alley behind the Casino." Hansen let the implication settle.

"Shit," said Iggy. "He was set up on a delivery or a pickup," he exclaimed.

"Yeah, we think so," said Hansen. "An autopsy revealed a high concentration of cocaine in his body. Plus, we found a folded piece of paper with the rear address of the Casino in your friend's pants pocket along with the notation 7:00 pm on it. And get this, the letterhead on the paper is Joey's Auto Body Shop."

"Then that nails them, doesn't it?" asked Jake.

"This is all just circumstantial evidence, Jacob. We have no witnesses. Your friend could have obtained this information from anybody at Joey's place and for any number of reasons. We need more proof."

With that, Detectives Hansen and Riley rolled out their plan to the young musicians, which would mean a trip to Vancouver to do some undercover work. The boys quickly realized they were getting into something out of their league. Still, they felt they could trust the two cops and if everything went as planned, there shouldn't be any problems.

Travel costs to Vancouver would be handled by the detectives and they felt it would be exciting to see that scene from a musician's viewpoint. So, the two agreed and it was decided they would drive to the West Coast mecca on Saturday in the Bug's Rambler. Riley made bookings for the boys, getting them registered into the Regency Motel in Burnaby on Dominion Street. Hansen gave his own and Riley's personal phone numbers to Jake and they agreed to check in every night at eight o'clock with one or the other of the detectives.

They were traveling under the names of David Kennedy and Joe Peterson, and they even had appropriate fake IDs and drivers' licenses to back up their pseudonyms. It was now Saturday, and they were on their way.

Chapter Fifteen

Saturday, July 17th 5:00 pm

UNKNOWN TO the detectives, Iggy had made a run yesterday to the Maritime Pub where he met up with Danny, the guitarist for High Tide. After a lot of running around and seeing some very sketchy places, Iggy's wallet was five hundred bucks lighter, but he now had a .45 semi-automatic handgun that gave him a lot more confidence for what lay ahead. Jake was not impressed.

It was raining when they arrived at the Regency in Burnaby. Close to the motel, in fact two blocks north, was the Grand Villa Casino Hotel and Conference Center.

The drive to Burnaby had been long and uneventful yet it was still awesome. West from Calgary, they traveled through the foothills to Canmore, then into the Rockies through Banff, Lake Louise, Golden, Revelstoke, Salmon Arm, and Kamloops. South to Hope, southwest to Chilliwack and Abbotsford, then west to North Surrey and finally to Burnaby, completing their trip.

The mountains were mind-numbing to the two Maritimers. The highest points of land Iggy had ever seen were the highlands of Cape Breton. For Jake it was possibly Marble Mountain in Newfoundland when he went skiing there once with a friend who lived in the nearby town of Corner Brook. Never had he seen anything like this! The dark green, fir-covered approaches changed to hazy, slate blue colored cliff faces, which then soared thousands of feet to the most dazzling white snow-capped peaks. Amazing to see in the middle of summer. They would definitely have to return to these places this winter. It was strange to watch snow blowing off the desolate peaks high above them as they traveled in the heat of the valley floor in Bug's Rambler that had no AC.

They had not conversed much along the way as they marveled at the scenery around them. When their route flattened and they were in North Surrey, Iggy sensed Jake was pissed off at him about something.

"What's on your mind, Jake?" he asked his friend.

"Jeez Ig, I'm thinking about that gun you bought. I never thought things were going to get this heavy."

"Look Jake, we're in the big leagues now, buddy. You've seen how Joey and Frank operate. I don't know about you, but I don't have any qualms about using the gun to protect us from these assholes," he said. Then, in an attempt to downplay the situation, he continued. "Anyway, if we play our cards right, we shouldn't need to use it."

"Iggy, I hear you, but man, this is totally over my pay grade. My parents would freak if they knew what I was into right now."

"So, don't tell them. It's all cool, brother. Trust Iggy. Deal?"

"Yeah, I guess so," said Jake. But he was still worried about whether or not their plan would work. Their involvement called for Iggy and Jake to contact one Johnny DeSota, a blackjack dealer at the Grand Villa Casino. DeSota was an informant for the Vancouver police who had been *persuaded* by them to introduce the boys to Mr. Giovanni "Dino" Martini. Iggy and Jake were pretending to be a couple of up-and-coming drug dealers who were looking for work and had heard of the Martini connection from Joey back in Calgary.

If the boys were questioned by Dino about their relationship with Joey and Frank, it would be their story that as far as they knew, Joey and his guy were small time players who couldn't be trusted. Further, they were to mention that Joey and his man were being considered as suspects in a murder that had been recently committed in the city.

It was felt by Hansen and Riley that the mobster would buy this story since their sources had informed them Dino, of late, was very suspicious that Joey was ripping him off. If not Joey himself, then probably Frank, his underling. This was an opportunity to plant the seed in Dino's head that they were looking at Joey for the murder of an unknown druggie who was probably running a pickup for him. The more Hansen and Riley discussed this scenario, the more they liked it. If Dino were to think along those lines, he would probably be more apt to bring the boys into his sphere of influence and thereby have them keep an eye on the situation with Joey until they, Iggy and Jake, could be trusted.

Unfortunately, what Iggy and Jake did not know, was the fact that both Dino and his assistant were *not* aware they had not killed Frank. This would give them a lot of grief later on.

Hansen and Riley had no other suspects in Bug's death. If the boys could really get deep into Dino's organization, maybe they could find out more about that particular crime, but at the moment, their focus was on Giovanni's drug operation. Yet, it would be a huge bonus for the detectives if in fact they could nail Dino for the murder of the kid from back East.

It was now eight o'clock and the two young musicians had just finished unpacking their gear after arriving at The Regency and Iggy had just placed his first check-in call to Hansen back in Calgary.

"Iggy here, detective. We've arrived in Burnaby, and we're checked in at the Regency. We're planning on going over to the casino now to see if we can meet this Johnny Desota character. He knows we're coming right?"

"That's right. Just be cool and our guy should set up the meet with Dino. He better. We've got a ton of shit to hit him with if he doesn't play ball, and he knows we mean business. Just say that Hansen sent you."

"One thing, Hansen," said Iggy. "You're still not sure who stabbed Bug, are you?"

"Not really. Hell, maybe he was caught trying to steal the pickup and it actually was Frank."

"In that case, how are we supposed to *spy* on Frank for Dino? As you know, I'm not in Frank's fan club."

"Let us give that some thought and we'll talk about it tomorrow night, okay?"

Iggy had no comeback for that at this time if, that is, they wanted to continue in their hunt for Bug's killer. They both knew they were getting involved in a life-or-death situation with a criminal who had mob connections in L.A. But they were also unsure of where things fit with the two detectives and whether or not they could trust them. If Frank did kill the Bug, did these cops have their backs? And if it wasn't Frank, then who did it? There was only one way to find out.

They left for the Grand Villa Casino at nine pm.

Chapter Sixteen

9:00 pm
Grand Villa Casino
Vancouver, B.C.

GIOVANNI "DINO" Martini held an executive penthouse suite in the Grand Villa Casino Hotel and Conference Centre. He was permanently "comped" by the owners of the Casino who happened to be two of the most notorious drug capos in the U.S.: Alberto "Big Al" Gabrazzi and Vincent "Vinnie" Fellino. Their operation in Canada was held jointly, as were many others they owned in the States, but their Western sectors in both countries were Vinnie's responsibility. He in turn basically delegated full reins on the operational side of things to his nephew, Dino.

It was nine pm on a busy Saturday when the boys arrived at the casino, and while Johnny DeSota was nervously keeping an eye out for two guys pretending to be criminals, Dino was sipping on a glass of red Merlot in his penthouse. He was accompanied by one Grigori Ivanov, his Russian hit man.

"Grigori," said Dino, as he patted his lips with a napkin, "you are certain nobody saw anything the other night in Calgary?"

"Right, boss" replied Ivanov. "I was very careful. Do not worry yourself with this thing."

"You mistake me, Grigori. I do not worry. I simply want you to know what my associates here may say or do to you if something has gone wrong," Dino said and watched as the Russian's face turned even paler.

Ivanov enjoyed a good living with his mafia employer, but he had seen firsthand on several occasions just how brutal these people could be in their displeasure for poor work. Dino, for his part, knew it was necessary every now and then to issue veiled threats to the Russian who tended to take his job a little too casual at times.

Meanwhile, downstairs, Jake and Iggy approached a blackjack table where a scrawny individual with greasy, slicked-back hair and a thin moustache was dealing cards to a solo player. The dealer matched the description given by Hansen, so they waited away from the table until the player left, then went over and placed some chips they had purchased on the table.

"So, Jimmy," said Iggy. "They tell me you're the man to get us in to see Mr. Martini."

"Sez who?" said DeSota.

Jake decided to take the upper hand. "Look, asshole, we haven't got all night. If Hansen finds out you're giving us the gears, you're in trouble. So, what's the score?"

"Yeah, yeah, I got it. Let me cash in my table and take a break." They followed him to an office down a hallway and waited outside until he came out with another guy who they assumed was his replacement. They left the table with DeSota's replacement, then went with him to a house phone where he made a quick call and came back to them.

"You're on and man, if this goes south, I'm dead. So, no more contact with me, okay? As far as Mr. Martini is aware, when you were at my table, you simply asked for the owner and made a hint about wanting to move some product. Go to the 35th floor, Penthouse West, and he'll see you."

~ * ~

After hanging up the house phone in his suite, Dino came over to Ivanov. "That was Johnny on table five. He's sending up a couple of wannabes who say they have an idea about how they can move some product for us. Or maybe they're just here for a job interview." They both chuckled. "Stick around, Grigori. This might be worthwhile. I told Johnny to be on the lookout for someone who might be able to take on a position with us."

Grigori went to the door when the soft chime sounded, and he ushered in Iggy and Jake. When they saw the large Russian, they were immediately intimidated. Grigori had that way with people. His hooded eyes stared blankly at them as they introduced themselves as Dave Kennedy and Joe Peterson and requested to see Mr. Martini. When Grigori ushered them into the penthouse suite, they saw Dino standing in front of a floor-to-ceiling, room-length window gazing out at the magnificent view of the Vancouver skyline to the west. With his back to the boys, he said "What's your game, boys, and don't bother trying to bullshit me."

Iggy took the lead. "No sir." he said to the *capo's* back. "We are here to fill a hole for you in your sales force."

"What hole?" asked Martini, as he turned from the window to face the boys.

"The hole that's about to be created by Joey Delano and Frank Trueblood when they are arrested for murdering some guy who was making a pickup for them at the Casino Calgary last week."

"And how do you know this?" asked Dino, looking questioningly at the Russian.

"The Body Shop is a small bar, sir. We heard it from friends."

"So, why do the cops suspect Joey?" asked Dino.

"Everybody around that bar has known for some time that Joey and Frank have been ripping you off, sir. It's common knowledge. The poor schmuck who got stabbed never knew what he was getting himself into. They know Frank and Joey are greedy."

"Oh, and by the way," Jake added. "They have a witness who saw Frank following the druggie when he left to do the pickup. When they approach you for a replacement of their purchase, Joey and his assistant are no doubt planning to tell you their "delivery man" was either mugged or was caught playing a scam with somebody else."

Dino took all this in while looking aside at Grigori. Unknown to Dino, Grigori had never met Frank, so both Dino and Grigori had naturally assumed it was Frank who had been stabbed. And now both of them were surprised to find out it was *not* Frank that was stabbed that night. All they knew was that they were right in suspecting a scam, since the parcel Grigori had brought to Dino only contained paper. Of course, the Sears bag Grigori was carrying also only held paper. This, though, was not mentioned to the two wannabe dealers.

"I still don't get it," maintained Dino, playing innocent. "Why didn't they call me?"

"I believe the police raided The Shop early the next morning as soon as they received their anonymous tip about Frank. They were both arrested immediately for questioning and probably got lawyered up with their first and only phone call."

Dino could understand that. He also knew neither Frank nor Joey would be willing to talk to the cops about the connection they had with him. So, the best thing to do at this time was to either wait it out or maybe even see if these two characters from back East might be able to find out more information for him. On second thought, it might even be wise for the four of them to make a trip to Calgary, tie up some loose ends, and test the loyalty and intentions of these two at the same time. Then, depending on what they learned, they could meet with Al and Vinnie on Monday the 19th as arranged.

Dino hated this part of the operation, but that was why he had Grigori as a helper. Also, he didn't think there was a need to bother Vinnie with their plans at this time. Dino was confident Vinnie trusted him to handle this area of their operations and he did not want to appear uncertain to him. That would not be good.

"Well, gentlemen," he said, having apparently come to a decision. "We're all going back to Calgary. Grigori, go with David and Joe to pick up their stuff and come back here. I'll call ahead and have the Lear readied for takeoff."

10:35 pm

Iggy and Jake now had a problem. How and when were they going to be able to get in touch with detectives Hansen or Riley? Things were moving too quickly for them, but they really had no choice. They just had to hope that they might be able to tip off one of the cops before Dino talked with either Frank or Joey. And Iggy still wasn't fully satisfied that Hansen and Riley had the two musicians' best interests in mind. One other item concerned them, which was the look Dino had given the Russian earlier during their talk at the penthouse, when they told Dino that Frank and Joey were being considered as suspects in a homicide. They sensed something was being held secret by them which only added to the unease.

The Lear jet departed Abbotsford Airport at ten-forty pm and approximately one and one quarter hours later they were landing at Calgary International Airport. With the change in time zones, it was now one am as they drove downtown toward the Casino Calgary in a rented Lincoln Mark V.

"Say, Grigori, could you drop Jake and I over to our apartment so we can grab a change of clothes? I'm feeling a bit grubby, man." said Iggy. Ivanov looked for a slight nod of confirmation from his boss and took 32nd Ave NE south after he received directions from Iggy.

When they arrived at the apartment, Dino told Grigori to accompany the boys while they changed clothes, just to "keep them honest." *Shit!* thought Iggy, there goes any chance of calling Hansen. While they went into their bedrooms to change, Grigori waited in the living room. When they came out the Russian was holding a 9mm Glock 17 levelled at them. Without saying anything, he motioned them to stand against the wall while he quickly and expertly searched them. Fortunately, Iggy had left his .45 semi in his backpack which was now in the trunk of the rented Lincoln.

As the four men started down the hall in single file toward the exit door, they passed a series of pictures hanging on the wall to their right. Jake noticed Grigori pausing to take a long look at one of them.

When Jake saw what had captured the Russian's attention, he was mortified. There, standing with a group of people in some downtown bar, was the Bug with both arms hung around a young attractive girl in a tank top. The Bug with that ear-to-ear smile holding court. The boys had missed seeing the photo on the way in and now they might *have some 'splainin to do* as Ricky would say.

As they drove in silence back to the Casino Calgary some things started to add up for the boys. From what they had seen and heard from both Dino and his Russian aide; it was becoming obvious they were involved in the Bug's death. They couldn't prove this yet. But just the way Dino looked at Ivanov when they told him Frank was arrested here in Calgary for murdering some druggie...and when they observed Grigori's reaction as he saw Bug's picture in the apartment...man, they knew it was only a matter of time before these bad guys were on to them!

The trick, at least for the moment, was to keep Dino and his friend under the belief that they were just a couple of guys from back East wanting to get in on some drug action to make a quick buck.

Grigori, for his part, now wasn't sure who he actually stabbed that night because he had never met Frank, and therefore didn't know him from the Bug. The picture on the wall of the apartment they had just left certainly bore a resemblance to the guy he killed. So, the Russian figured the boys had to be connected to this guy or maybe they just knew Frank through the guy whose picture he had seen on the wall. He decided to hold this information from Dino until he was sure what was going on.

They climbed into the Lincoln and headed back to Dino's suite at the Casino Calgary. Iggy made a point of asking to get a pack of smokes from his backpack in the trunk before they took off.

Chapter Seventeen

Earlier the same evening
Calgary
11:00 pm

AT ROUGHLY eleven pm, Hansen and Riley had still not heard from the boys. A call to the Regency Motel simply revealed they were not in their room, but a call to the front desk had confirmed that they had not checked out. The detectives decided to go over to The Body Shop and interview Joey and Frank.

When they arrived at The Body Shop, things were in full gear. Loud, blaring metal music assailed their ears and they wondered how half of the kids there could hear anything. The whole scene wasn't new to them, but no matter how often they visited this type of joint, they felt so out of step with the social norms and music trends that it was almost embarrassing. Plus, of course they stood out from the regulars like sharks in a trout pond. They may as well have COPS! stamped on their forehead.

They made their way to the bar and asked to see the owner after introducing themselves. As was the case with Iggy and Jake, the barkeep summoned Frank Trueblood and the Metis native showed up a few minutes later. He was wearing a large gauze bandage wrapped around his nose.

"Run into a door?" asked Riley.

"Somethin' like that," replied Frank as he scowled at the officers. As he did the other night with the two musicians, he took the detectives down the hallway to Joey's office, and they all entered to find Joey pretending to be hard at work sifting through various billings, receivables, and other documents.

"How can I help you guys?" asked Joey and directed the cops to the two leather chairs in front of his desk.

"Well, to start with, Mr. Delano, we are investigating the death of one Douglas Canning, known locally as Bug. The Bug was a regular patron of your bar, and we just thought you guys might be able to tell us if he was around last Thursday night."

"Detective, I'm a busy man!" Joey shouted. "I don't have time to socialize with my clients, so if you can excuse me?" He stood and started to lead the officers out of his office.

"We understand he was instrumental in getting a lot of bar people coming here for after-hour drinks and fun," said Riley. "We haven't yet looked into your license and permit conditions, and we would just as soon not get into all that, okay?" Joey had not bothered to get an after-hours license. Besides, the license would only stipulate that yes, they could be open after 2:00 am, but only for late night dancing and hard partygoers. No alcohol could be served.

"Detective, you're not suggesting we serve liquor after hours, are ya?" he chuckled. "Anyway, what does that have to do with the Bug's stabbing?"

"Who said he was stabbed, Joey?" The police had not released this detail to the press and Joey's mistake was a big tell.

"And something else. Bug's body was found in the alley behind the Casino Calgary. We've been following the whereabouts of Mr. Giovanni "Dino" Martini and we know he was with his heavy Russian hitter at the casino the night of the murder."

"So?"

"So, we know you and Dino have a relationship regarding the ownership of your joint here. And yeah, you are no longer on title, but you are an employee. Further, the lawyer who handled the sale for you is also named as a principal shareholder of a numbered company that now owns your place along with several other establishments in Vancouver and LA, all of which are connected to this same holding company."

"Detective, I'm busy. Get to the point! What does all this financial crap possibly have to do with me?" shouted Joey.

"Here's the thing, Joey. One of the best ways to clean up dirty drug money is to run it through an account with regular bar sales. We can certainly have a forensic audit done to see what we might find. Do you want that?"

"Christ, you guys! Busting my balls when all I want to do is make an honest living!"

"Gimme a break, Joey," said Riley, who up to this point had mostly been on the sidelines. "You don't know the meaning of an honest living!"

"Maybe we should take this conversation downtown, Joey," said Hansen. "Can you account for your whereabouts last Thursday night?"

"C'mon man! Are you arresting me for murdering this Bug? Detective, you're barking up the wrong tree man. I might go over the edge on some things, but no way could I have ever done anything like that." Joey had a desperate look in his eyes and Hansen noted sweat beginning to run down his neck, despite the AC on high in the office room. There was definitely something this character was hiding.

"Hey, Frank, how about you?" Riley asked, now directing his attention toward the Metis native. "We can talk to a lot of people here. You never know, maybe somebody saw or heard something that night."

"I was working here all that night. Check with as many people as you want to." There it was again, that look of desperation the detectives had seen earlier, now in the eyes of both Joey and his man, Frank. Hansen decided to press the issue and went for it.

"Frank, I happen to know you drive a late model Ford 150 half ton with plates, let's see," he said, as he reached into his side pocket "numbered 402 DIR. And damn if I don't have a witness who tells me he saw that vehicle leave here last Thursday. The night our victim was murdered."

Frank suspected the cop was bluffing, but yet Hansen must know something, otherwise how or why did he have his truck data with him?

Riley decided to go after Joey. He asked Hansen for the note paper that contained banking data given to them by the two musicians. He referred to it and said, "Okay, Joey, we know you make deposits to your commercial account number 7005499 in the name of a numbered company 5000710 Alberta Limited at Scotiabank on 6th Ave SW."

The detective waved his arms to encompass the building. "We want to take down the owners of this shit hole so if you want to cooperate, maybe we can talk to the DA about dropping charges from murder one on the Bug down to manslaughter, or..." here he made a point of looking at Frank's nose and said with a smile, "self defense?"

Chapter Eighteen

Midnight Saturday, July 17th to 1:45 am Sunday, July 18th

WHEN THEY reached the casino, the three of them left the rental with the hotel's valet service and headed toward the elevators. Iggy was worried about the way the Russian kept staring at him with those dead-fish eyes, not saying a word.

After entering Dino's office, the boys sat on two separate easy chairs facing Dino who was situated across from them behind his desk. The Russian sat behind the boys on a sofa making it difficult for them to move into action if need be.

"So, boys," asked Dino. "Tell me where and how you plan to move some product for me. I know this town pretty well, and I thought I had most of the hot spots covered."

"Ever been down to the Maritime Pub on Heritage Drive in the Southeast?" asked Iggy. "The place is filled with a lot of people that we know, or at least, they're from our part of the country. I happen to know the owner, and I can tell you sir, there's a real opportunity here. I think you should let us get in on it before somebody else does."

"Okay, let me think about it. In the meantime, tell me about yourself. What's your background? Ever been in stir back East?"

"Nope," said Iggy, "Nor has my friend Jake here. We're both musicians, we played the bar circuit back home for a few years. I've done construction work, also worked for my old man at his auto body shop. Jake here was a banker."

"A banker?" said Dino, turning his attention to Jake. "Now that's interesting. What type of banker were you?"

"Commercial lending, mainly to the small business sector." said Jake. *Shit*, he thought. *Where is this leading?*

"Actually, Jake, I may have some other plans for a man with your background. My associates are always looking for some experienced financial people." Dino turned his attention to the Russian behind the boys.

"Whaddya think, Grigori? Why not give these boys a trial run and see what comes of it. Tell you what, boys, we've got a few things to take care of. First, let Grigori take you back to your apartment. Give your number to him and we'll get in touch in the morning. Then we'll see what kind of salesmen you are with your friends at the Maritime Pub, *si*?"

When the two young men had left his suite, Dino called his colleague in Vancouver and the fates of Joey and Frank were confirmed.

~ * ~

It did indeed sound to Iggy that these hoods were buying their story. So far, things were looking good. The sooner they got home, the better they would feel, and they were both looking forward to talking with the detectives.

They left the casino and went back to Bug's apartment. Not a word was spoken by Ivanov on the way there. When they got home, Iggy gave Bug's number to him and when they were both out of the Lincoln, Grigori rolled down the passenger window and called them back to the vehicle.

"Hey Maritimers," the Russian said with a smile that did not reach his shark eyes, "not to leave town, eh? I'm looking at you." And he sped off in the early morning.

"That guy gives me the creeps," said Jake. "Dude, what are you getting us into here? And why did you tell the man I was a banker in my past life?! Now I'm probably gonna have to get into their laundering game."

"Relax, Jake. Trust the Igster. This could work to our benefit. Now let's try to reach our cop friends again."

Hansen's phone rang four times, and the call was then sent to his answering machine. Iggy left a message asking them to get in touch, things were happening. He then called the Maritime Pub and asked for Greg, the bassist with High Tide. Fortunately, they had just completed their last set and Greg came on the line.

"Greg, it's Iggy Miles from back East. Jake and I talked to you and

Danny last Sunday?"

"Right on, man. What's up?"

"Many things my friend, some very heavy things. Can we meet now before you crash? This is serious and involves the Bug. You and Danny can really help us out if you're up for it."

"We're in," said Greg.

Iggy grabbed his backpack and he drove south down MacLeod Trail with Jake in the Bug's Rambler. Twenty minutes later the four musicians sat together in a booth at the pub.

"Thanks for seeing us at this late hour, Greg," said Iggy as he and Jake sipped on beers with the two musicians they had made friends with the previous week. "This is all very weird and almost incredible but hear us out. I told Danny on Friday that I needed a gun to protect Jake and me from some unsavory dudes we had run into. Danny didn't ask for any more info at the time, but now you need to know.

"Since Friday we have come across information that would lead us to suspect an after-hours bar in the Northeast called The Body Shop may be selling hard drugs to their clientele and laundering the proceeds through their bar sales. We have further determined that somehow the Bug may have gotten himself mixed up in this which probably resulted in his murder."

"Whoa, man!" said Danny. "This is heavy. You told Greg you wanted our help, but I don't know how or what we can do," he added doubtfully.

"Let me tell you this in confidence, guys," said Iggy. "We have been speaking with a couple of *hardened* Calgary police detectives about all this, and they have given us some of the information regarding the drug laundering operation. It involves players in Vancouver and possibly Los Angeles, definitely big time. The two cops, for personal reasons, have requested our help and as of Friday we signed on. We believe they have our backs and they have set us up with phony IDs. This has enabled us to go undercover and work for a drug boss, a Dino Martini, from Vancouver via LA," finished Iggy.

"We have told the detectives, as part of our cover, that we are confident we can arrange your help in allowing us to put a sting in play through the pub to nail these guys," added Jake. "I know this is a lot to take in, but we really want to get the assholes who killed Bug. He did not deserve to go that way. The cops have a bigger agenda in mind, which is an international drug bust, but the two things, we believe, are connected."

"If you guys trust the cops, then we can make it happen," said Greg. "The owner of the pub is away on business in Toronto for a week. He's a nice enough dude but may not buy into this scheme though. So, we'd have to do this on our own."

"Okay," said Iggy. "That could still work in our favor. We have to get back to our place and await a call from a bad actor by the name of Grigori, a Russian hood who works for Dino. Do not speak to him, or anyone for that matter, about this under any circumstances, until you hear back from us. We also have to talk with our detective friends about bringing you guys on board."

"So, if we happen to show up with the bad guys, just play along, right?" said Jake. "And if you get a call from the police, you can confirm everything we have just discussed."

Chapter Nineteen

2:30 am
July 18th

IGGY AND Jake drove back in the Rambler to the Bug's apartment for some much-needed sleep. It was now 2:30 am on Sunday July 18th. Before crawling into their beds, Iggy said to Jake, "You know man, this whole thing is starting to get to me. If we don't hear from the detectives soon, maybe we should rethink everything and catch a flight to the West Coast with the money we have left."

"Let's see what the morning brings," said Jake. And they were soon sleeping like the dead.

3:00 am
While Jake and Iggy were just starting to nod off, Detectives Hansen and Riley were leaving The Body Shop feeling pretty good about things. They had managed to scare the shit out of Joey and Frank. With the data given to them by Iggy and Jake, and some pretty cool bluff work, the two detectives had managed to convince the small-time criminals to agree to cooperate with them regarding Dino. That all said, neither Frank nor Joey mentioned anything to the detectives yet about what Frank had witnessed at the casino last Thursday night.

So, while the cops were no further ahead with their murder investigation, they were going to meet with Frank and Joey midafternoon downtown at the precinct. They expected to get some good leads on the "Martini Project," as they now called it.

As they were exiting the bar's parking lot in their cruiser, a black Lincoln Mark V was pulling into the entrance of the lot at the far side further up the avenue. It was 3:10 am and the after-hours club was starting to rock.

3:30 am

When Detective Hansen entered his small two-bedroom condo in Buona Vista Downs in the southeast part of the city, he saw his answering machine blinking. After listening to the message from Iggy, he was tempted to call him then and there, but given the late time, he decided to wait until the next day.

Things were really starting to happen. Hansen had a good feeling about where they now stood with Joey Delano and Frank Trueblood. He was convinced they were washing drug money for Dino Martini and being able to break that open would be a major score for himself and Riley.

As well, he was aware from the material he had been sent by the Vancouver police that it didn't end here. His colleagues in that city were particularly interested in two other crime lords, namely Alberto "Big Al" Gabrazzi and Vincent "Vinnie" Fellino. These were big players and man, who knew where it could all lead. It was international in scope, and he, Detective Jack Hansen, could very well earn back the respect and dignity in his Calgary department that he so dearly coveted.

Hansen climbed into bed and instantly fell sound asleep.

Chapter Twenty

THE PHONE rang piercingly next to Jake's ear and rudely woke him from a very erotic dream he was having about his old girlfriend, Sharon Donovan, back home. *It is time to get off my butt and meet some new ladies,* he thought as he picked up the phone.

It was Detective Hansen calling to tell Jake they had a breakthrough in their laundering investigation. Jake in turn told Hansen they had made some progress in their undercover work, and it would be best if the four of them could get together, the sooner the better. It was agreed the cops would be at their place in a half hour and Jake immediately went into Iggy's room and roused his buddy from a dead sleep.

"So much for the thought of going to Vancouver," grumbled Iggy. Then he realized with some alarm that they had a small problem. "We've got the cops coming here and hey, what about our Russian friend? Christ, if he lands while Hansen and Riley are here, he'll obviously smell a rat."

As often happens in these moments, serendipity occurs. The phone rang and Iggy picked it up. Sure enough, it was Grigori and he wanted to speak with "Mr. Joe." For a minute, Iggy forgot they had given bogus names to the criminals.

"Yeah, just a sec," he said and passed the phone to Jake, raising his eyebrows and mouthing the Russian's name to him.

"Mr. Joe, Mr. Martini is tellink me we should go see your friends at the Maritime Pub today," he said.

"Yeah Grig," said Jake. "I was expecting your call about this and in fact, just before you called, I was speaking with my friend. He wants to meet with us today as well, but he has some other things to do first. He said he can see us around suppertime, is that okay?"

The Russian reluctantly agreed to the late meeting and hung up. While they waited for Hansen and Riley to appear, Jake and Iggy made some coffee and had some toast, bacon, and scrambled eggs from the few groceries they had purchased on Friday afternoon. It was going to be a busy day.

2:45 pm

Detectives Hansen and Riley were visibly shaken when they finally landed at the Bug's apartment. The reason, as told to the boys, was that just before they left the station around noon, they received a call from the precinct captain telling them to go to a crime scene in the southwest sector where a homicide had occurred. The actual scene, though not told to the boys, was The Body Shop.

Upon arriving at Joey's bar, they had soon realized their case against Dino Martini et al was about to vaporize before their eyes. This was mainly because their two star witnesses were hardly in any shape to testify. It's difficult to say much when your throat has been sliced from ear to ear.

The crime scene was Joey's office, and it was horrific. The detectives had never seen so much blood in a confined area. Moreover, the nature of the injuries that had been inflicted upon Joey Delano and Frank Trueblood had to have been conducted by an insane individual. Not only had their necks been slashed, but their tongues had been rudely pulled downwards through the cavities now available in their throats...classic Sicilian neck ties. It was obvious they had been murdered by professional killers.

The detectives relayed none of these details to Iggy and Frank. It would have only served to remove them from the scene when they were now needed more than before. So, when queried by the boys as to what was happening with Frank and Joey, they simply told them that they were unavailable at the moment but that they had reason to believe The Body Shop was definitely operating as Iggy and Jake suspected.

The boys told them of their meeting with Dino and the Russian and how they had convinced the two criminals that it would be profitable to set up another drug laundering operation at a bar in Southeast Calgary called the Maritime Pub. And finally, they went over the details of how this was

74

accomplished with the cooperation of their friends who were with the High Tide band currently playing there. They were now seeking the go ahead from the two detectives to set up a sting on Dino and Grigori.

Iggy then told Hansen and Riley about his suspicions regarding the Bug's killer being related to either Dino and/or the Russian. To the detectives, this seemed to jive with the recent murders of Joey and Frank, but nothing was said to the boys.

"The Russian will be here to pick us up later this afternoon, probably around four thirty. We will be leaving here and going to the Maritime Pub. Our friends Greg and Danny at the pub have been told you guys will protect them in this sting. The owner of the pub is away in Toronto on business for a few days, so no one else needs to be involved. How do we proceed?" said Jake.

The detectives truly admired the grit and determination of these boys. There would be hell to pay from their captain if something bad happened to them during this venture, but then it was a good plan and if properly executed, their superiors need not know all the details.

So, Hansen laid out the details and when the four of them were satisfied with it, they called Greg at the pub and arranged to meet with him and his fellow musician, Danny, in twenty minutes. It was now three thirty-five pm and they left the apartment with the promise to Iggy and Jake that they would be fully protected at all times.

"Here we go, Iggy," said Jake. "Man, this is getting scary. I don't know if I can even get in the same car with this Russian who now seems to have had a part in Bug's murder. He'll be here in an hour and then we're on our own. I wish we had the "Duke" riding shotgun with us." He was referring to his screen idol, John Wayne.

Then Iggy, in another great impersonation of their hero said, "I wouldn't make it a habit of callin' me that, son."

Chapter Twenty-One

4:37 pm

SEVERAL LOUD raps on the Bug's apartment door announced the arrival of the Russian. Iggy opened the door and led Grigori ahead of him down the hall to the living room. He keenly watched while the man paused at the picture hanging on the wall.

"Friend of you?" asked Ivanov. He pointed at the Bug and the blonde girl having a good time at some bar.

"Yeah, from back East." Iggy decided it was time to go *mano a mano* with this prick. "Too bad about him. He was recently found in a back alley behind the casino. Some lowlife stabbed him, and the cops say it was probably just another drug deal gone bad."

"Much danger for people who get mixed up in drug world," said Grigori, staring with his dead eyes at Iggy. "Maybe good lesson for this young man's friends, no?"

"Too true, Grigori," replied Iggy, holding the Russian's gaze.

"But then, my friend here was actually a naïve kind of guy. I mean, the Bug, as he was called, just wanted to have a fun life, and he thought everyone else was on the same trip. Man, I'd surely like to run across the slime ball that murdered him." They were both still holding each other's eyes.

Then Iggy decided he had enough of Grigori at the moment. He raised his arms in a "what-the-hell" gesture with a big grin.

"Hey, what're we waiting for?" Iggy asked as he suddenly dropped the stare game, and they entered the living room where Jake was waiting.

"Let's hit the road," Jake said as he tossed a backpack to Iggy and draped his own over his shoulder.

While they got into the Lincoln, Grigori was thinking that he was now certain he had stabbed the frail blond guy whose picture was on the wall in the apartment. Some guy they called Bug. But what did it matter? He was able to carry out Dino's prime directive last night at The Body Shop when he took care of both Frank and Joey. It was all too easy. These western idiots who think they are so tough. *Grigori Ivanovich would show them how to be tough!* And what about these two punks who were now in the car? There was something about the taller guy, David Kennedy, that caused him concern. *Not to worry, Grigori Ivanovich,* he admonished himself. He had survived a long history of dealing with desperate people across Eastern Europe and he was confident these two young Canucks were not about to pose problems.

Following Iggy's directions, Grigori soon arrived at the Maritime Pub. The parking lot was relatively empty. After all, it was still early on a Sunday evening and the Calgary Stampede had officially finished last night. Most of the younger set in the city were still nursing hangovers from the binge drinking that always accompanied the annual festivity.

"So, where's your boss?" Iggy asked Grigori.

"He had some other business. Not your concern," said the Russian. "Where are your friends?"

"They should be here, let's go," and they entered the pub.

As expected, there were many empty tables in the dark interior of the building. Over to the right, they saw two young men sitting in a booth facing the door with a couple of pilsners they were nursing. They looked like a couple of tough bikers. There was only one other booth occupied and that held a couple of older men who, dressed in dirty jogging pants and windbreakers, appeared to be down-and-outers.

When they approached the booth holding the bikers, Greg rose and gave Iggy a bear hug. "Davie Kennedy, my long-lost friend! How's it hangin' brother?" he said. Iggy was pleased with the welcome. Hansen had apparently coached the boys well for the scene they were about to play out. "I see you're still draggin' young Joe around," Greg continued, and he slapped a high five to Jake in a biker style greeting.

"Y'all remember my good bud, Danny, from Sydney, right?" he said.

"Couldn't forget that ugly face, dude," replied Jake as he shook hands with Danny.

"And this man, my friends," said Iggy, gesturing to the Russian, "is gonna make a ton of cash for us. Say hello to our new friend, Grigori. Say, can we get a drink?" The boys tossed their backpacks into the booth.

A cute waitress appeared at the booth and took their orders. Soon she returned with a fresh round of four beers and a double vodka for the five men and the meeting began. "Dave" outlined the plan to Greg and Danny, the same as he had earlier told the detectives and the two drug suppliers. Here was an opportunity to move a lot of cocaine to patrons of the Maritime Pub and wash the dirty proceeds from the sale of the drugs with regular bar sales. It was too easy.

"Are you two ownink this place?" asked Grigori skeptically. Greg immediately stood up, obviously very offended.

"Davie," he said, "I thought this guy was a friend of yours."

"Whoa, whoa people. Let's be cool," Iggy said. "Grigori, I apologize for not filling you in with some background on my good pals here," he added. "Greg and Danny have built up a nice little nest egg for themselves since coming West five years ago. You can check the title to the pub here when you want, but it's all legit. Sorry, but I just assumed your boss would have already looked into this aspect of the deal, given he's a bona fide businessman and all," he said defiantly to the Russian.

Of course, he knew it would not have been possible for Martini to do that since the scheme was only proposed on the weekend. The Land Title Registry Office wouldn't open until tomorrow, Monday the 19th.

The Russian was confused by "Dave's" statement, and he was quite unsure of how to proceed. He did not trust the so-called owners of the pub. But then Grigori did not trust anybody. Ever. Yet, he felt his boss held a liking for the two boys; at least he thought Dino might have a place for them in his organization. Therefore, he decided to cede to the moment and go along with "Dave."

"I apologize if I offend your friends, Mr. Dave. Let us proceed with our discussions."

It was on. The deal was set whereby two kilos of cocaine, as a starter, would be available for pickup sometime next week. The sooner the better, the bikers stated. Greg and Danny would meet Grigori, who would be accompanied by Iggy and Jake, and they would purchase the coke at wholesale prices for ultimate retail sale to the pub's clientele at extremely good margins.

Profits from this illegal activity would then be included with regular bar sales and thereby laundered. It was fully expected that the introduction of coke to the Maritime crowd would certainly increase business at the pub and create a false sense of increasing the pub's regular cash flow in the eyes of their bankers or other authorities. And hey, Iggy and Jake planned to work their music into High Tide's genre and hopefully, to Grigori and Dino, this would seem part of the overall plan.

"Greg, excuse me for a minute while I talk with Grigori," said Iggy. He took the Russian aside and said in a conspiratorial voice, "Let me have some time with these yahoos and get this deal cemented." He spoke just loud enough for the others to hear him. Grigori was not aware that the "double" vodka he had ordered earlier was actually a quadruple as part of the scam. His brain was too fuzzy to pick up on the ruse that Iggy was now running.

"If you're okay to drive, Joe and I will get a lift back home when we finish here with the guys, if that's okay. Hey, you Russians can handle your vodka, correct?"

"Your wodka like piss" slurred Ivanov. His national pride and masculinity were at stake to some degree and, as hoped by Iggy, he stormed away.

After the Lincoln left the parking lot, they all breathed a sigh of relief and ordered another round of beers. The two older men who were sitting in the booth on the opposite side of the room came over to the booth. Each of them carried a beer. The tallest guy, with a black beard and a dirty Calgary Stampeders ball cap spoke first. "Nice work, guys, I'm gonna nominate you all for an Oscar this year!" Then Hansen removed the fake beard and ball cap. Riley also removed a fake pair of glasses which were held together with a piece of gauze tape. He also took a ratty brown wig off his head.

"Well, Greg, I guess you and Danny have met detectives Hansen and Riley." They all clinked their bottles to a successful meeting.

"Okay, gentlemen, let's do some math," said Hansen. He reached under the booth and deftly extracted a device which he had affixed to the underside of the table before the arrival of the Russian with Iggy and Jake. He then plugged it into a small recorder, and they all listened to the conversation which had been outlined only minutes earlier.

"Hot damn!" exclaimed Riley. "Two kilos for the first score. That's excellent, Iggy!"

"What's the big deal?" asked Greg.

"Well, my friend, you buy this much coke at today's prices, it's gonna cost you five grand a kilo, so ten thousand dollars, right?"

"Yessir, a big outlay!"

"Yeah, but here's the amazing part; after it is stepped on, that is mixed with some flour, baby powder, or whatever, the product is increased by weight immensely whereby one kilogram becomes sixteen kilograms. So, your two kilograms are now thirty-two thousand grams. And in case you upstanding young men didn't know it, the street price of blow in Calgary today is fifty bucks a gram!"

"Holy crap!" yelled Jake. "One point six million." His banker's mind was quick with the numbers.

"Yeah, so you can see that not all of the proceeds from the sale of the drugs could go with your bank deposits. It would be too obvious to the bank and the authorities. So, a good portion of the money would be raked in by Dino and placed in various holding companies."

"But it would be our money. How can they just do that?" complained Danny.

"Come on, Danny, don't be so naïve," said Iggy. You're dealing with crooks here, not straight up businessmen. They'll do whatever the hell they want."

Then Hansen decided it was time to lay out his part of the scam. "Relax, boys. I know you were starting to see a way to make a quick retirement for yourselves, but that ain't gonna happen. Here's what we have in mind." And so, the "great sting" enfolded while they ate steaks.

Chapter Twenty-Two

Tuesday, July 20th

IGGY AND Jake were sitting in the apartment on Tuesday night, rehashing their role in the plot that Hansen and Riley had laid out to them on the weekend. According to Hansen, the money to finance the drug purchase was probably going to be handled by Dino or his superior, Vinnie Fellino. More likely the latter. It made sense. Iggy and Jake and the other two musicians were only going to be used as dealers and launderers.

They would soon find out, since the Russian had called them yesterday to tell them they were heading south first thing Wednesday morning. To Los Angeles, no less. They had repeated this to Hansen, and he was elated. Of course, as they figured, this squared with the main focus of the detectives' attention, which was to score an international bust, first and foremost.

But Iggy and Jake were still mainly thinking about how they might be able to gain some knowledge on what part Dino or Grigori had to play in Bug's death. They were positive there was a connection but short of directly confronting the killers, they had no real proof. It was extremely frustrating. Iggy suggested they should hit the sack, given it was going to be an early day tomorrow, and they would need all of their faculties. Jake was reading *The Calgary Herald* which he had folded and thrown on their sofa. As Iggy watched this, he saw Jake's eyes grow wide.

There on Page two of *The Herald* was a storyline that had captured Jake's attention.

Calgary Police Make Grisly Discovery in Northeast After-Hours Bar

Jake passed the newspaper to Iggy who read the article in horror as the full description of the mutilations and how they occurred was related with all the gory details. It was hinted the killings were a style of execution favored by mafia drug gangs as a way of sending a message to anyone in the business. Silence was broken only at an extreme cost.

His feelings of horror turned to anger when the story revealed the names of the two deceased victims and the expected time of death, which was sometime between three and five am on Sunday.

Both Iggy and Jake were totally pissed at the detectives. Why didn't they let them in on this information? There was no way they could not have been aware of the killings. But instead, they had lied to them and had implied that the crime scene they were called to earlier was in the Southwest, a separate homicide.

But how did this connect to their own investigation, if at all? Maybe it was some other bad characters that Joey and Frank had crossed, but there was no time to look into that now. They needed their rest and so they both crashed. What a mess they had managed to get into here. But perhaps things might finally come to a head tomorrow when they picked up their product.

Wednesday, July 21st

Dino and Grigori were on their way to pick up Jake and Iggy. Dino said to the Russian who was driving, "So, Grigori, everything has been handled?"

"Yes, Boss" Grigori replied. "I have called Lewis at the Calgary International Airport as you instructed. He is to pretend he is takink the Lear jet with two "look-likes" of the Maritimers to L.A. He was to file flight plan with tower in case the police check to confirm."

"Very good, my friend. That should keep them busy while we go on a different route. But just to be on the safe side, let's do a quick run by the apartment to make sure the police are not hanging around there, okay?"

Dino knew if he had Grigori mention to the boys that they were going to Los Angeles, they would tell this to the police. But in fact, they would be going to Whitefish, Montana, a popular ski resort where they planned on picking up their product then smuggling it back into Canada with the Lear. They had done this before and for the right price, their guy at the Vancouver International Airport would help. They had changed vehicles from Dino's Lincoln rental to a Jeep Cherokee, more befitting the trip to mountain country, and they had packed hunting and fishing gear to satisfy any curious border patrol people.

A drive past the apartment indicated nothing amiss, so Grigori turned around and came back to the Bug's at six forty-five. Grigori went to the door and was quickly let inside by "Dave Kennedy" who yelled out, "Hey, Joe, Grigori is here. Let's get moving."

When Grigori saw that the boys were wearing T shirts and cut-off denim shorts, he told them to change into regular jeans and hiking boots and to bring a couple of heavier shirts. Change of plans. Not going to LA but Montana.

Shit! thought Iggy. *Now what?* Hansen and Riley were expecting them at the airport anytime soon. Iggy had even remembered to copy the tail number of the Lear for easy identification, and he had given this to Hansen. When they were leaving the apartment, the Russian turned to Iggy as they passed by the picture of the Bug in the hallway and gave him one of his "Fuck You" smiles. *So, this was it, the gloves are off,* thought Iggy. The first chance they got, Iggy and Jake were going to have to look for a way out. But if it came down to it, they both knew they were prepared to do whatever was necessary to protect themselves.

The Jeep took them south from the City on Highway 2 through the two communities of Okotoks and High River, then all the way to the border town of Carway. It wasn't much to see. Just one building with officers on either side. The right lane looked after Canadians going south and, on the left, U.S. traffic was processed as people came into Canada. After showing their IDs along with their passports and a quick explanation about where they were going *trout fishing in Whitefish, we should only be there a few days,* and they were on their way again.

Jake could now see why they called this Big Sky Country. Far ahead of them, they saw the mountains, but other than a huge expanse of azure, spotted here and there with fluffy cirrus clouds, that was it. Not the same majesty as The Rockies, thought Jake, but still very awesome. High mesa type vertical formations in various sizes provided an irregular tabletop mosaic not seen in the Canadian Rockies. And rather than the blue slate coloring they were familiar with from Alberta and B.C., here there were varying shades of brown, red and orange.

They drove south on U.S. 89 to Browning where they hooked up with U.S. 2. They then continued southwest to a small town called Singleshot, where they turned almost in a horseshoe northwest to Pinnacle, then due west on to West Glazier. The country in which they were now driving was more mountainous. Finally, Jake saw a highway sign that read Whitefish 2 miles.

It was going on two in the afternoon when they entered the ski resort town. Since they were all hungry, they decided to go to the hotel, check in, and get something to eat. The boys were impressed with their rooms at the Grouse Mountain Lodge. The hotel had a heated pool, access to canoes on the lake, which was only a five-minute walk away, and a huge buffet offering anything you could think of in the way of food. Dino then told them they were going to eat at a bar called Sam's in downtown Whitefish. It was there that they were expecting to meet up with a "mule" who would be bringing their product to them. The boys were told to keep their mouths shut and to lose their attitude.

That was fine with Iggy and Jake. They were hoping to go along with their ruse as long as they could until Hansen and Riley showed up. They had to get word to them, but how could they with Dino and the Russian hanging to them like dirt on a blanket.

Sam's looked nothing like the lodge where they were staying, but the boys knew this joint would kick ass come ten or so tonight. The building itself was a simple one-story rectangular construction built of old barn boards. Inside the building, the bar followed the same style of structure. It was made of sturdy oak and was lacquered so many times over the years that it now carried the color of ten-year-old bourbon. It bore the ravages of time as well, including cigarette burns and the odd knife markings of some long-forgotten love vows. Placed around the bar there were bowls of roasted peanuts-in-the-shell to which the patrons were busy helping themselves. The bar was three quarters full, and everyone was cracking open the salted goodies and tossing the empty shells behind them on the floor, all the while steadily drinking Coors and Buds, their thirsts driven by the salted nuts. The entire floor of the bar was a mess and now and then a couple of cute waitresses would come out with brooms and buckets and clean up the boards.

Behind the bar, two very talented barkeeps kept pace with the busy drinkers. The guys were amazing, able to toss quart bottles of whiskey, rum, or whatever was required, back and forth to each other within the bar area. They flipped them end over end in the air, even juggling two or three bottles at a time prior to mixing shots and going on to the next customer. Very cool. Every now and then an appreciative crowd of young drinkers would give them a hand. Iggy and Jake knew these guys would be a huge hit and make a fortune in tips at any bar back home.

Since they had nothing better to do, the boys decided to get closer to the action at the bar, telling Dino they'd stay within sight of the table if they were needed. Jake felt Dino was still taken by the two of them and that he was willing to trust them to a certain extent. The Russian however was another matter altogether and they were going to have to do something to somehow take him out of the picture.

As they began making small talk with the bartender, Roscoe, about the local scene, an idea came to Iggy. Jake had asked Roscoe where they might be able to score some pot, and they were informed that wouldn't be a problem.

"In fact," said Roscoe, "if you guys are into something a little more exciting, say some acid, that could be arranged," he added, eyebrows raised. Iggy thought for a minute then called Roscoe over, whispered something to him, and gave him a twenty. Incredibly, two minutes later a couple of small red tablets wrapped in tinfoil soon appeared beside the next two Coors Roscoe had placed before them. Iggy quickly shoved the tabs in his pocket.

Chapter Twenty-Three

Wednesday, July 21st, 2:15 pm

WHILE THE four had been driving to Sam's, Detectives Hansen and Riley were becoming extremely frustrated. They were sitting in their 1967 Chevy Impala just outside Private Gate 5 at the Calgary International Airport, closely watching the pale blue Lear jet with tail number PNB 5069.

They had been staking out the plane since noon. At one time they saw a pilot entering the craft with two males dressed in Tee Shirts and cut-offs. While they didn't get a close look at the guys, they assumed they were Iggy and Jake. And there they sat for the next two hours.

Finally, just after two, the jet taxied out to the runway and was soon heading south to L.A. Seeing this, the detectives then went into the terminal and contacted the control tower where they confirmed the Lear Jet with tail number PNB 5069 was indeed on its way to Los Angeles. *All right!* thought Hansen and gave a fist pump to the air as he went to the closest pay phone and called his contact with the LAPD. Things were about to happen. It was going on four in the afternoon when he dropped Riley off at the precinct downtown and he went home to his small flat in Buona Vista Downs Southeast. He was only there a few minutes when the phone rang. It was Detective Fernandez from the Los Angeles Police Department, Drugs and Vice Section.

"Yeah, Hansen, I think you got taken, man. Simply no sign of your party at our end. The flight plan had been entered as you said, but it was cancelled one hour after takeoff."

"Fuck!" said Hansen. "Okay, detective, I appreciate your help anyway. We'll take it from here and keep in touch. Our guys are definitely in jeopardy out there somewhere and all we can do at this point is wait in the hopes that somehow, they can contact us."

5:30 pm

Well, in one sense Detective Hansen was correct in his earlier assessment of the situation. Things were about to happen all right, just not in the manner he was hoping and expecting. That morning it had been pre-arranged by Grigori that Lewis, Dino's pilot, was to call Dino at the lodge when he arrived back at Calgary International Airport following his faked flight to Los Angeles. Prior to leaving for Sam's bar, Dino had spoken with Lewis and confirmed the detectives had been duped into thinking everyone was now in LA, so Dino then instructed his pilot to fly the Lear to Glacier Park International Airport, only a ten-minute drive from where they were. It was his intent to pick up their dope as soon as their mule arrived with it, then hustle back to Vancouver and meet up there with Vinnie.

Dino and Grigori were now at Sam's awaiting the arrival of their carrier, one Carlos Milago, and he was late. Dino was not amused as he again checked the briefcase lying beside his right leg under their table. The case contained ten thousand dollars in used bills, mostly fifties and twenties, all U.S. currency.

The deal called for Iggy to "test" the product to ensure they were purchasing top grade coke, and this was to take place in their suite back at the lodge. Iggy and Hansen had arrived at this part of the scam together. When Iggy said he was going to need to be convincing in his role, Hansen agreed to provide him with a kit that was used by the police to grade the quality of cocaine that had been seized. He had this now in his backpack and he was ready to play the role.

At approximately five o'clock, two sketchy looking individuals approached their table. The taller of the two was a dark-skinned Latino who wore faded jeans, a white tee shirt and black leather Wellington boots. He carried a tan-colored expensive looking leather briefcase, and he was the image of Terry Malloy from *On the Waterfront*, except for the vivid scar which ran the full length of his left cheek. His partner was a short, stocky older man, probably in his mid-forties with grayish greasy hair which he wore in a long ponytail. This guy was probably the tough one of the two, thought Iggy, and he stored these thoughts away for future reference if and when he might need them.

"Ah, Carlos, you finally made it. I was beginning to become concerned for your wellbeing," said Dino to the Latino as he rose to greet the two carriers.

"Yeah, well we ran into a snag coming in on number 5 just outside Sacramento. Huge pile up on the highway and it was closed for two hours. What a pain in the ass, man! Say, this is Dennis," indicating his partner. "Where you wanna do this?" he asked, cutting right to the nut.

"We'll go back to my suite at the lodge. By the way, this is my helper, Grigori, and these two boys are new to our team. They are from New Brunswick, Canada." With that, Dino settled the bill, and they made their way back to the lodge.

When they were settled in Dino's suite, Dino said to Iggy, "David, please be so kind as to let us know what you think of this product." While Iggy went to his backpack to retrieve the kit that Hansen had loaned him, he heard Carlos say, "What the fuck is this? You think Al is gonna rip you off or something? Besides, what would this yahoo from New Broomstick know about anything?"

"Carlos, please be cool. Simply good business, you know how it works, yes?"

"Yeah, yeah, just do it, man," he grumbled. Iggy appeared and took out a glass ampoule that contained a clear liquid along with a paper chart on which there were six horizontal blocks ranging in color from pure white to dark maroon. He broke the top off the ampoule then, gesturing toward the briefcase that Carlos was holding, he held out his palm.

Carlos opened the tan case in which two large plastic bags, each containing a white powder-like substance, were revealed beside a set of silver miniature weight scales.

Iggy chose one of the bags at random and took a small paring knife from the kitchen drawer. He made a small incision in the bag and dipped the knife tip into it. He then let a small amount of the powder fall into the top of the ampoule which he vigorously shook so the liquid and powder mixed together. In a minute, the solution turned a deep reddish maroon color and he smiled. Placing the paper color chart against the ampoule he simply stated, "Not bad. About 90% grade. You're cool, Mr. Martini."

Carlos quickly rifled through the bills passed to him by Dino and the deal was solid. At that point Carlos and Dennis prepared to leave. Dino took Carlos aside and gave him the keys to his rental Jeep and they were gone. It was arranged that Dennis would drive the Jeep to the closest Avis shop nearest Highway 2 and drop it off on behalf of Dino who was returning on the Lear to Vancouver.

Jake, then acting as Joe Peterson, told Dino that by stepping on it, he should be able to get around sixteen times more volume for street sale. A total of thirty-two thousand grams for the two kilos at fifty bucks retail per gram.

"Do the math," said Jake. "One. Point. Six." At that point "David" and "Joe" became an actual part of the team. Iggy and Jake felt both relieved and horrified.

"Nice work boys," said Dino. "From here we go to Vancouver, and you will meet my associate, Mr. Fellino."

"We'd be honored, sir." replied Iggy. *Christ*, he thought. *What did we just get ourselves into?*

Chapter Twenty-Four

7:00 pm

IGGY AND JAKE were on an adrenaline high after the deal was made and the two carriers, Carlos and Dennis, were on their way back to LA with the ten grand in cash for their boss, Al Gabrazzi. The complete process was totally unnerving. Neither of them had ever had any experience with hard drugs before. Sure, Hansen had provided some coaching before they left Calgary, but still...man they needed a beer now badly. They just wanted to chill out and Sam's seemed like the best spot to give them what they needed.

But more than a couple of beers, what they really needed was to make a quick call and bring Hansen up to date on their endeavors. They begged off for a couple of hours of relaxation at the bar. Apparently, Dino felt they could be trusted but still, he insisted they take the Russian with them, just to keep them company. It was mid-week, early in the evening, so not much was happening at this time when they arrived at the bar. It was getting on nine pm when three guys came on the stage and started tuning up. They were the house band; a rock cover group called The Jets.

Jake loved their sound from the outset. They were very efficient, being only three guys: bass, drums, and guitar. They had a huge sound, utilizing all the latest in accessories such as "wah wah" pedals, distortion or "fuzz" box add-ons, and a kick-ass speaker system. They were using homemade custom bins which Jake suspected held twelve-inch Bose units. Awesome! And even better, the first song they laid out was the two-in-one 1970 full edition of *I'm Your Captain (Closer to Home)* by Grand Funk Railroad.

For the rest of the set Jake and Iggy were in heaven. They could not get over how good this group was, and they simply had to tell them in person.

90

Grigori could not have cared less. He was sipping on a vodka and when he got up to take a leak at the end of the set, Iggy felt it was time. Without giving it another thought, he carefully nudged Jake, showed him the two tabs of LSD he took from his shirt pocket and quickly dropped one of them into the Russian's drink. Then they followed the members from The Jets as they made their way to the bar for a beer break.

"Man, I gotta say, that GFR tune was simply awesome. You guys sound great." said Iggy.

"Thanks," replied their lead singer and guitarist. "Glad you liked it."

"You boys local?" asked Jake.

"Nope, came here last week from Calgary. Awesome bar, dudes. You guys know how to party down here."

"Whoa, man. Unreal. But we're visiting from Calgary ourselves." He looked hard at Iggy for a beat and somehow was able to mentally confirm something with him. His decision made, he went on with his conversation with their new-found musician friends.

"You won't believe what we've gotten ourselves into down here," said Jake. "Seriously, you would be doing my bud and I a real solid if you would let us buy you boys a beer and expound on that for a couple of minutes." The three Jets looked at each other then made room for their new friends and intros were made all around. Donnie, Jared, and Brad. The three were from Grand Prairie, a small city in northern Alberta.

Jake and Iggy then told their story to the three spell-bound fellow musicians from Canada, all the while checking their table to see when Grigori was going to return. They spent the next ten minutes with the guys at the bar modestly telling them how they were just a couple of musicians from Saint John N.B. looking to get into a rock group, blah, blah, blah. It's amazing, thought Iggy, how easy it was to meet and get along with fellow rockers. At that point, they saw the Russian angrily gesturing to them to get their asses back to the table. On the way back, they smiled at the Russian as he took a big gulp of his vodka.

When they had finished telling their wild tale to The Jets, Iggy had formulated a plan which he first wanted to share with Jake before presenting it to Hansen and Riley. He now looked carefully at the Russian.

"Hey, how are ya doin'?" asked Iggy. "Can I get you another vodka?"

"Ya. But just a double. I drive." Iggy wasn't sure what he was supposed to be looking for in the way of reactions from the LSD taking effect on a person. But very soon it was becoming obvious something was happening in the Russian's mind when Iggy looked again and noticed Grigori staring intently at the center display of flowers on the table. Iggy went to the bar and when he came back with the vodka drink, Grigori looked at it as if it were a foreign substance or maybe some new discovery. *He is out of it*, thought Iggy.

Leaving the Russian who was sitting by himself, muttering and looking around the bar in amazement, they discussed their plans. Iggy then found a pay phone and called Hansen.

By the time he got off the phone and they were both back to the table, Grigori was totally out of it. The boys were able to simply ignore him.

"Everything's set up," said Iggy. "When Hansen first came on the line, he started giving me shit about not contacting him. I quickly told him, 'Yeah, like you were so up front with us about Joey and Frank and their little mishap at The Body Shop. That shut him up a tad."

Just then The Jets came back on stage. "Hey, we're back!" said Donnie, lead vocalist and guitarist. "We've got a little treat for y'all. Since it's only Wednesday, we thought a small break in our routine might be in order. There are a couple of fellow Canucks here tonight and we think you'll wanna hear them do some CCR cover work with us. Y'all okay with that?" A loud applause from the crowd and Jake knew this was going to be a very cool night.

The boys hopped to the stage and Donnie gave Iggy his spare guitar, a Gibson Les Paul Standard. Jared, the group's bassist loaned his Fender Precision to Jake while he grabbed a tambourine off the front of Brad's drum kit. As Iggy plugged the Les Paul into an Ampeg speaker box, he grinned at Donnie and asked, "Okay if we do this one in G boys?" and on a four count they slid easily into "Who'll Stop the Rain". Then on with "Bad Moon on The Rise," "Born on The Bayou," and finally "Fortunate Son."

After a huge round of applause, Iggy and Jake reluctantly left the stage and returned to their table. With all of the bar crowd following their every move, Grigori was in a total state of paranoia as they tried to move him out of the bar. For a moment, the boys thought they might need to call an ambulance, but for some reason the Russian suddenly became lucid, and he asked them where they were going. "Home," said Iggy. Then he said, again in a very good John Wayne accent, "Life is tough, Grigori, but it's tougher if you're stupid." He looked at his buddy Jake and said, "Sands of Iwo Jima," 1949, and winked. Grigori just stared blankly at Iggy.

By the time they got back to the lodge, Grigori was still somewhat fucked up. He couldn't explain to Dino what was wrong but clearly the Mafioso boss was becoming concerned with the Russian's inability to hold his vodka. Jake mentioned he had, maybe, three drinks at the bar, but wasn't sure. Dino shook his head, more in embarrassment for Grigori than anything else.

11:45 pm

When Hansen got off the phone after speaking with Iggy, he immediately called Riley. He explained what he had just learned from Iggy and where things were headed. These guys kept surprising them with their tenacity and wherewithal. It was amazing they were still alive let alone setting up what could turn out to be the drug bust of the century. He outlined his plan to Riley and then called his colleague in the LAPD to keep him current on this extremely liquid operation.

Next on Hansen's agenda, he had to make flight arrangements for himself and Riley on the earliest possible trip to Vancouver tomorrow. This turned out to be Flight 440, an 11:04 am Air Canada flight that would arrive in Vancouver in just over one and one-half hours. So, make it 11:39 am PST after the change in time zones.

Chapter Twenty-Five

IGGY WAS the first to rise the next morning, and he quickly snuck into the fridge and made a vodka and orange juice drink for Grigori. It was what he called a morning "picker upper" after the Russian's hard night. Unknown to the Russian, he had also slipped in a little extra punch in the form of the remaining tab of acid he had saved from the previous night.

Dino was the next to come into the kitchen and he was in good spirits, mainly due to the confidence and street creds shown by the young musicians last night. He was certain his uncle Vinnie would approve of his new addition to the team. The boys were young and full of energy. They had that attitude of today's youth and showed a lot of *intelligenti.*

Smiling at Iggy, Dino called Lewis on the Lear's phone and told him to prep the jet for takeoff. They would be at the small airport within the hour.

Shit! Iggy was not expecting to be leaving so soon. Yesterday, when Dino told them they would be flying to Vancouver today, for some reason Iggy was thinking it would be at least one, maybe two pm before they landed there, and this was the info he passed on to Hansen. Damn, it seemed every time they thought they had a plan that might get them out of this mess, something happened, or they overlooked some small detail that could prove deadly.

Whatever, it was too late to do anything about it now. The boys would have to play the cards they had been dealt. To date, they had managed to get through it alive. But would their luck hold out?

Grigori then entered the kitchen looking very hung-over, strung out, and not quite with it. "Good morning, my Russian friend." exclaimed Iggy. He handed him the glass of vodka and OJ with that little extra kick. "This'll get you back in shape," he said.

The Russian scowled stupidly at Iggy and obediently downed the cocktail, shouting, "*Nostrovia!*"

The flight from Whitefish, Montana to Vancouver, B.C. would take approximately four and one quarter hours. When they deducted the one-hour time zone lag, that would mean they would arrive in Vancouver around 11:45 am PST.

Neither team was aware of how close together their arrival times were going to be, assuming flying conditions and departure times were the same on each end. This should be an interesting flight, thought Iggy, as they packed their gear together and made ready to leave for the airport outside Whitefish. He was keeping a close eye on the Russian, wondering how he was going to react on the plane.

They drove past Sam's bar on the way. The two boys gazed at the building which housed some of the best moments of their brief lives so far. The short time spent with The Jets was way beyond anything they had experienced musically, and they were hooked. This was definitely the lifestyle they craved, and from this point onward, their focus would be on establishing just that...a good manager, a popular venue from which to build a base of followers, and most of all, their own playlist. The ultimate goal, of course, was to obtain a record label willing to take them on. *Was it all dream work?* thought Jake, as they neared the airport.

One thing was certain, even with the dangers surrounding them. They were going to make sure they obeyed Rule number 2 in The Plan: Enjoy the Ride.

Chapter Twenty-Six

Thursday, July 22nd
10:55 am

AT TEN thirty, the Lear touched down at Vancouver International Airport and they were greeted by the usual drizzle that seemed to be an everyday occurrence in this part of the country. When the weather in Vancouver was discussed, everybody always said "Yeah, it rains a lot here, but you get used to it." That was the summer seasonal response. The winter version was, "Yeah, we get a lot of rain, but you don't have to shovel it."

Bullshit. This weather sucks, thought Jake as he ran across the tarmac in the now pouring rain to a nearby hanger. Iggy had his backpack on with the .45 handgun in it. They had just committed a crime of smuggling arms from the U.S. into Canada, and nobody seemed to give a shit. Not to mention the two kilos of high-grade cocaine that Dino had somehow managed to bring with them into the country. Jake was sure Dino had someone on the inside working in Canadian Customs which would be another job for Hansen and Riley to figure out.

At the moment, their main concern was keeping abreast of how things were going to enfold once Martini met up with them at this hangar. Dino had directed them here and they were told to grab a coffee and relax until he returned. So here they were sitting in a grungy office sipping on lukewarm coffees which tasted like dishwater.

"Where did the Russian get to?" asked Jake.

"That boy is baked." said Iggy. "The last I saw, he was tagging along after Martini like a lost little boy while Dino went with Lewis, the pilot, to declare anything of interest at Canadian customs." This was a crucial part of the game in which Jake had hoped to be able to get involved.

"Yeah, as if," replied Jake sarcastically. "It would be cool to be a fly on the wall of that customs office," he continued. "Hansen would really like to be able to arrest whoever's being paid by Martini in aiding his scheme here."

"You know it, man," said Iggy. Just then, they were interrupted by the Russian as he came wandering into the building. He was carrying his suitcase in front of him with both of his arms extended, like the bag was some kind of sacred covenant. He had a terrified look on his face and approached the two boys.

"You must keep this hidden from them," said Ivanov. "It is a very dangerous thing!"

"What is it?" asked Iggy, feigning seriousness.

"A bomb," Grigori said, in a reverent tone. "It is set to detonate at the least provocation. Where is Mr. Dino?" he asked the boys in a quavering voice. Jake thought the Russian was about to start sobbing.

"Here, let me take the bomb for you," said Iggy. "I'll be very careful." Then he tossed the old suitcase haphazardly into the office and went looking for Dino, leaving the LSD depraved Russian in Jake's hands. Jake started to object but decided he better just go along with Iggy's decision, given the state of mind the Russian was in.

As he stepped out the side door of the hangar, Iggy spotted a familiar figure slipping behind a cartload of luggage. The man lifted his head when he saw Iggy and sure enough it was Hansen, dressed in a brown leather bomber jacket. A black watch cap covered his head, and a pair of faded jeans completed the warehouse look he was attempting to convey.

Iggy motioned to Hansen to have him follow behind as he led him across a deserted alleyway to a spot that was protected from the wet weather and other eyes.

"We just flew in from Calgary," whispered Hansen. "Riley is tailing Martini at customs as we speak. We can probably make a case right now and make it stick."

"That may be so," said Iggy, "but Dino mentioned to us on the way here from Whitefish that we'd be meeting his "cook" after landing in Vancouver. I think we're about to make a run to some backwoods joint where they probably step on their coke and prep it for the street. Wouldn't it make sense to break up that part of the operation while we're at it? Also, you can then get credit for a much larger bust in terms of straight dollar value, no?

"And another thing. Dino told us earlier that we were going to get to meet his uncle, Vinito "Vinnie" Fellino. I figured you'd want a shot at this dude. So, there you have it." Iggy was making a play to Hansen's ego, and he knew it was working. The problem was every new twist to the scheme was an added danger to them.

Hansen listened closely to the suggestion Iggy had just made and, of course, it made perfect sense. The bigger bust, the better.

"What the hell!" exclaimed the hardened detective. "We're into it this far, why not go for the gold? We'll wait and grab the whole lot of them. The cutting farm employees, the customs worker, the pilot, Dino Martini and the Russian, and most importantly, Vinnie Fellino."

"Okay, your call," said Iggy. "Jake's babysitting our Russian friend. It's a long story. Right now, he's a puppy."

"Okay," said Hansen. "Me and Riley will tail you guys to wherever you're going to doctor the dope. Depending on what happens at that scene, we may or may not make the bust there. We'll play this by the book and make sure you guys are protected."

Iggy took this to mean that both he and Jake, aka David and Joe, would be arrested as part of the sting, and it would probably be easier to maintain their cover when they were back in Calgary. Hansen then gave Iggy a fist bump and he crept back behind the luggage cart to await Dino with presumably Riley close behind him. Iggy returned to the hangar where Jake was playing crazy eights with the Russian.

"Man, he keeps trying to cheat. Given his state of mind, you'd think he'd be incapable of that," said Jake, giving the Russian the snake-eye.

"It's hard-wired into his psyche" explained Iggy. "He could no more play fair at anything than he could refuse a drink of vodka."

After several hands of bad cards, Jake decided he had enough. Besides, the Russian was starting to get somewhat straight, and they had to come up with a plan. *Would he remember what he had been through?* Jake wondered. If not, they would have to simply return to their earlier subservient behaviors and see how it went.

It was too late to dwell on the matter because right at that point, Dino and his pilot entered the office. They each wore big smiles and Dino carried his briefcase with its valuable stash.

They decided to celebrate their re-entry to Canada with a nice meal, so they prepared to head downtown to the English Bay area. Miraculously, it had stopped raining, and everyone was happy as they piled into the rented Lincoln limo. Lewis stowed away the suitcases for Dino and Grigori in the over-sized trunk and left them to return to the Lear. The boys kept their backpacks with them in the rear seats of the Lincoln.

When Lewis had thrown Grigori's suitcase into the trunk, Jake watched the Russian's actions with interest, wondering how Grigori was going to react to the careless handling of the "bomb," But Grigori didn't seem to care one way or the other how his suitcase was being handled and this gave Jake concern, since it looked like he was becoming clear minded once again.

His fears were soon set aside however, when he realized Grigori's focus was now centered on his driving. Jake could imagine the Russian would probably start having flashbacks from the hallucinogenic drug that had been screwing up his head for the past day and a half.

So, Iggy figured Grigori should be fairly easy to handle for the next while, at least as long as he was driving. It wasn't difficult to imagine this guy was responsible for the death of their friend. It was harder to understand how he and Jake were capable of maintaining a working relationship with this monster. What was this saying about their own states of mind? Were they becoming hardened criminals themselves? These questions plagued Iggy's mind as they drove to the downtown core, and he vowed to bring all of this low life to justice.

Chapter Twenty-Seven

2:47 pm

THE DINNER was fabulous. They ate at El Grotto, an Italian restaurant overlooking English Bay, downtown Vancouver. Jake dined on plank salmon, sautéed potato wedges sprinkled with sprigs of parsley, carrots julienne and creamy asparagus. Iggy, of course, insisted on having lobster. The Russian stuck with his usual; a ten-ounce sirloin, rare. Nino, who knew the waiter, ordered a seafood fettuccine alfredo. When they finished, they walked down to the marina and admired the bay full of expensive yachts.

Dino advised they were to meet with a man who was responsible for cutting their product. He told them this was an extremely dangerous part of the operation. Where they were going, they would be able to see how the coke was treated with relatively benign products such as sugar, flour, or cornstarch. Sometimes, dangerous chemical additives, such as caffeine, laxatives, or even kerosene were used. By "cutting" the relatively pure cocaine with these additives, the product quality was lessened, but the volume of the drug was increased many times over, hence, the more valuable it became to Dino.

Also, he told the boys, his chemical chef might add very dangerous substitutes to the product after it had been stepped on. This might be done to maintain a similar reaction for the user as the higher-grade cocaine, but the subs were usually low-cost opioid products such as Procaine, Lidocaine, or Fentanyl; all highly addictive and often fatal.

"This is not a gentleman's league." he stressed. "We must be extremely careful with whom we deal." Suddenly, the boys felt sick to their stomachs. This was a part of the operation they had not expected to see, and it bothered them greatly that they could be held responsible for being

100

complicit in such a deadly activity. Should they not be successful in busting this operation, they would feel the guilt of their actions today for the rest of their lives. With that in mind, they again silently vowed to each other that they would do everything possible to get these guys behind bars. It was going to be a long day.

Dino told them all this information as they drove first in a south easterly route on the TCH to Abbotsford, then more northerly to the city of Chilliwack. Outside of Chilliwack, they followed a one lane road that soon turned to gravel. Before long, they were in a fully forested area that appeared extremely remote. There were no telephone poles, and no buildings were seen for the next five miles. The gravel road had become no more than a logging road, rutted badly from the earlier heavy rains that spring. The further into the woods they drove, the denser the forest became. Just when the boys were certain Grigori had taken an incorrect turn somewhere, they drove into a large, cleared area that contained two big wooden shed-like structures.

From one of the buildings, a chimney emitted a foul smelling, white colored smoke. One of two doors to the building opened and a man wearing a black leather apron over denim overalls and a red plaid shirt came out to meet them. He was probably in his mid-forties with bright blue eyes and a glistening black beard. What little hair he had was greasy and covered by an old green and white John Deere ball cap.

"Ciao, Roberto," said Dino. "Come, meet some new friends." Introductions were made to the boys, then "David" and "Joe" were given a tour of the cutting plant by Dino's chemist. It was quite impressive, given the operation was very basic in needs with very little overhead and was run by only Roberto and his wife. The smaller building to the right of this one served as living quarters for the chemist and his wife, Gina, whom they met soon after the tour. There were also several extra bedrooms in the side building along with a common kitchen and large meeting room which all in all could be used to entertain guests, as was the case tonight.

It was now going on nine pm, and it was beginning to get dark outside. Iggy and Jake kept a wary eye out for movements of any kind, half expecting the detectives to jump out of the trees like gangbusters and place them all under arrest. It was very tense.

Jake was glad when Roberto came into the great room with Gina and offered everyone drinks. The tension in the room decreased substantially after the second round and Iggy was pleased to see the Russian had once more gone back to drinking double vodkas. Too bad he had used both hits of acid to keep the asshole in line. Oh well, at least Grigori was intent on drinking himself into his normal drunken state. The boys, if need be, could use that to their advantage.

Around eleven fifteen, Jake decided to take a walk outside, "To get some fresh air." The night was pungent with the smell of pine resin. This far from any neighboring towns or cities gave the night sky a spectacular light show. Jake looked at the heavens in awe. Every now and then, a meteor would race across the horizon and Jake was tempted to make a wish. *If only it were that easy,* he mused. Just then he heard a soft snap behind him, and he saw Hansen emerge from the edge of the clearing.

"Nice night," the detective said in a low voice. "Everything going to plan?"

"I would say," said Jake. "The cutting process has been done and everyone's chilling out for the evening. Supposedly, we are going to meet with "The Man" tomorrow. Is Detective Riley with you?"

"Yep. He's in our cruiser. We can maintain radio contact with the precinct that way. Captain wants us to bring the whole thing to a conclusion ASAP. By the way, he's not happy that you guys are part of the operation, as you can guess, but given where we're at in the operation, it was felt we could continue the sting so long as we were able to keep a close eye on you and Iggy. What's it feel like to be a star?"

Jake could almost taste the envy coming off Hansen, like some bad body odor. "Relax, detective. We're not in this for any glory," said Jake. "We said straight up we wanted to help and so far, we've managed to keep safe. You and Riley will get all the credit and don't worry, you won't get into any trouble with your boss, at least not because of us." He secretly enjoyed adding the last part of his statement as a qualifier.

"You're right, of course," said Hansen. "My apologies. Sometimes this job gets to me. Another three years and I'll have my twenty, then it'll be *sayonara, baby!* And Jake, we do appreciate what you guys are doing here. It takes guts, man, to take something like this on. After it's all over, let's talk about what's in your future. Seems to me you two almost have a calling for the force."

Jake couldn't help it. In his best John Wayne drawl, he evoked a line by his hero from a 1965 flick, *In Harm's Way*: "Well, Hansen, all battles are fought by scared men who'd rather be somewhere else."

He bid goodnight to Hansen and returned to the guest house. The group were now into their third drinks, but he noted Iggy was nursing the same beer he had started earlier.

"Well, gentlemen, it's been a long day so I'm hitting the sack," said Jake. Dino, half drunk, grunted goodnight.

"Yo, Dave, I'm right behind ya," said Iggy. *Good job. Iggy is sober*, thought Jake. *I keep forgetting to use our pseudonyms.*

He walked slowly past the Russian who was loafing sullenly on a lazy boy chair. As he walked by, Grigori looked up at him and mockingly said, "Need to get your beauty sleep, 'ay Canuck?"

He had a mean look in his eye and Jake could tell he was dying to egg him into a fight. There would be lots of time for that, Jake assumed. A quick look at Iggy, who gave him an undetected head shake, confirmed he was doing the right thing by actually doing nothing.

The boys knew the Russian was pissed at something. Whether it was because he had further suspicions as to their real identity, or if he was perhaps jealous of how his employer had taken to them, they were unsure. Another day, another night.

Chapter Twenty-Eight

July 23, 9:15 am

THERE WAS little conversation the next morning. The Russian was again pissed off about something and Dino had to keep placating his aide to avoid a deterioration in his mood. Iggy wondered how long Martini would put up with this asshole. The boys thought the Russian must have some kind of ace in his back pocket to keep testing his employer the way he did. Not their problem yet, though, so they ignored Grigori as much as they could.

When they were packing up to leave, Roberto came into the room carrying two large sports bags, similar to the Adidas bag that Iggy took with him when they went to the gym in Saint John. Alberto opened the bags and placed them if front of Iggy and Jake for their inspection. *Well, well,* thought Jake. *Now we are going to get some respect.*

"Hand me the grader and charts, Joe," said Iggy. Jake took the apparatus from Iggy's backpack, mindful to keep the .45 hidden from view, and passed the dope kit to Iggy. Iggy then picked two plastic wrapped packages at random, one from each Adidas bag. There were now sixteen parcels in each sports bag, individually wrapped in one kilo plastic packs. The boys were still amazed at the illegal money that was generated by these guys. And this was just a "trial" run to convince Dino he had made the right move in taking on the Canucks! Looking at Roberto, Iggy said, "Nothing personal, my friend," as he stuck his small knife in the first kilo package. Dipping a small amount of the white powder into a glassine ampoule, and then shaking it well, he watched as the clear liquid turned a dull orange. "There we go," he said. "52.8 percent. Roberto, tell me you hit this with some decent subs. The homies will want some bite in it 'kay?"

"Yes sir," said Roberto. "I..."

Iggy cut him off. "Don't gotta know the details man. As long as it

104

will get the job done, know what I mean?" He then repeated the same procedure with the other random sample he had removed from the other sports bags. As expected, that package returned a rating of 51.5%.

To complete the sham, Jake took out the mini scales and weighed a couple of other bags at random to verify weight, and they scored well on the scales. The boys looked at Dino and told him they were good to go. Now it was a matter of getting back to Vancouver and meeting up with the head dude, Fellino. Then the big bust. The sting was finally coming to an end, and it wouldn't be too soon as far as the boys were concerned.

The drive back to Vancouver was relatively uneventful. On the way, they stopped in Chilliwack for lunch and a gas refill. Dino made a call on a pay phone, presumably to his uncle Vinnie, before they left the gas stop, while Jake anxiously scanned the traffic coming and going on the highway. They had seen no sign of the detectives since leaving the cutting farm.

When Dino returned to the vehicle, he was in an extremely good mood. The Russian, as usual, was sullen, and they continued their drive with their own thoughts. After a while, Dino interrupted the moment by saying, "Dave, who did you say the pub was owned by?"

Shit! This caught Iggy totally by surprise. He groped in his memory to recall what he had told Dino from when they first met, which seemed ages ago.

"I didn't, Mr. Martini. Far as I know, the business is owned by my friends, Greg and Danny from back East. We can check that out when we get back." Iggy thought they may as well play it casual for now. Hopefully, Dino was asking this on a whim, and not at the suggestion of his uncle.

Now and then, Jake checked the side mirrors for any sign of Hansen and Riley but there was nothing to be seen. If they could have been hiding in a tree back at the farm when they left, they would have seen the detectives pulling out of a pile of bushes which served as a camouflaged makeshift hide-out for them. They were cautiously following the Lincoln and they were obviously good at this part of the job.

Now, maintaining a speed of seventy miles per hour as they tailed their quarry, Hansen was relating his little meeting with Jake last night.

"These guys crack me up!" said Hansen. "I mean, come on. Here we are in a life and death drug roust and these boys are actually having fun, quoting lines from old John Wayne movies. I tell ya Riley, there's a place for them in our training academy, for my money," he added.

The plan from here was to stay with the Lincoln until they met up with Vinnie, then check in with their Captain. It looked like they would be able to nail these bad guys for some serious prison time, but first they'd probably have to get them for actual trafficking. This would mean another mini sting at the Maritime Pub, where Hansen presumed was where this would all end up. He didn't see where that would pose a problem.

"Hopefully, these mopes haven't yet checked out the ownership title to the Maritime Pub," Riley said. "I mean, if the regular owner is back from Toronto and he's approached by them, what will that do to our bust?"

"Well, so long as they haven't done that yet, we should be okay," said Hansen. He just had a thought. "In fact, why don't you give a shout out to Cap right now on the radio and get him to contact the owner. Have him explain what we've done to date and how we're going to need his cooperation for a tad longer." It was a good move and Hansen could feel everything starting to come together for them. "Man, how sweet it is," he murmured to himself.

The drive northwest through the lower mainland of B.C. continued. By four-twenty they were in North Surrey, then they drove past Burnaby and eventually down to the Grand Villa Casino. At close to five they parked their cruiser on a side street down from the casino as they watched the four men get out of the Lincoln and walk to the entrance. A valet service took care of the Lincoln while Hansen and Riley followed the men at a safe distance as they approached an elevator. The detectives watched from a safe distance as the elevator took the group to the 35th floor Penthouse West. They decided to hang out at the bar which was close enough to see them when they came back down.

Thirty-five stories overhead, the four men left the elevator when it arrived on the penthouse floor, and they proceeded to the suite that was continuously "comped" to Dino by the Casino. When they entered the penthouse, they were surprised to find Vinnie Fellino and his bodyguard already there, enjoying drinks as they watched a soccer match on the fifty-inch wide-screen TV mounted on a wall in the living room.

After a cordial embrace from his uncle Vinnie, Dino introduced the two boys to the drug magnate. Vinnie Finello was a short stocky man of sixty-five or so. His face was well tanned, and his smile exhibited perfect teeth that only the best dental care in North America could produce. His jet-black hair was combed straight back in the Mediterranean style, and he wore a pale cream silk shirt against light tan slacks and oxblood tassel loafers. The boys knew this was a man of class who appreciated the good things in life and suffered for none of them.

"So, David and Joe, my nephew tells me you have managed to impress him with your street smarts and your confidence in the matter of handling a certain part of our business," said the crime boss. It was obvious he was choosing his words carefully, no doubt concerned the boys might be wired.

The boys picked up on this and as a way of gaining his confidence, Iggy and Jake, as if on cue, walked over to the big bodyguard and took off their shirts as they stood in front of him with their arms in the air.

"Hector," said Vinnie to the bodyguard, as he began the usual pat-down, "I don't think that will be necessary. Our friends here are obviously clean. Gentlemen, can we get you a drink?"

Soon the boys were enjoying a couple of cold beers and they began discussing how they would approach their buddies, Greg and Danny, at the Maritime Pub, regarding the distribution of the cocaine in the two sports bags in front of them. They also talked at length about the best ways of laundering profits from the sale of the drugs and here Jake, aka Joe, was able to add his banking knowledge to the operation. Things were moving according to plan. Then Dino, giving a side look to his uncle, said to Jake, "Joe, why not call your friends in Calgary and start to set things up?"

This move was made by Dino, no doubt as both a test of their loyalty and also to demonstrate to his uncle that he was in control of the show. It took the guys by surprise, and they could only hope that Danny and Greg would be able to sense they were in a tense situation.

Chapter Twenty-Nine

Friday July 23rd
9:10 pm

AT DINO'S request, "Joe" made the call to Danny at the Maritime Pub in Calgary. While he dialed the number for the pub, Dino walked over to his desk and quietly picked up on the other extension. Jake watched in horror as Dino gave him and Iggy the signal to remain quiet.

"Hey, Danny," said Jake. "This is Jake and I'm calling you from Vancouver," He spoke to Danny in a monotone, totally unlike the normal street banter that they had developed in the short time they knew each other. He was hoping Danny would clue in on the fact that he had another party listening on another line. As soon as he started the conversation with his pal from back East, Jake was grateful Danny had remembered the fake names that had been established earlier.

Also, he was greatly relieved when he became aware that Danny and Greg had apparently already been briefed by Hansen as to what they should say. This was important because a dumb response by Danny to Jake's comments could quickly bring the deal to an end, including themselves. In fact, just in case there may be other people listening to their conversation, Danny went on to say that the owner of the pub, a Mr. Gerald MacKinnon, originally from Truro, Nova Scotia, was now back from business in Toronto, and was anxious to meet the boys. This was a bonus from Danny and now they need not worry about that aspect of the sting. Apparently, Hansen and Riley had brought the valid owner into play as well. To complete his credibility, again on the assumption that others may be monitoring their conversation, Danny said, "Remember the other day when I came onto the Russian pretty hard? Tell him I'm sorry. I just wanted to let him think Greg

108

and I were the owners. Showin' off, you know..."

"No problem, Dan, I thought you guys were the owners myself. Just so long as the owner, MacKinnon, is keen to do some business, we're cool."

"Yeah, like I said, Joe, MacKinnon is cool. We've gone over the numbers with him, and he is anxious to get it going."

After Jake's conversation with Danny was finished, Dino approached him with a big smile and gave him a huge bear hug. Vinnie watched this with amusement, and they settled back in their lounges to finish their drinks while the Russian called Lewis at the airport and told him to get the Lear ready for a quick trip to Calgary. *Man,* thought Jake, his heart rate running high, *this is not the way I'm used to doing business. Banking was never like this.*

At ten to eleven, the group of six made their way from the elevator lobby to the casino entrance where the Lincoln limo awaited them. The group included the drug lord Vinnie Fellino, his nephew Dino Martini, the Russian Grigori, Vinnie's bodyguard Hector, and the two boys. Hansen and Riley were quick to lay their newspapers aside and get back on the job of tailing them. They tailed the Lincoln back to the Vancouver International Airport and watched as the group left the vehicle and strode toward the Lear jet which was warming up for its short trip East to Calgary. While Hansen and Riley expected this, it was still necessary for them to confirm this with the air traffic control tower.

"Fool me once, shame on me, fool me twice, fuck you," said Hansen aloud to himself as they left the tower. This time, they made sure they saw the actual flight plan in printed form by the controller who, under threat of losing his job, was judged to be telling the truth. They immediately called in an update to their captain. He was not happy to get the call at his home and be interrupted from his usual Friday night sexual foray with his lovely wife of ten years.

"Well, excuuuuse me!" said Hansen, in a fair impersonation of Steve Martin, an up-and-coming standup comedian, when he hung up the phone. Riley didn't get it and Hansen didn't bother explaining. They were in a hurry, and they ran over to the regular terminal where they bought two very expensive one-way tickets to Calgary. They would have to retrieve their cruiser at a later date.

"Shit, this bust is going to cost the good citizens of Calgary a few bucks," noted Riley.

"D'ya think?" Hansen sardonically replied.

Fortunately for the detectives, they were able to book an Air Canada flight to Calgary which was scheduled to leave in fifteen minutes. AC Flight 405 was approximately one hour and twenty minutes in the air and touched down at Calgary International at one thirty-five am, Saturday morning, local time. The private Lear made good time as well, and both parties were heading towards the Maritime Pub, after exiting the Avis rental lot at the airport in the Southeast sector by 2:10 am.

"I'm getting too old for this shit," exclaimed Hansen, as they followed the rented white Ford van. Fortunately for the detectives, their Captain had arranged for them to be met at the Calgary airport by Sgt. Blakely of the Calgary PD. The sergeant was equally pissed off at having been roused from a good night's rest at his home. He uttered a loud yawn at the two detectives as they sped along MacLeod Trail south to the pub. They kept a safe distance of a block or more behind the van as they drove in the unmarked police car.

Chapter Thirty

Saturday, July 24th
2:27 am

WHEN THEY arrived at the pub, it was going on 2:30 am The parking lot was empty, and it was necessary for Sgt. Blakely to drive with his lights off to a secluded area on a side street.

"There they are," whispered Riley, pointing to the rear end entrance of the pub where they watched the group leave the van and enter the building. Hansen and Riley stealthily crept toward the building, leaving Blakely to occupy the cruiser. Before leaving their vehicle, Hansen told Blakely to call in backup but to have the team approach silently with no flashing lights.

This is it, thought Hansen. Finally, after approximately two weeks of planning and hard work, traipsing around the country, losing sleep and drinking bad coffee, it looked like they were finally going to make a bust. He couldn't wait to see the surprised look on the faces of the two high rollers from the U.S. and their henchmen as they threw cuffs on them.

"Yeah baby, let's roll," he whispered to Riley, and they snuck closer to the bar area with their guns drawn. They entered quietly through the same door the group had just taken and they managed to get to the food preparation area of the pub unseen. They could now hear voices and then saw, through a dirty window in the kitchen service door, that the six from the van were all sitting around two circular tables. They heard them speak with three other men who they now recognized as the two musicians, Greg and Danny, along with their employer and pub owner, Gerald MacKinnon. *This is too good to be true thought,* Hansen.

Laid out on the table were the two sports bags Jake had told him about, filled, Hansen assumed, with packs of dope. They listened while

Iggy/Dave was "selling" the plan in his role as a dealer to the three eager participants. He was explaining how it would be necessary for the two musicians to develop a following of "clients" which could be accomplished by the owner converting the pub to an after-hours facility. Further, Jake/Joe then proceeded to advise the owner how to successfully launder the proceeds from the sale of the cocaine and how it would be necessary to open a new "numbered" account in the name of a holding company.

At this point, Dino entered the conversation and made his pitch with a very reasonable compensation package for the musicians. Everyone was happy. The nine men were toasting their successful meeting when all hell broke loose at the Maritime Pub.

Back on the side street, Sgt. Blakely was watching three cruisers appear in his rear-view mirror and immediately sent a prearranged two-beep alert to the detectives on their hand-held radio phones. At that point, Hansen and Riley had just finished witnessing the deal being finalized by the group of nine at the two tables inside the bar area. The detectives burst through the service door, guns drawn yelling, "CALGARY PD! EVERYONE ON THE FLOOR! THIS IS A BUST!"

To their surprise, all involved dropped to the barroom floor. "Hands on your heads where we can see 'em!" he yelled again. God, he loved this part of the job.

The detectives held the nine men under gun cover while the three teams of policemen arrived on the scene and began placing handcuffs on the criminals. It was a major arrest and police photographers were there to capture the moment on film. The detectives were posed like the famous Eliot Ness during an alcohol raid in the thirties. They stood beside the drug cache laying on the two tables, looking all business for the cameras, and all the while the detectives were struggling not to appear joyous. When they frog-marched the group outside to the waiting police vehicles, they put Fellino and his nephew Martini in the rear of one car, the Russian and Fellino's bodyguard in a second, Iggy and Jake in a third, and the two musicians with the pub owner in the last cruiser. The four police cars, along with the detectives and patrol policemen then left the scene *en masse*.

It was an impressive sight, this cavalcade of law enforcement, as it made its way north to the Calgary Remand Centre on 85th Street NW. The facility housed approximately two hundred inmates at any given period. The guests were there either pending trial, awaiting further charges or simply awaiting transfer to Spy Hill prison or some other long term correctional centre.

As they were driving away along the route, with Riley driving, Hansen turned to the two boys in the back. "Well done, gentlemen. Just a few more scenes at the Centre to complete the ruse. We'll make sure we break you all up, so they won't know for sure which cells have been assigned to you.

"None of these actors may have been in the Centre before and therefore they may not know the drill, but better to be safe than sorry. They will obviously suspect somebody has ratted them out, but that can't be helped. We will be discussing your roles in the upcoming trials, then we can talk about the witness program that is available to you, and which is highly advisable."

Hansen noted the looks of alarm on the faces of the two boys. They had clearly not given much, if any, thought to a trial or having to testify before a jury against these animals. Time to allay their fears, thought Hansen.

"Look boys, I know you're frightened, and that's nothing to be ashamed about. Just as Riley and I will be required to testify, so shall you guys. Your testimony is a vital part of this operation. With the evidence we now have, we can put these *gumbas* away for decades, which for a couple of them will equate to life. We must, however, have your full corroboration behind the evidence in order to get a conviction. Remember, you will be receiving full police protection, twenty-four-seven, both before and during the trial process. We'll keep the press to a minimum and it'll be over before you know it, okay?"

"No, not okay, Hansen," said Iggy. "But I guess we don't have much choice in the matter, do we? Yeah, I suppose we could simply take off, maybe head back East. I don't know about Jake here, but there's no way I want to spend the rest of my life looking over my shoulder."

"Nor I," said Jake. "Plus, these guys gotta do serious time. The Bug would have wanted us to do this much for him, I guess, since we've come this far."

"My point exactly, Jake. Do this for your friend. We still don't have sufficient evidence to charge them with murder, but trust me, I know our government will want to send a message here, considering the drug problem we have. So, I expect we'll see them in prison for a very long time."

It was obvious Jake and Iggy were reluctantly going to cooperate in their roles as witnesses for the prosecution. Hansen easily read the fear in the faces of the two young musicians. He knew from experience that it was going to be a difficult road ahead for the two boys. Given what was at stake for the drug lords, extra security precaution would have to be continuously first and foremost on the minds of the authorities as they proceeded through the upcoming trial phase. It was too bad he was not able to convince the Crown Prosecutor to bring charges of homicide against Giovanni and the Russian. *What the Hell,* he thought, *you can't win 'em all.* And so began the long process of their experience with an international based trial which the Calgary Herald announced as *The Drug Trial of the Century.*

PART II

Chapter Thirty-One

Monday, September 20, 1971
9:25 am

ALL JAKE and Iggy wanted to do was to play music and return to their former old lifestyles. They were tired of having to watch every move they made when they ventured outside the Bug's old apartment. It had now been almost two months since the arrest of Vinnie Fellino, his nephew Dino Martini and the hired hand, Grigori Ivanov. In spite of this, Detective Hansen was very reluctant to remove the ever-present police protection service which was becoming very problematic in the lives of the musicians. They felt constantly confined as to where they could go, who they could see, and what they could do. This was not working.

A meeting with Hansen and Captain Miller of the Calgary Police Department was scheduled for later that morning at 11:00 am, and they were eager to hear if any news might be forthcoming in regard to a trial date. They dreaded having to provide testimony in support of evidence obtained by Hansen and Riley, yet it seemed this was the only way to get these guys behind bars.

When they left the apartment for the precinct, they said good morning to Constable O'Hara, the cop on babysitting duty today. "Good luck, guys" he said. "Hopefully our office will have some news for you today. I'll see you over there."

Traffic across town to the precinct was light for a Monday morning and they arrived early for their meeting. Hansen and Riley greeted them at the front desk and brought them to the inner part of the robbery/homicide department. They proceeded to Captain Miller's office and upon entering, Riley closed the door and they got down to business.

"Well, boys, you must be getting anxious to get matters rolling, eh?"

the captain stated. He was a stout man in his mid-fifties, Jake figured. He maintained a no-nonsense military air about himself, which was accented by his silver and grey crew cut and a small moustache of similar color. Immediately after Vinnie, Dino, and the Russian had been incarcerated, Hansen had arranged to have Jake and Iggy meet personally with the captain. He had praised them highly for their actions in helping the detectives in the sting. That same day he told them he would be very interested in offering them a place on the Calgary PD once everything was settled with the case. The guys just shrugged it off, but Miller promised them he would be talking to them at a later date regarding his offer. He now looked at the pair appraisingly as they met in his office.

"Captain, we will be so glad to get the trial underway," said Jake. "Any news in that regard?"

"Well, how does this Thursday sound?" replied the captain.

"Now we're talking," said Iggy. "Tell us what we need to do, maybe give us some sort of expectations, you know?"

"Actually, that's why we wanted to see you today, guys. We want to introduce you to the Assistant DA in this case, Mr. John Newell. John has been around the system now for a decade and he would like nothing better than to nail these bastards, excusing my French," said the captain. "We will take you down to see him now and he'll fill you in. Sound good?"

"Let's get at it then," said Jake and they were led down the hall to a separate part of the building where they came to a bank of elevators. They took one of them to the third floor and were immediately in a totally different environment. Where chaos and noise were the main elements three floors below them, here there was a serenity that was palpable. The captain led the group to a door that simply announced any visitors to:

Office of the Asst. District Attorney, Calgary Branch
John Newell, Q.C.A.D.A.

They entered the office after a soft tap and were greeted by a tall individual with flowing blond hair that came to his suit collar. He had a huge walrus-style mustache that drooped over a full mouth that was grinning affably and went with his bright blue eyes. He was already taking stock of the boys as he welcomed them to his domain. *Here is a guy who is very confident about himself,* thought Jake. *He draws you into his personality and gives you comfort. This is a guy he could trust.*

After introductions were made, Captain Miller and the detectives excused themselves and left Iggy and Jake in the capable hands of the Assistant District Attorney, John Newell.

"I've been wanting to talk to you for some time now, guys. You worked for about a month with the scum who are presently residing as guests at the Calgary Remand Centre. From the report I read that was prepared by Hansen and Riley, you boys are the stars of this sting. They were both very high on you, so congratulations on a job well done." He gave them a firm handshake. "Just so you know, the perpetrators have been told their trial will begin on Thursday. They are not certain you are part of the system that will be bringing them down, but we should assume they strongly suspect this. They will, therefore, not be surprised when they see you on Thursday and when you are called as witnesses for the state.

"I want to get inside their heads. You can help me do this. We'll spend the next three days in role plays, Q&A's, and a lot of psychobabble.

"You should also know that we do not have sufficient evidence against the Russian to bring homicide charges against him. I know this is a letdown to you, but we are at least hopeful we can get him a stretch of ten years minimum for his role in the drug operation. Also, there is always the chance we can flip Dino and have him testify against the Russian if it means a reduction in his own sentence..." the young prosecutor left the possibility open. If nothing else, it should at least give the boys some hope.

And so, the coaching, teaching, and mentoring of Iggy and Jake began in earnest. Over the remainder of the day and the next two full days, the boys were subjected to mock trial work that was both enlightening and frustrating. By the end of their training sessions, the assistant DA felt confident enough to present them as solid witnesses. It was going to be a very high-profile case, one which ADA Newell was very much looking forward to getting his teeth into.

Chapter Thirty-Two

Thursday September 23, 1971
9:30 am

"ALL RISE!" The court secretary loudly announced the presence of the Honorable Judge Raymond B Stickley, and the "Drug Trial of the Century" was officially initiated.

The defense team for the plaintiffs sat on the right front of the court. There were five separate lawyers representing Fellino, Martini, and Ivanov. The other felons, being Lewis the pilot, a custom's officer at the Vancouver airport and Hector, Fellino's bodyguard, had earlier last week all plead guilty to lesser charges and were already serving much lighter sentences at the Spy Hill Correctional Centre. The RCMP in Hope, B.C. had made a raid on the farm in that area where Roberto and his partner had been apprehended. Further investigations into the operations of the drug lord, "Big Al" Gabrazzi were being conducted by the LAPD, the Vancouver PD and the Calgary PD, but nobody was holding their breath in that case.

The crown prosecution team sat on the front left pews. Iggy and Jake were both seated directly behind the ADA's table, and the two musicians from the Maritime Pub were also there with the boys, as was the pub owner, Gerald McKinnon.

When the criminals were escorted into their respective positions, it was necessary for them to pass directly in front of the boys and the other three witnesses. Because of the leg shackles that adorned the accused, their movements were restricted, and it seemed to take an eternity for the three accused to shuffle by them. As they did, each of the Mafia bosses glared at Iggy and Jake.

The Russian, however, was different. His stare seemed to get to the two musicians more than his bosses. Jake knew it was because of those hooded, reptilian eyes. Devoid of any real emotion, really. Just an absolute certainty that things were not yet over for him.

Never in Jake's short life had he been subjected to such looks of sheer hatred and venom coming from the three defendants. He was simply grateful they were all under restraints and there was no way any harm could come to them in this type of setting. However, the experience was very unnerving, and it was necessary for Jake and the other witnesses to steel themselves for the ordeal they would be facing over the extent of the trial.

Chapter Thirty-Three

Thursday, October 25th, 1971
to Thursday November 18th, 1971

THE TRIAL was originally estimated to last approximately four weeks. Almost by design, the prosecution and defense counsels presented their closing arguments on the morning of October 25th, four weeks and four days after the commencement of the trial. Iggy and Jake performed their roles in commendable fashion as witnesses, as did the two detectives, the pub owner MacKinnon, and the two pub musicians, Greg and Danny. All told, the prosecution presented what was described by the press as a "solid, airtight case."

The jury was instructed by Judge Stickley as to the possible outcomes on how they might find the three defendants, and they left the courtroom to ponder their options at eleven ten that morning. At three thirty-two that afternoon, the jury returned, and an excited throng of people crowded into the court venue to hear what was expected to be a newsworthy announcement, one way or another.

At the outset of the trial, the lawyers for the accused had argued for bail, but their request had been quickly declined, given they all represented very strong odds of flight risk. The three accused appeared drawn and haggard, dressed in orange prison jumpsuits, and it was obvious that the two Italians, at least, had not fared well in their confined environment over the past month. Their hands were cuffed and remained shackled to a belt around their waists. Leg chains on their ankles permitted them only short steps as they shuffled into the courtroom. They calmly took their seats in the pew. Both Fellino and Martini stared at the jury panel while the Russian turned and gave a chilling smile to Iggy.

When requested, the jury foreman handed a note to the bailiff who in turn passed it to Judge Stickley. Stickley then thanked the jury for their services. He instructed the three defendants to rise. He read each of the names of the defendants aloud, then solemnly spoke to them.

"A jury of your peers has reached a verdict in this case. Before reading the verdict, do the defendants have anything to say on their behalf?" Stickley asked. The three simply stared at the Judge.

"I'll take that as a no. This court finds the defendants guilty as charged." pronounced Judge Stickley. With that he slammed his gavel on his desk. "This trial is adjourned. Bailiff, please escort the defendants to cells." After consulting his calendar, he told the court he would meet again with the felons to pronounce sentencing on November 19th.

The commotion in the courtroom was immediate. As the crowd of reporters rushed to the exit doors to call in the news to their awaiting editors, the general public cheered and there were congratulatory handshakes among the prosecution team, the detectives Hansen and Riley, and of course, the various witnesses for the prosecution.

The three felons were then escorted out of the courtroom to be taken immediately to the Calgary Remand Centre where they would be held pending sentencing. The lawyers for the defense were presently occupied by several court reporters, vehemently protesting their clients' innocence and the fact that they would be filing appropriate appeals in due course. This, of course, was all bluster, since the case against the three was solid and it was well presented by the talented young Assistant District Attorney.

Iggy and Jake left the law building to meet with Hansen and Riley at a bar on 6th Ave SW, about a block from the Courthouse. It was called The Lock, Stock & Barrel, and it was favored by law enforcement men and women across the city. It provided that segment of society a safe haven to temporarily rid themselves of internal demons and share a common bond.

When they entered the bar, the young men were given high fives and words of praise from the two detectives, as well as many other police officers, the majority of whom they had not even met. It was a great feeling, and they spent the rest of the afternoon basking in the success of their lengthy ordeal. It was a long time coming.

For the next three weeks, Iggy and Jake spent their time working on unfinished tunes that Iggy had started ages ago, in another lifetime. They were eager to get a group together and to start making some money. And while the Bug's apartment had been convenient for them at the time, it was not their own, and now they wanted to find a place that gave them room to practice their craft that was at the same time more aesthetically pleasing to their liking.

They had become so involved with these pursuits that they had almost forgotten about the sentencing for the three criminals that had been such a disagreeable part of their lives. It was to take place tomorrow, Friday, November 19th.

Chapter Thirty-Four

Friday, November 19th, 1971

THE CALGARY Law Court Building was nothing like it was a month ago, when a frenetic crowd had filled the courtroom to hear the outcome of "The Trial of the Century" surrounding the drug lord Vinnie Fellino and his cronies. Today, save for a couple of court reporters and lawyers for both the prosecution and defense teams, the courtroom was practically empty. Apparently, drama was not expected to be found at this event. The players had been determined to be guilty and whatever punishment was to be meted out by Judge Stickley, the local citizens of Calgary could apparently care less. Jake and Iggy, however, were there and keenly awaited the Judge's pronouncement with bated breath.

Once again, they were subjected to vicious stares of hostility from the three convicted criminals as they were escorted into the courtroom.

"Do the accused have anything to say before my sentencing is made?" Judge Stickley asked the three. In response, he received nothing but sullen looks. "Again, I'll take that as negative," he said.

"I have considered the vile nature of the crimes you three have committed against the populace of our communities, particularly the high disregard you have displayed for the health of the youth of our nation," said the Judge. "Including the extreme risk that you place on our law enforcement people who try to keep our communities free of the vices you so blatantly throw upon our society, not to mention the rash of crime that has followed as a spin-off of the nature of these drugs.

"It is therefore my judgment that the three of you be hereby sentenced to a term of not less than thirty years to be served at the Spy Hill Prison facility," and his gavel descended on his bench with the full authority of the law.

Wow! thought Jake. This was better than they expected and though it fell in the category prescribed by previous judgments, it was still a big deal. The two older defendants would probably be in prison for the rest of their lives, unless they turned out to be model prisoners and could somehow receive leniency in their old age at some future date.

The boys were elated with the sentence handed down and they held no sympathy for the convicts whatsoever. They had knowingly participated in the preparation and sale of drugs to many young people who had either overdosed in the streets or had their lives ruined because of them. The three were only victims of their own greed.

They were especially glad to see the Russian receive a similar sentencing as his bosses. He was one bad actor, and they still shuddered every time they recalled the look of evil he gave the two boys just before he was escorted from the building.

They had finally reached a climax to the perilous journey they had undertaken a lifetime ago. Although it was fraught with danger, they had met a number of good people along the way, and they were anxious to build on these relationships.

Detectives Hansen and Riley had received appropriate commendations from their captain for their persistence in following leads and the excellent police work displayed by them over the past several months. On a number of occasions, Iggy and Jake had been approached by crime reporters from the *Calgary Herald* who were pursuing rumors the two boys had been working as undercover amateur cops for the police. The boys denied such rumors and preferred to remain out of the spotlight regarding the affair.

When Iggy and Jake met up with Greg and Danny after the trial and sentencing, they learned their two friends had gone through the same grilling from reporters as they had. The two pub musicians were only too happy to get back to their gig work at the Maritime Pub, and so they avoided the press as well. They did, however, put out an open invitation to Iggy and Jake that they could perform whenever they felt like it at the pub. To this end, the two boys had deferred, preferring to continue to work on their own tunes in the strong conviction that this was what they needed to do.

At the same time, they were very mindful of the cold, hard reality of their financial plight. Winter would soon be approaching, and they would need to get some kind of cash inflow happening. The good news was that the general economic outlook for Calgary was very buoyant. The boys were at the beginning of a boom, thanks to the oil and gas sector. If you wanted work, it was available. The population of the city was just under four hundred thousand in 1970 but was soaring like the high-rise towers which were emerging against the city skyline daily. It was party time in Calgary. It was time to rock and roll.

Chapter Thirty-Five

Friday, December 9th
4:00 pm

OUTSIDE THE ranch style bungalow, a cold wind was blowing off the mountains approximately thirty miles to the west. The boys hardly registered the wind as they lounged in their living room beside a cozy fire that blazed in a floor to ceiling stone fireplace.

"Whatcha think, Jacob?" asked Iggy. "Do you like this tune ending in minor A? It kinda leaves you wondering about the message of the song a bit more, I think." It was late Friday afternoon, and the boys were getting comfortable in their new residence in Cochrane.

Jake agreed wholeheartedly with Iggy's use of the minor chord. Iggy had a way with words and his ability to find chords to suit the written word was amazing. The way he explained this to Jake was that Iggy had always assigned certain colors to key words in his lyrics. He did the same thing with certain notes. To Iggy, it was simply a matter of matching up the colors.

Last week, they had moved into a house rental situation just west of the city in a community called Cochrane, population 1064 and incorporated as a town the same year they moved there. The small town was exactly what the boys wanted and needed. Only a fifteen-minute drive from the city, it allowed them to go to Calgary when the urge hit them.

Calgary was quickly becoming a place of too much craziness. It seemed half of the Maritimes had moved west to Alberta, and they all wanted to live in the city. Working up North in the oil patch was a common pursuit. The jobs for most of the Maritimers only lasted for the winter, long enough for them to make a bunch of money then return to the city in the spring to party it up and spend everything they had. Most of the guys from back East drove half ton pickups, drank hard whiskey, and wore cowboy boots and ten-gallon Stetsons. They listened to Waylon Jennings and Charlie Pride, and they collected pogey in the summer. The only difference from back home were the glass high rise buildings and the new concrete highways that were appearing everywhere.

This was not the lifestyle that Iggy and Jake had in mind. One day, when they were scanning the papers for rental accommodations, they spotted the ad for a four-bedroom ranch house on three acres. It had a large, empty barn, a very cool fireplace, two separate bathrooms, and an eat-in kitchen with all appliances included. The place came fully furnished with real leather chairs and sofas, and a year's supply of split hardwood that had been seasoned for three years. It was simply a dream come true for the boys. The owners of the property were a young couple who had recently decided to move to Ottawa.

They learned later that the husband was in the oil industry, and he had recently accepted a position with the government. Unknown to the young professional at that time, he would later be a part of the Trudeau regulatory group which would soon thereafter be responsible for removing tax incentives in Northern Alberta for major exploratory oil firms. This in turn would lead to ninety per cent of these companies leaving Canada for the U.S. and other countries, such as Nigeria, Oman, and Venezuela. By the early eighties, the economic result of that would be disastrous, but for now, all was financially well in this "boom or bust" province.

As part of the deal, the boys had actually purchased the property under a "rent-to-own" agreement, whereby the rental payments they made to the owners for the first year would be counted as their down payment toward the purchase. They were hoping to be settled in their professional musical career by the time it would have been necessary to obtain a mortgage to complete the purchase.

They had already made a couple of trips to Banff, where Jake introduced Iggy to the sport of alpine skiing at Sunshine Mountain and Lake Louise. There was nothing like it for Iggy. He was immediately hooked, and the sport came naturally to him. Maybe it was simply the rhythm of the turns and anticipating the mogul bumps. Whatever, he became adept at skiing, and he had quickly graduated from the Bunny Hill. He was now eager to tackle the Black Diamond runs.

Jake, for his part, was equally in awe with the difference in the quality of the snow here, compared to the smaller hills back home. Here there was actual powder, compared to the ice packed runs at Poley in New Brunswick, Martock in Nova Scotia, or even Marble Mountain in Newfoundland. And there were no annoying lift line ups here, whereas back East you could count on waiting a half hour in line while young brats raced over the backs of your skis on snow boards. Finally, there were at least a dozen or more excellent groomed trails always open. They were in heaven. But first they needed to find work, so they focused on the Banff bar scene.

Cochrane was only an hour's drive to Banff. The only problem was that in the winter it was common to run into some very bad snowstorms. Actually, the winter weather in the mountains could start anytime from October onwards.

Today was an excellent day for their trip so they had made hotel bookings at the Sunshine Village Ski Resort for the next two or three days. It was reasonably priced, and, in any case, they were hoping to only be there for the weekend. It certainly wasn't the CPR Banff Springs Hotel, but it would serve their purpose.

They had set off for Banff just after 5:00 pm and when they arrived at the lodge, the sun was setting behind a gorgeous mountain crest, spilling soft winter light over seven or eight runs that were quickly becoming empty of skiers. Everyone's attention was being drawn to the Big Bear Lounge where a live band was warming up. The boys joined the flow of young people to check out the action, and they were able to grab a table for two near the stage, order two pilsner beers and some hot chili potato skins, and get settled in. They were completely taken by surprise when one of the musicians on the small stage came running over to their table.

"Hey, dudes. What the hell are you guys doing here?" the young musician cried as he gave them each a large hug.

"Wow! Iggy, remember the guys at Sam's down in Whitefish? It's Jared, right?" asked Jake.

"Yeah, man, so good to see you two again. Donnie and Brad are backstage, and they'll be out soon. You guys gigging around here?"

"No, we wish that were so," said Iggy. "Actually, we're here to check things out and see if we can get something happening, you know?"

"This is awesome. Listen, we know the owner here pretty well, and more importantly, we happen to know that the regular house band has just broken up. We're filling in until another group can be found. We'd take the gig ourselves, but we're committed to a tour for the next three months in B.C. and Oregon starting the first of the week. This could be your lucky night boys."

10:00 pm

They could not believe their good luck During the break after the first set, The Jets took them to a small office at the rear of the bar and introduced them to John Dowl, the pub owner. He seemed like a cool guy, somewhere just north of thirty with a dirty blond beard, blue eyes, and he had that great tan everyone here in the village seemed to easily acquire.

He was sorry he wasn't able to retain the services of The Jets for any longer than the weekend, but he was willing to hear how Iggy and Jake sounded, especially when The Jets gave the two Maritimers such a glowing recommendation.

The pub owner was not to be disappointed. At the beginning of the second set, Donnie brought the two boys up on stage, and, after introducing the pair, he left them with their drummer, Brad.

Iggy told Brad he wanted to do the Jackie Wilson version of "Your Love Keeps Lifting Me Higher."

"You're familiar with the tune, Brad?" Iggy asked.

"Yeah, I think so. It simply requires a brisk four-four tempo bongo intro, with Jake coming in on bass on the second bar, right?"

"You got it. Then I'll follow Jake."

It was awesome. Iggy came in after Jake, playing his high D major bar chords. He knew if he and Jake had a chance this weekend to show what they had, this was definitely the tune he wanted to do. It was currently getting lots of radio play and this crowd was eating it up. Donnie and Jared could not contain themselves. They jumped onto the stage and joined in harmonies, with Jared adding some extra percussion with a tambourine.

The owner came up to the stage at the end of the tune amid loud cheers of, "More! More!" from the crowd. He quickly realized a winning band when he had one and grabbed the mic from Iggy. "Folks, these guys are gonna be here as your new house band starting next week. Am I right guys?"

"We would love nothing better, John." said Iggy. "By the way, folks, you are so lucky to have The Jets appearing here tonight. These boys are on their way to fame and fortune as they take off Monday on tour to our neighbors to the west, B.C. and Oregon. Let's all wish them a good run and you can probably expect to hear an album is in the works, isn't that so Donnie?" There was another loud round of applause as Iggy and Jake basked in the centre of all this praise. "Oh yeah," he shouted over the noise. "We're from Saint John, New Brunswick and we're called Fusion!"

The crowd roared their approval, and it was a large win-win for all involved...The Jets, Fusion, owner Dowl, and certainly the crowd. After The Jets finished their third and final set, the musicians all had a couple more beers, discussed things in general, the highlight of their talk being the now well-known drug bust that they had earlier discussed with the band members. The musicians shared stories of different venues they had experienced, and their talk lasted well beyond two in the morning when they finally decided to call it a night.

When they got up in the morning, they found it had snowed the previous night and a fresh five inches of powder greeted them on the slopes. They spent the rest of the weekend skiing and hanging out with The Jets.

Things now seemed so far removed from the situation they had been in during the previous summer. Every now and then, however, they were reminded of the effects that cocaine was having on society. Coke now seemed to be the drug of choice for the elite. Iggy could see this every so often when a group of well-dressed young skiers would come into the bar. Usually, the loudest of the group would start holding court, bragging about this or that, throwing his money around and looking with wild eyes at every cutie that passed his table. Like he was going to take her right there and then. The same dude would make frequent trips to the men's room and return with a stupid grin on his face, wiping his nose, sniffing, even giving the bar manager a sly wink. *Where was Billy Thompson when you needed him?* mused Iggy.

It was all familiar stuff from other days and Iggy mentioned it to Jake. They agreed to be wary of what they observed and did, who they hung out with, and all that. They had to keep that shit a long distance from themselves. They were on a good run now and there was no way they wanted to screw it up.

As the weekend quickly came to an end, the boys felt they had made a very successful trip. The owner of the Big Bear Bar was convinced the two could bring in the après ski crowd which he knew from past experience could be very fickle. Yet the boys knew they were good as a duo, but if they wanted to continue in the same genre, they knew they must very quickly acquire a good drummer. With that in mind, they decided to head back to Cochrane and maybe make a quick trip into Calgary to try and pick up a good drummer. Perhaps they could check with Greg and Danny who had been around for a while. They knew the score in the city and, more importantly, they could trust the two from back East to not lead them astray with just any percussionist who might be looking for work.

It was starting to snow again lightly when they left Sunshine Village with a promise to Dowl that they'd be back first thing Monday morning. As they left his office, it was 10:05 pm on Sunday. They failed to see the tall Latino who was closely watching them as they finished their conversation with the bar owner at a table in the restaurant area of the bar. The dark-skinned Latino sat on a bar stool having a drink with the bar manager. He wore a small black mustache and dreadlocks that fell over a red bandanna he was wearing around his neck. A long vivid red scar ran down his left cheek.

Chapter Thirty-Six

Sunday, December 11th
11:15 am

THE PHONE was ringing insistently while Alberto "Big Al" Gabrazzi mixed a champagne and OJ drink in a tall, frosted highball glass. His lady friend, one Juanita Cortez, was lazing on his sofa dressed in a see-through lilac nightgown that she had worn the previous night, if only for a brief time. This morning she was feeling rather strung out.

Big Al swore as he slowly moved toward the phone from his kitchen. He picked up after the sixth ring and fairly shouted into the mouthpiece, "This better be good!" as he admired the woman lying before him, especially the black silk thong she wore underneath her nightgown.

"Sorry to disturb you, Mr. Gabrazzi, it's Carlos. I have something to tell you that I think you may want to hear."

"Quickly, Carlos. I am not a patient man."

"Sir, I am still in Banff, Alberta at the Big Bear Bar. I have just seen the two young men who were responsible for the arrest of Vinnie, Dino, and the Russian. I am certain it is them. They have just been hired as the house band for the bar here. This is a gift. The operation we are setting up here is working out well and now we also have an opportunity to exact revenge for your family, no?"

Normally, Al would have been harshly critical of Carlos for having the stupidity to speak of such things on the phone. But this was indeed big news. But before he sanctioned any form of action on behalf of his partner, Vinnie, he wanted to speak with him first.

"Leave this with me, Carlos," he said. "I will get back to you no later than Monday. In the meantime, keep a close eye on the two *ragazzini, si*?" He was keeping a close eye on Juanita. She now had her back to him as she bent over the table holding a rolled up fifty against the two lines of coke lying there. Her nightgown and thong were laying on the sofa.

Carlos was also happy. He somehow knew the two young men were not the real thing when he saw them last summer at the cutting farm. Now he could kill two birds with one stone, so to speak, and he chuckled softly to himself.

1:37 pm

The boys made a quick stop at their ranch house in Cochrane to pick up a few changes of clothes and their backpacks, which included Iggy's .45 semi-automatic. Better safe than sorry, Iggy thought. Jake called Greg at the Maritime Pub and after outlining the purpose of his call, they quickly got on the road again for the short run to the city.

Greg was just finishing a coffee with Danny when Iggy and Jake landed at the pub in his Beaumont. They greeted each other warmly, rehashed a few of the highlights from the trial, and got down to business. "When you told us you were looking for a drummer, we immediately thought of Roger Theriault, from the band No Exit that played in Halifax at My Apartment for a couple of years straight. Guys, I can tell you Roger's a solid percussionist, with no luggage, and a guy who simply wants to make beats, no bull shit, right?" said Greg.

"Sounds like our man," said Jake. "I remember the group; they did a lot of straight up rock and had a good tight sound. What's he doing out this way?"

"That's just it. Nothing, man. We spoke to him right after you called, and he told us he's ready to roll in a heartbeat. He's living with a stoner up in the Northeast and really wants to get out of that environment, know what I mean?"

"Tell you what, Greg. Why don't you call Roger now, tell him we are in a spot, and we want to pick him up, like, in a half hour. If he can get his gear together, we can throw it in the Beaumont and head out. Make it clear that it's a trial run, though. We'll need to work through our charts for the next couple of days, and if it goes okay, he's got a steady gig at the Big Bear Bar in Sunshine."

"Man, that'll be a given for Roger. I really think this will be a good match for you dudes, the guy is good and he really deserves a break. He was planning on returning to his hometown in Truro, Nova Scotia, if he could break away from his old lady."

Greg made the call to Roger, and he told Iggy the new drummer was ecstatic. He gave the boys the address in Falconridge, and they headed out. They took Highway 1A East over to 68th Street NE and this took them straight north into the drummer's community.

It was a beat-up section of the city, and the boys became wary of what they were doing when they saw the building that was situated at the address they had been given. The grey stucco bungalow sat between two older cement five-story apartment units. It had seen better days. Loud music was blaring from a broken window and as they approached the building, a door was quickly opened and a short, long-haired guy of thirty-something came running out. He carried drum cases in both arms and was being chased by a girl of an indeterminate age wearing denim overalls, a black ZZ Top tee shirt and hiking boots.

"You guys here from the pub, come to save my sorry ass?" he shouted with an infectious grin that was both impish yet sorrowful at the same time. In the meantime, the girl who was standing behind him began yelling at him, cursing all the while, and threatening him with all manner of harmful acts.

"Well, if your name is Roger Theriault, then we are your saviors," said Iggy.

"Here, grab these and I'll get the rest of my gear," Roger shouted as he handed a couple of the drum cases to Iggy. After several trips back and forth from the bungalow to the Beaumont, all the while having to listen to a very irate woman venting her obvious distaste for her departing partner, the three musicians eventually loaded up Jake's car. As they sped away westward on McKnight Blvd. NE, they picked up the John Laurie Blvd NW and were soon on Highway 1A West going to Cochrane.

"Well, that was a dramatic exit, man," said Iggy. "Ironic, eh?"

"How so?" asked Roger.

"The name of the last group you played with. No Exit, wasn't it?"

"You might say I had something to prove," laughed Roger.

At least the guy had a sense of humor, thought Jake, and then they were entering Cochrane.

Chapter Thirty-Seven

Monday, December 12th
11:20 am

VINNIE FELLINO was not yet accustomed to being told when he could receive a telephone call, where he could take it, nor under what conditions. But the Spy Hill Correctional Centre had their own opinion of that normal civic right. The call was finally put through Monday morning after several attempts, much bureaucratic bullshit, and a high degree of aggravation on the part of Big Al Gabrazzi. The room where Vinnie took the call was somewhat away from the general prison population, but it was still very difficult to hear his partner over all the shouts and normal activity of a high security correctional facility.

After his discussion with Gabrazzi, Vinnie felt a bit vindicated. Throughout his career in crime, he lived with the credo of the mob. Nobody ever ratted against the family and lived to talk about it. That was written in blood and even if Vinnie grew soft in his golden years, once his partner had brought the news about the sighting of the two boys to his attention, it was now absolutely necessary for him to save face and sanction the hit against the two musicians who had so blatantly abused his trust in them. This was the way of the Family. The truth was, Vinnie was not that impressed of late with his nephew Dino. Dino was not doing his time well and he feared he might be getting ready to rat on his family and seek a reduction in his term at Spy Hill.

With that in mind, Vinnie would meet with Grigori in the exercise yard today after lunch *without* Dino's knowledge and pass on some information to the Russian. He was impressed with the long reach of influence his partner in L.A. was capable of exercising and the plot that Gabrazzi had lain out for him sounded doable. He would soon see just how effective the plan he was about to share with Grigori would be. Bold, and creative. That was certainly Big Al Gabrazzi. No matter, at the appropriate time, the Russian would either be successful, or he would not, in which case he would be dead. It was all beyond Vinnie's control.

As noon approached, the prisoners gathered in a central mess area where they were served pretty good food, for prison fare. Today it was to be lasagna. Not bad, thought Grigori. He looked forward to the meal and a nice walk around the perimeter of the exercise yard to settle his stomach. So much for tough living at Spy Hill Prison, thought the Russian. This was a piece of pie compared to some of the *gulags* he had spent time in while traveling across Eastern Russia over the years.

As he strolled along the edge of the ten-foot-high wall, he was pleasantly surprised to see Vinnie Fellino coming across the prison square to meet him. The two walked together three times around the yard while two armed prison guards in lofty towers took note. The guards had no idea of what was being discussed by the two inmates, which was just as well. For if they had overheard their conversation, their comfortable nights' sleep would have been no longer possible.

The Russian carefully replayed all he was told by Vinnie in his mind, as he was escorted back to his eight by twelve-foot cell. Hopefully, this would only be his living arrangement for the rest of the week. The plan, as related to him by Mr. Fellino, relied on the participation of an inside prison employee who had a son that was currently in need of help. Well, "help" was one way of putting it. The son, who was a regular at the Big Bear Bar in Sunshine Village, was in need of drugs, as simple as that, and he had agreed to talk his father into doing a few things over and above his job description. At precisely six o'clock on the morning of Saturday, December 17th, the Russian was to complain vigorously about chest pains. He would be taken to the sick bay, a low security environment, where he would secretly be given a handgun by the prison employee, the father of the druggie in Banff. Grigori had been watching the sick bay area all afternoon, carefully studying the layout, watching the officials who came and went, noting times.

He was able to determine that a certain doctor changed shifts with another colleague at seven am each day and, from this, the plan was further expanded. Next Saturday, Grigori would simply walk out of the prison while it was still dark, dressed as the doctor and with bogus credentials also provided by the employee. He would be home free. As back up, he would have a loaded .38 pistol and a homemade shiv hidden in his under shorts. Once out of the prison he would get some civvie clothes, a bottle of vodka and maybe a local whore. Then meet up late Saturday with Carlos, the Latino mule he had met in Whitefish a while back.

To add to the plan, the prison employee had agreed to start a small fire in a closet beside the sick bay area. The resulting alarms would serve to pre-occupy the guards and at that time of day, security was expected to be at a minimum. Ivanov was impressed with the plan. It involved a lot of people and no doubt Mr. Gabrazzi had to put out a lot of money to bankroll it.

While all of this was playing itself out in the Russian's mind, Carlos was sharing a drink with the bartender at the Big Bear Bar. He had received a call in his hotel room at the lodge from Big Al telling him of the plan to have the Russian escape from the Spy Hill Prison. He was told to await the arrival of Grigori some time next Saturday afternoon or early evening in the bar at the ski lodge. The two of them could then formulate their own action plan as regards the demise of the two musicians. Big Al promised him a large Christmas bonus should they be successful. He did not have to mention the alternative payback.

Chapter Thirty-Eight

Tuesday, December 13th
3:15 pm

"THAT SOUNDS pretty good, Roger," said Iggy. He was impressed with the style of the former No Exit drummer. They had just finished a second run-through of "Light My Fire" by The Doors and Roger had nailed it. He was everything Greg had promised and then some. The former No Exit drummer was certainly capable of taking a solo drum break if required, but he was not the type to overplay his role; actually, if one had to describe him, they would say he was a tad on the gentle side as drummers go.

They had been practicing for two days straight now, and their act was coming together. Every now and then they received favorable feedback from the owner, John Dowl, when he happened to be around. Also, most of the service staff at the bar were often dropping in to take time on their short breaks and enjoy the show. The band was not due to officially start until Thursday the 15th, so they still had lots of time to tighten things up.

As they popped a few beers, Jake now took the opportunity to tell Roger of their plans about getting more into their own songs. Roger was excited to hear this, and Jake then asked Iggy to do his favorite, "Rocking in Whitefish," a simple three chord rock ballad inspired by their brief meet-up with The Jets last summer. Roger took the lead in proposing a straight four-four tempo with some cool accents that Iggy and Jake really liked. They were on their way and Jake had the feeling nothing could stop them now. Fusion was like the Phoenix rising from the ashes and they were going to kick ass Thursday night.

Thursday, December 15th
10:00 pm

"Wow!" exclaimed Roger, checking out the large crowd that had come out to hear them. "Man, this is great. Iggy, do you know there is a table of young ladies over by the right exit door that are truly wanting to chat us up?"

"In your dreams, Roger. Just be cool, bud. There will be plenty of time for babes."

In truth, Iggy himself was getting anxious to meet some lady with whom he might be able to develop a more lasting relationship than he had been having since coming to Alberta. One-night stands were the norm, and they were starting to wear pretty thin. He wasn't looking to get married, or even anywhere near a live-in type of thing. Still...

His thoughts were interrupted by loud shouts and cursing coming from the entranceway. Iggy looked over toward the activity in that area and was able to see several young preppy types acting up at the entrance to the bar. The bouncer, John Lang, was arguing with the young men. From what Iggy could tell, John was certainly capable of handling himself, but he seemed to lack the diplomacy required to deal with difficult customers. And because he was outnumbered in this instance, it could get nasty, so Iggy and Jake walked over to the area and Iggy asked, "Hey, John, what's the problem?"

"Hi, Iggy. No real problem. Yet." And here he looked at the main object of the confrontation; a tall, thin collegiate-looking guy who was clearly upset about something. As well, he exhibited all the signs of cocaine use that Iggy and Jake had previously witnessed in the months leading up to the trial. Iggy leaned close to the guy and made eye contact. Speaking in a quiet, intense voice he said, "Dude, don't make us call the police here. I know you're carrying coke in your jacket and believe me, you do not want them to catch you with it. So, here's what we're gonna do."

Iggy turned to the bouncer and said, "John, how about giving these boys tickets for tomorrow night's show, on our tab. And guys, please don't come in here high. This is a one-off deal."

Whether it was the way he said this to the three guys, or maybe it was the fact that they simply had to take the offer made because everyone close by distinctly heard what Iggy had said to the college guy, Jake didn't know. But he was relieved when the three took the proffered tickets from the bouncer and turned away from the opening. The situation had been resolved.

When the small crowd around them dispersed, Iggy again went over to John. "Didn't mean to upstage you there, John, or anything like that, man. These guys only would have ended up in jail, furniture here would have got busted up along with your knuckles. Not worth the aggravation, right?"

"You got that, Iggy" John replied, then the bouncer went on his way back to the bar area.

"Nice play, Iggy," said Jake.

"Well, stay tuned. This kinda shit is just starting," he said in a rueful way. They couldn't seem to get away from the problems that cocaine was bringing their way.

The remainder of their first night at The Bear, as it was called, was uneventful. Actually, word spreads quickly in a small community, and it did not take long for the incident with Iggy and the way he handled the three preppies to get around. The regulars at the resort were proud of the stand Iggy and the band as a whole had taken against hard drugs, making them that much more popular.

Sunday, December 18th
1:00 am

By the end of their last set on Saturday night, the boys were in a great mood. They had excellent feedback from the crowds that week and the owner was also very complimentary about their sound. They were looking forward to practicing the following week and getting some new tunes down prior to the Christmas weekend. It had been a long day, so after packing their gear in the Beaumont, the group decided to call it a night.

On their way back to their room, a couple of shady characters passed them in the hallway and Iggy had a bad feeling as soon as he saw them. The lighting was dim, and it was very brief, but he thought he recognized one of them from somewhere. The guy with the dreads...where the hell had he seen him before? Then Iggy realized something. It wasn't the dreadlocks he had seen before, because they were new. But the new hairstyle was blocking what he *had* seen at another time, and that was the vivid scar on the Latino's cheek. That memory came flooding back to Iggy now: the scene last July at the ski lodge in Whitefish, Montana when they had picked up the two kilos of ninety percent grade cocaine from Al Gabrazzi's mules...the Latino with the scar and the attitude. He turned around to get a better look at the two that had passed them in the hallway, but they had disappeared. Damn!

This is not good, thought Iggy. As soon as they got back to their room, Iggy checked his backpack while Roger used the bathroom. He made sure his .45 was still there and he shoved it in his jacket pocket. He then put a finger to his lips in a "be quiet" gesture to Jake and called the Calgary police, asking to speak directly to Detective Hansen.

"We've got a situation here in Banff, detective," said Iggy, as soon as Hansen came on the line. "I'm positive I just spotted one of the mules who brought the two kilograms of cocaine to us when we were undercover in Whitefish. You gotta get up here, man."

Detective Hansen then told Iggy something that was even more frightening. Apparently, earlier on Saturday morning there was a major event at the Spy Hill Correctional Centre in Calgary. The Russian had escaped from prison by posing as one of the prison medical doctors. The bona fide doctor was in fact taken hostage during the escape, and the Calgary police are trying to find the Russian's whereabouts along with the doctor and his vehicle.

This latest news was disastrous. How could they take the chance that the Russian was not already here at Sunshine Ski Village Resort seeking them out? He was definitely the sort of psycho who would want revenge after the scam that Iggy and Jake had pulled. Besides, he was now positive that the Latino he had seen in the hallway was Carlos. And that was no coincidence! They had to get out of here, right now. The decision made, Iggy relayed this to Detective Hansen. The detective told them to go to the ranch house in Cochrane, stay in their house, lock all doors, and they would probably be there in Cochrane before them.

The three young musicians packed the few sets of clothes they had in a hurry and raced down to the Beaumont. Iggy was worried that his worst fears were about to happen, but he was hesitant to get into the whole business with Roger, whom they had just met. It just wasn't the right thing to do. So, while Roger was using the bathroom, he had quietly asked Jake to keep this from their new drummer, at least until they got home safe and sound, under the protection of Hansen and Riley.

Chapter Thirty-Nine

Sunday, 4:25 pm

THE SNOW was now falling heavily. Hypnotically, the flakes flowed toward Jake as they made their way home to Cochrane from Banff. Fortunately, Jake had changed the summer tires on the Beaumont over to snow treads and because he had been given plenty of advice from Greg at the Maritime Pub. He also took the extra precaution of adding chains to the Beaumont's rear wheels.

By the time they arrived home, it was getting dark, and the intensity of the storm had increased. Their driveway was covered in at least six inches of wet, heavy snow. The temperature was decreasing steadily, and the radio weather station was calling for a full-blown, major winter storm for the next twelve hours. This meant traffic in the area would be basically non-existent.

When they pulled behind the barn, they saw hidden from view the welcome sight of Hansen's police vehicle. The detectives told them to quickly enter the house and act normal. They would stay hidden from anybody coming onto their property and make sure the musicians were protected. With that in mind, Jake decided to park the Beaumont in the driveway where it could be seen, and they went into the ranch house.

Although Iggy and Jake had earlier agreed with each other to not bother getting into the whole sordid business with their new band mate, it was obvious Roger suspected something weird was happening. The trip home in silence, the insane speed that Jake drove to get here, and now a police car with two officers sitting in it right outside them behind the barn. Roger was now beside himself with a number of sensations, namely anger, fear, and confusion. "Hey, you guys. What gives? Talk to me!" he shouted.

Iggy put a container of coffee on the stove and decided to tell him everything. When he was finished, Roger was flabbergasted.

"Are you fucking kidding me?" he exclaimed. "Man, this is a trip."

"We're sorry to get you involved in this Roger, but we were sure this was all behind us! Just when we get a couple of good breaks, now everything is going to hell."

"At least we have the cops here to protect us," said Roger. "Don't worry guys, I feel safer here than back in Falconridge, no longer having to contend with Helga of the SS."

The three drank their coffees and huddled around the kitchen table. Jake got a good fire going in the living room fireplace and they sat making small talk, too afraid to go to bed.

Every now and then they stole a glance out of their kitchen window, but visibility was practically nil. The only sound they could hear was the wind as it howled around the corners of the house and the crackling of flames from the fireplace. Suddenly the telephone shrilled, frightening the musicians.

"Hello?" said Jake.

"Yeah, Hansen here...trust all is well?"

"As well as can be, detective."

"It's been over an hour since you guys landed. How about we split up into shifts for the night? I can't imagine them trying anything in this storm, but I guess you never know. I was thinking I could wait here in the vehicle and keep an eye out while Riley joins you for some sleep."

"Sounds like a plan," said Jake. "We can do something similar here in the house. Then see what the morning brings, I guess."

Detective Riley was soon at the door with his side arm drawn. He was introduced to the new drummer then Roger went with Jake to two separate bedrooms where they each tried to catch a nap. Detective Riley said he would stay up with Iggy for a bit more before retiring himself.

Riley and Iggy had decided to turn off all the lights in the house and they were now sitting in the large leather chairs in the living room facing the comfortable fire. It was eleven twenty when Iggy heard a strange scratching noise at the kitchen window, and he cautiously got up to investigate. When he moved the lace curtain aside, he could clearly see where somebody or something had removed a layer of frozen snow from the window. When he rose on his feet to look down in the blackness toward the base of the house, a large face suddenly rose up five inches in front of his own. The face was wide-eyed, totally in shock at seeing Iggy on the inside of the glass looking out at him, and the vivid scar on his left cheek was unmistakable.

Suddenly, the figure outside was raising his arm toward Iggy and it contained a gun with a silencer attached to the end of the barrel. Iggy could see a grin forming on the Latino's face when abruptly he heard a loud POP over the noise of the howling wind. Simultaneously, the face he was looking at became a red mist. Iggy ran to the bathroom, violently ill, while Detective Riley ran outside to investigate.

Riley saw his partner standing over the body of a man who was clearly dead. Hansen was checking out tracks in the snow which were quickly becoming obliterated with the continuing snowstorm. "Call it in, Gerry. I had to shoot the fool before he got Iggy. Is he okay, by the way?" Hansen asked, as he walked toward the end of the driveway, carefully checking the area.

"Yeah, he's in the process of losing his supper but he'll be fine." Riley walked with Hansen, and they could see where another vehicle had recently been parked and snow had been thrown up when it had left in a hurry.

"I guess they came in here with their lights out," said Riley.

"Yeah, well, one of them's gonna be *leaving* with them out too," Hansen replied. They went back into the ranch house where they found Iggy, Jake, and Roger huddled around the warm fire.

"We've got a coroner and a forensic team on the way, boys. Sorry you had to witness that, Iggy, but there wasn't really an alternative..." Hansen explained.

"Detective, you saved my ass. You are the man!" Iggy said.

"The guy outside resembles the description you gave me when you called earlier. He did have an accomplice, but that guy managed to get away. For what it's worth, we'll cover the vehicle tracks with a tarp and maybe the crime scene guys can make something of them. Why don't you guys try to get some sleep and we'll talk about future plans in the am?"

Iggy went to his kitchen cupboard and brought out a bottle of dark liquid. "I bought this the other day to treat Christmas guests if we had any," said Iggy. "I guess this is as good a time as any." He arranged five glasses on the table. He then free-poured double shots of Newfoundland Screech. It was a dark rum which was brewed in St. John's, the capital city of that province. Many tourists who visited any of the many pubs in St. John's for the first time were always told of being "screeched in." It was an ancient tradition there where the newcomer was required to bolt down a large drink of the dark rum, followed by kissing a cod fish. The young musicians and the toughened detectives then drank the fiery liquid together and they wished each other well.

"Don't worry, detectives, we're out of cod fish," joked Jake.

After the toast, the two policemen covered the vehicle tracks as best as they could and then returned to the ranch house to wait for the other teams to arrive. A half hour later the whole yard was lit up with bright halogen lights as the forensic team did their work. Carlos' body was removed by the coroner and the drill for "Officer Involved in Shooting" began with Hansen and Riley as they went over the incident with Captain Miller and an Internal Affairs Officer.

When the boys arose in the morning, they were impressed with the amount of police activity surrounding them. They were also somewhat surprised to note the Assistant District Attorney, John Newell, was on hand, along with Captain Miller.

Detective Hansen took the three boys along with his captain and the ADA into the den. They made brief re-introductions and got down to business. "Well, gentlemen," began the ADA, "you are still in the sights of some nasty people, I see. So, to show our appreciation for what you have been through up to this point, and to ensure it does not happen again, we have a proposition for you," he said.

Chapter Forty

Wednesday, December 21st,
11:15 am

FOR THE past hour the three boys had listened intently to the Assistant District Attorney as he outlined a plan that was designed to keep the young musicians safe, allow them to lead normal lives, and give them the option of exiting this plan as and when the extremely dangerous external forces now at play were eliminated. It was called the Canada Witness Protection Program or CWPP.

As explained to the guys, all three of them would clearly meet the criteria set out in the act for such participants. It was a program that had been established through the RCMP but was available to any law enforcement group in Canada.

They would be taken to a place suitable for them to establish new identities, new employment, and a certain amount of financial compensation. The last benefit mentioned was available, but it depended on how long the program was expected to last. In that regard, the ADA was confident that the matter of rounding up the remaining criminals would be sooner than later, given the assistance they were now receiving from their law enforcement colleagues in the U.S.

ADA Newell was explaining the details of the program to the boys and naturally, the three wanted to know where they would be transferred and what they would be doing to make a living. The Assistant D.A. would only say, "All in due course, boys, all in due course." In the interests of security, they would be flown to their destination where everything else would be fully disclosed, "Far from prying eyes and ears," he said. At a later date, the Government would arrange to transport Jake's vehicle and their musical equipment to their new address. At that point in the discussion, all three of the musicians stood up and vehemently demanded that they be allowed to bring their musical gear with them. The Beaumont could stay here, if need be, but their guitars and drums had to come with them. It was nonnegotiable.

It all sounded so surreal, like something right out of a B movie. Well, a new surrounding wouldn't be so bad, the boys thought. The more they thought about it, the better it sounded. The boys had seen close up what was at stake for them personally, and at this point they were willing to do whatever was necessary to protect themselves. As they were finalizing things with the ADA, Hansen's beeper went off and he told them he had to make a call to Banff.

When he got off the phone, Hansen rejoined Captain Miller and the others in the den. "That was Constable O'Hara in Sunshine Village Ski Resort, Captain. As you know, he's assisting us there with the search for the unknown accomplice regarding the attack here last night."

"Yes, detective. What's up?"

"Well sir, there have been some developments. Just outside the village, a couple of hikers came across something." He looked sideways at the three musicians. "It appears they have found the vehicle belonging to Dr. Jeffreys from the Spy Hill Medical facility. Sir, it's not good."

"And...?" prompted the captain.

"Sir, the vehicle has been burned extensively but the team there were able to determine the owner ID from the raised numbers still visible on the burned plates. It's the doctor's car, no question. They have also found the charred remains of a body in the vehicle, and we are now awaiting results from the medical examiner's office in Calgary."

They all knew what the outcome of the dental comparisons would be. Undoubtedly it was the doctor, and the Russian was on the loose. There was every indication he was the unknown accomplice in last night's attack here in Cochrane. There was now no reason at all to ponder over the offer of protection being made by the authorities to the musicians. For the members of Fusion, it was a no-brainer.

In view of the imminent danger now posed by the apparent closeness of the Russian in their midst, it was decided to fly the boys to their new destination tomorrow afternoon. Jake's Beaumont would be put up in storage by Hansen who jokingly promised Jake he wouldn't drive it over one hundred miles per hour in the winter season.

By 2:00 pm the following day, they were all at the Calgary International Airport with what luggage they owned along with their musical equipment. Hansen took them to the Executive Flight Centre at Calgary FBO where they were met by a young-looking pilot outside the gateway. Hansen helped them lug their gear aboard a small Cessna, then gave them each a hug and they were gone.

Iggy and Jake left with mixed feelings regarding their relationship with Hansen and Riley. One thing they knew. They would definitely miss them.

Chapter Forty-One

Thursday, December 22nd
4:10 pm

THE FOUR-SEAT single engine Cessna 172 aircraft slid almost noiselessly through the darkening skies in south central British Columbia. The snowstorm that had ravaged that mountainous part of the province yesterday had all but disappeared, leaving a peaceful flight for the pilot and the three passengers aboard. As Jake looked through the window on his right, he was able to detect the lights of an airport runway as they appeared now and then through the light cirrus layer of clouds beneath them.

From what he could determine, they had flown in a southwesterly direction for about an hour, but since he did not have a map, nor was he familiar with the area, he was at a loss as to their whereabouts. Try as they might to gain information from the pilot, he was under strict conditions to remain silent and would only give them a grin and silently shrug his shoulders when asked. The Cessna was now making its descent, so they would know very soon. As they approached the runway lights below them, a large lake became discernible, and the outline of a medium sized city was visible. It looked inviting from the air. They could see clean, wide streets and avenues with no industrial areas of any size, only houses in neat patterns with swimming pools in most of them.

The pilot helped them with their gear which included their musical equipment along with their clothing. A van with an RCMP insignia on the side panel along with the iconic gold, blue, and white striping sat idling at the end of the runway. A uniformed officer quickly introduced himself to the three musicians as Constable Henway and they loaded the gear into the van. As they sped away from the airport, Iggy had a chance to look at the terminal building on his right as they went by it. *Welcome to Kelowna* the sign on the front of the terminal read.

Constable Henway was a young man, not much older than the boys. He knew little of their situation and told them he was not in a "need-to-know" status, so they should only divulge matters concerning their exit from Alberta to higher authorities. That was good advice as far as the boys were concerned. Consequently, their conversation as they drove toward the city was limited to the weather, what happened in Kelowna (yes, Constable Henway did tell them they were going to be living in Kelowna), and when they might be able to get something to eat. They were starving.

Henway told them there was great golfing here in the summer, lots of beautiful lakes to test their fishing skills, and there were several ski hills close by. The city and surrounding area were in the Okanagan Valley which was best known for its fruit agriculture and wine production. It was also an attraction for well-to-do senior citizens from all over Canada. *Jeez, that sounds exciting.* thought Jake, a little sardonically.

It was now fully dark as they entered the parking lot of the Kelowna RCMP detachment on McIntyre Rd. Henway told them there were three other offices and they all closed at 4:00 pm. They were going to meet briefly at this office with Sergeant White who would fill them in with all the necessary details and answer any questions they had. Henway would wait outside for them in the van and drive them to their new residence after the meeting with Sergeant White was finished.

"Okey dokey," said Iggy to the serious young cop. He was beginning to get a feeling for the place. It was not a sense of fear. Not apprehension either. Boredom maybe? Before prejudging anything though, he told himself to give the place a chance. Apparently, there was some good fishing and skiing here, so it couldn't be that bad. Who knew what was in store?

It was now 5:45 pm and they had just finished their meeting with Sergeant White. It was explained to them that the RCMP had federal jurisdiction of the CWPP. To this end, a number of "safe" houses across the country were maintained by the federal government and the unit in Kelowna was just one of them. They would have the place to live in, free of charge including utilities. As well, there was a 1969 eight passenger Dodge van that was theirs for getting around. There was one other financial incentive that would be provided, which, as they were pleased to find, was that the feds would make the "rent-to-mortgage" payments on their existing property in Cochrane. For a while. Other than that, they were on their own. They would need to pay their own food bills, transportation costs, everyday incidentals.

But one nice, final tidbit: the local RCMP were aware the boys had their own band and so they had arranged to introduce them to a local nightclub owner where perhaps they might be able to get work, depending on whether or not the owner was satisfied with their abilities.

They would, of course, all be given new identities. *Shit*, thought Jake, *I still have to remember to use the ones we got last time around.* In addition, it was vitally important that they never tell anyone of their backgrounds. They must not call their parents or any of their friends. Letter writing was permitted but no return addresses were to be given to any of their recipients. So it was that Iggy/Dave became Eddy Ross; Jake/Joe was now Mark Driscoll; and Roger had the new moniker of Freddy Allmand. Roger was actually excited about having a new name, thinking he could claim to be one of the Allmand Brothers. Jake didn't bother to tell him they were *The Allman Brothers*, no "d."

When they arrived at their new residence, they were quite surprised to find it was a modern four-bedroom, brick, split level bungalow. In addition to a large living room with a fireplace, there was a finished rec room in the basement with a wet bar and a regular sized pool table.

It had a paved driveway, a detached garage, a small backyard complete with a BBQ pit and a five-foot-high fence around the perimeter. Of course, everything was white with snow at this time of year, still...

Jake could envision the three of them in the spring, lying on the lawn, sipping on some pops with a few burgers on the barbie. Not a bad scene. He wondered what the neighbors were like. They unloaded their gear, got settled into the bungalow and rolled a blunt to christen their new digs.

Chapter Forty-Two

Friday, December 23rd
1:25 pm

THE BOYS entered the parking lot of The Emerald Lounge, a high-end restaurant/bar establishment on the west side of the city, sitting on the very edge of beautiful Okanagan Lake. The premises advertised fine Chinese cuisine, a conference hall, three separate dance floors, live entertainment, a DJ, and a separate karaoke area for the venturesome. They had called earlier in the day and had arranged an interview with the owner, Mr. Ken Chou. The owner of the establishment had been expecting their call, having already spoken with Sergeant White of the RCMP. *So far, so good*, thought Jake.

As the boys introduced themselves to the slight Asian owner, they were impressed with his courteous manner toward them. He said he was hoping they might be able to fill a spot left vacant by a trio who had gone back to Vancouver last week. The band to be replaced was a doo wop trio that specialized in older fifties and sixties tunes by groups like The Drifters, The Marcel's, The Four Seasons, and the like.

"So, you boys do this doo wop? Doo wop very big here. Older peoples like very much."

Uh oh, thought Iggy. *But, really, how hard could it be?*

Before Iggy could respond, Jake stepped in and said "Uh, sure Mr. Chou. We do doo wop"

Christ, he was even having a hard time pronouncing it.

"That good then. It settled. You call me Kenny. Not Mr. Chou. You start next Thursday night; play Thursday, Friday, and Saturday only. See Miss Lee at front for details, please."

"Well, that's great Mr. Chou, but don't you want to hear us?" asked

Iggy. "What if we're not good enough for you?"

"Miss Lee. She know if you good enough or not."

Okay, that was cool. Now all they had to do was come up with enough tunes to fill three sets over the next week. Next, they met with Suzie Lee at the front office, and Jake immediately fell in love. She was the prettiest, cutest, smartest, funniest girl he had ever met. A petite thing, maybe five feet with a short bob haircut. Plus, she seemed to like him, the way she smiled when he practically drooled over her. She told them what their starting pay would be, and they were pleasantly surprised at how much more they would be making here compared to what they had been used to receiving back East at The Trade Winds and even at The Bear. Once again Fusion was on a roll. Jake invited her to come over to the bungalow later that evening to hear them work. As part of the "hiring process" he quickly clarified. Suzie laughed. Iggy picked up on the connection between the two and scowled to himself.

Keeping in line with their change of identities, the boys decided to change the name of the group. They wanted to make this new venue their home for a while and felt they could perhaps accomplish it with some practice. So, they wanted a name to fit the new genre they were getting into. The Shuswap Doo Wop Band was born! Kelowna was about an hour's drive from the Shuswap Lakes, a region known locally for its legendary lake monster, Ogopogo. The creature was purported to be much bigger than the Loch Ness Monster. This was something they could probably bring into the act at a later time.

Iggy felt that even if they could nail down seven or eight crowd favorites from that genre, they would be able to get by with the number of easy listening tunes they had kept in their repertoire. But they still had their work cut out for them, and so they returned to their bungalow to get at it.

When they got home, Iggy decided to have a man-to-man chat with Jake. "I saw the way you got goonie over Suzie there, Jacob," he said. "For what it's worth, I think you should focus on the task at hand, dude. She's cute and everything, but there's a conflict of interest here. Man, she's basically our employer. It can't work."

Jake took the advice from Iggy somewhat reluctantly. If the truth were known, he still harbored strong feelings about his break-up a couple of years ago with his former steady in Saint John, Sharon Donovan. Iggy saw the infatuation with Suzie Lee as just that, love on the rebound. Almost like puppy love, for God's sake. Well, Jake would have to learn the hard way. So long as this business didn't start to screw up the new band.

Jake in turn told Iggy he was a big boy, and knew what he was getting into, so in other words, *back off, Nat!* When Jake addressed Iggy using his proper name, Iggy knew he had hit him in a sore spot. Ah well, they'd work it out.

9:15 pm that night

The Shuswap Doo Wop Band was finishing their second run through "The Wanderer" by Dion Dimucci when Suzie landed at their door. She came into the bungalow all smiles, saying she could hear them outside while walking down their driveway, and she thought they sounded great. She said all this while staring wide-eyed at Jake. Jake immediately welcomed her in, got her a coffee, and acted like a fool. It was very obvious to the other two musicians how heart stricken he was with the beautiful little Asian. When Jake was not looking, Iggy just looked sadly at Roger and shook his head to indicate his feelings about where he saw things heading with Jake.

Within an hour, the boys finished putting final touches on another four tunes and they felt good about the progress they were making. Suzie was clearly impressed with their talent. She said the band that was leaving was quite good, but they were older and frankly, the regulars coming to the bar were getting a bit tired of them. They always played the same songs, night after night for the past three years. This was good information for the boys to have and they would endeavor to insert several new tunes a week, at least for the first couple of months.

Since they had worked hard all day, the doo wop band felt they deserved a reward, so they hit out for a quiet drink at a nearby piano bar where they could discuss the new tunes they had practiced. They could also draw up a set list for next Thursday night. Suzie begged off and decided to go home for the night.

As they were enjoying their beers in the half filled, darkly lit piano bar, a tall black man came on a small stage that barely had room for him. He pulled himself in front of his Yamaha electric keyboard and broke into

Mr. Bojangles, the 1968 classic by Jerry Jeff Walker.

For the rest of the set, the boys were held in a trance-like stupor by the man. He played with grace and style, often using anecdotal humor in an attempt to connect with his audience. He had a sincere passion for his craft, yet strangely, nobody else in the bar seemed to hear him, or even cared enough to listen to his show. The crowd rudely talked loudly while he was playing, or drunkenly shouted out requests for something stupid, like "Knock Three Times" by Dawn.

The boys found themselves drawn to the performer, not because they felt pity for him, but because they couldn't believe he was not getting the attention and appreciation he clearly deserved. They had to meet him. Iggy approached the guy after the set was complete and invited him to their table for a drink. The soloist's name was Delbert Jones, and he was from Portland, Oregon. He was tall and lanky, about thirty, and he wore his curly black hair short, parted on the left side. Long sideburns and a pencil thin mustache accentuated a thin face with high cheekbones and coal black shining eyes.

He had a very modest manner for a musician. As the boys learned from their conversation, Delbert had been doing his one man show for a few years now, and while he found it tough at times, he was willing to give it another couple of years before giving up on his dreams to make it big.

Jake told Delbert there was no need for him having to put up with this kind of audience. "Delbert, man, you have raw talent and why haven't you simply hooked up with another band or cut records? Surely there are groups around this part of the country that could use your talent?" asked Iggy.

"Guys, I don't know how much you follow what has been happenin' south of the border here. We got ourselves in a real mess down in 'Nam. Nixon ain't gonna be doin' shit about it and seems we don't have much choice but to do his biddin.' Thas why I'm playing in your great country. I'm a draft dodger, boys. Too many of my friends and family have left their souls in Vietnam, and you shouldn't necessarily have to die for that to happen, know what I mean? I have yet to meet up with a Canadian group who are willing to take on a black man, much less a black draft dodger."

With that, Delbert rose to leave the table. "So, thanks for the drink and the good vibes, boys," he said. "Hope y'all enjoy the rest of the show."

The boys listened to Delbert for the rest of the evening, then Jake gave Iggy a look and then went on the small stage when Delbert was finished and said they wanted one last drink with him. When they were all sitting again, Jake made his pitch.

"Delbert, we want you to listen to a proposal. We are in a bind, man. We have a band, a trio, that was, up until today, a commercial rock band. Actually, a pretty good rock band. We did some easy listening, but truly we've never played much R&B, soul, disco, or doo wop. And now we've just been hired to play in The Emerald Lounge, but the owner is expecting a doo wop group, We have never even played with keyboards. But we really like your style man, and your talent. We know you can only make us better at what we do, and we think when you hear us, we can help bring out your talent as well. The last thing you have to worry about is any bad attitude from us toward you because of your color or the fact you don't wanna be in 'Nam. That is straight up." Jake took a deep breath and said, "So, whaddya think? Will you join us?"

"Man, you in the wrong game. You oughta be a preacher person." He pronounced it poyson. Delbert then let out a roar of deep laughter and ordered another round of drinks. He told them he would be happy to give it a try, but it would be under an unwritten agreement that he could leave the group at his discretion. He was not under any strict contract here at this piano bar so he could start anytime.

Just like that he became the fourth member of the Shuswap Doo Wop Band. And Delbert changed their sound dramatically! He was able to add so much to their group. Not only did the doo wop genre cry out for keys, but they were now able to get their teeth into so much more: Soul, R&B, blues, the list went on. Since they were to be paid quite a bit above what they had been expecting, the boys were willing to each take a smaller share so the four of them could be on a par, pay wise.

Delbert had followed them back to the bungalow that night and once they settled in, the boys trusted their better judgment and told their story to the new band member. How they happened to be here and what they had been through. If they couldn't trust Delbert in that matter, then everything else they talked to him about tonight was bogus. And Iggy realized it went both ways. He told Delbert all about the deal they had with the CWPP, and the overhanging risk Delbert would be under should the bad guys ever find out they were living and working here in Kelowna.

"Shit, boys, I figure this is safer than me havin' to go to fight the yellow man if I go back to the States. So, hey, I'm in," Delbert exclaimed.

Much more was discussed before they all went to bed. It was an opportunity for them to really get to know each other, so their opinions on the use of drugs and alcohol came up, as did their current relationships with other people (here Jake blushed profusely), their politics to some extent, likes, dislikes in music, books, and humor. On and on the night lasted, until the early hours of the morning. It was amazing how much in common the four men shared.

At three fifteen am the phone rang, and Jake was surprised to be speaking with Detective Hansen from Calgary. "Sorry to be calling so late, Jake, I was forgetting about the time zone, but still I would've been late anyway, I guess," then Jake cut him off.

"No worries, Detective; we've been up rapping. What's up?"

"Just thought you should know the Russian is still on the loose and there were a couple of sightings reported that may indicate he could be heading your way. We have just passed this info on to Sergeant White out there." Jake noted the detective was careful not to mention the city name of Kelowna.

"Well, thanks for the heads up, Detective. We'll keep our eyes open and be sure to keep in touch with you and Riley should the need arise." He was letting Hansen know that he was aware the RCMP held trump over the Calgary police in regard to any action with the Russian, but that they would certainly keep the two detective friends in the loop. *So many ups and downs,* thought Jake as he hung up the phone and was explaining the call to the others. This thing with the Russian couldn't go on forever, could it? After designating the fourth bedroom to Delbert and getting him fixed up with bedding, they finally retired for the night.

Chapter Forty-Three

Christmas Eve, 1971

THE FOUR band members, the lounge owner Kenny Chou, and his niece Suzie Lee all sat around a table at the restaurant section of The Emerald Lounge. Because it was Christmas Eve, the bar was closed. This was something new for Jake and Iggy, since they had normally become accustomed to the necessity of working in some bar while everyone else celebrated the season. Here it was different. It probably had something to do with the large section of retired people who made up the majority of the city's population. They no doubt had a say in the municipality's bylaws and that was okay with the band. They needed a rest, and it was a nice time of year to simply chill out and enjoy themselves.

There was nothing new regarding the search for the Russian. Jake and Iggy both thought he had decided to return to Los Angeles where he would have been able to hide from the law by getting some help from Big Al Gabrazzi. The thought that this animal was getting away with murdering their friend was very upsetting, but there was not much they could do about it.

Sergeant White had been around earlier during the week to check up on the boys, and he was impressed at how easily they had settled into their new environment. He was concerned with the lack of progress being made by law authorities on both sides of the border, and unless there was a breakthrough soon it was only a matter of time before the witness protection program for the boys would be terminated. *Too bad,* thought White. They really seemed to be taking to the community and it would be difficult to see them leave.

Now everyone was exchanging small gifts around the table. Iggy had received a new strap for his Martin acoustic guitar and Jake was admiring the newly released *Led Zeppelin IV* album that contained the hit single "Stairway to Heaven."

Jake watched in anticipation as Suzie unwrapped her gift that he had purchased for her. The gift exchange was supposed to be on a random draw basis where each of the six at the table were to pick names from a hat. Jake had arranged yesterday with the others that whoever drew Suzie's name, they were to give it to him. So, in exchange for Suzie's name, Jake had given Delbert's name to Kenny.

Suzie's face lit up when she opened the small packet with a silver charm bracelet inside it. The bracelet at this time only had one attachment. A miniature electric Fender bass guitar. She knew immediately who her secret Santa was and gave Jake (Mark) a short kiss in front of everyone at the table.

Delbert received a yellow, black and green Rastafarian hat from Kenny, and Kenny in turn received a black ball cap from Iggy with the words "The Boss" engraved in emerald, green embroidery on the front of it.

As the group were gathering up the wrappings from their gifts, they suddenly heard a loud CRASH! coming from the kitchen. Kenny jumped up and ran to see what had caused the loud noise. When he reached the kitchen, he saw a young man picking up pieces of smashed dirty plates, broken wine glasses, and silverware that had spread across the floor in front of him. Kenny recognized the man as Jimmy Chang, a part time bartender at the lounge.

"Jimmy, you okay?" asked Kenny, clearly concerned.

"As if you would care," the young man said sullenly. His hands were shaking, and he was obviously not well.

Only last week, Kenny had spoken with Jimmy, and it had been a serious discussion. Jimmy was the son of one of Kenny's cousins in Saigon and he had hired the young man as a favor to his relative. He recalled the talk they had and how angry he was to discover Jimmy was using drugs, in particular cocaine, that he had purchased from a bartender somewhere in Banff. The matter of taking hard drugs was a strong violation of the house rules Kenny had established with every employee right at the time of hiring them. Because of the connection to his cousin, Kenny had decided to give Jimmy a second chance at the time, but now regretted his decision.

"Look at yourself, Jimmy. You are high on drugs again, aren't you? I told you what would happen if you did not stop. Now you bring shame to the family. You must leave now!" He reached in his suit jacket for his wallet and gave the young man his final week's wages. With that, Jimmy threw his apron on the floor and ran out the back door of the building.

When Kenny returned to the group at the table, he apologized and explained the situation. Iggy was quick to pick up on the mention of the bartender in Banff who Kenny suspected was selling drugs to his cousin's son. *Another life in jeopardy,* Iggy thought. Man, things were getting out of control.

The incident brought sadness to an otherwise beautiful evening. It was getting late, so the boys decided to return home and they left Suzie to console her uncle. On the way home, Iggy said to the other three, "Y'all heard Kenny mention the bartender drug pusher? Anyone want to bet it's not our guy at the Big Bear Bar?"

Iggy was now really pissed off. Why didn't the authorities have a handle on this shit yet? It had been obvious to the band members when they were playing at the bar in Sunshine what was happening. Was everyone in that goddamn bar in on this? He was at a loss, so he decided to call Hansen tomorrow morning and have a chat with him.

~ * ~

Christmas Day, 1971
10:25 am

Gone was the seasonal good feelings of the previous night.

The boys had witnessed another soul lost to drugs that were being sold by the organization once under the control of Dino Martini. He, along with his immediate boss, Vinnie Fellino, was in prison. But the mad Russian was on the loose and no doubt he had met up with Vinnie's partner Big Al Gabrazzi in Los Angeles. The fact that a bartender in the Big Bear Bar in Sunshine might be selling was likely. He picked up the phone and called Hansen on his personal line.

"Hey detective, Merry Christmas," he said when Hansen came on the other end.

"Back batcha," replied Hansen.

Small talk was finished, and Iggy got into it.

"A kid at our new place of employment was recently fired because of using cocaine he had purchased from a dealer at a bar in Banff. I believe it was at the same bar where we briefly played, the Big Bear Bar in Sunshine Village. The kid left here pissed off at the owner. His name's Jimmy Chang, and I thought you might want to talk to him. I do not know if Sergeant White is aware of this."

"Okay, we'll look into it. Just so you know, the lab results came back on our vic in the burned out car found earlier. As you might have figured, dentals prove it was Dr. Jeffreys beyond a doubt. Poor bastard. Oh, and the tech boys also found a thumb print on a pint vodka bottle under the front seat which has been traced back to one Grigory Ivanovich. But you knew it had to be him. So, we're back to the Russian. Our friends in L.A. can't seem to find the guy and they simply don't have sufficient evidence against Gabrazzi to go to court. You are now up to date."

"Thanks, Hansen, guess we'll just have to go with the flow here. I don't understand why you guys can't get this asshole. I mean we're not dealing with a ghost, are we? How many Russians are there running around anyway? Jesus!" he hung up.

Christmas Day
10:33 am

While Iggy was speaking with Detective Hansen, Jimmy Chan was inhaling the last of three lines of coke off his wrist in the men's room at the Big Bear Bar. He had received his final pay from "Uncle" Kenny the previous day and immediately drove in his beat-up Chevy to the bar. What money he had was now gone and maybe he had just enough coke left to get him through the day.

He made his way to the bar and met up with the bar manager, Brent Wrigley. Brent was a preppy dude who had dropped out of college after three years chasing a business degree at Mount Royal University in Lincoln Park, Calgary.

His dad had been disappointed when Brent had decided to take a year off, but it was soon forgotten. His boy was just going through one of his things like a lot of the youth today, he figured, but he'd come out of it. In the meantime, though, he *was* getting tired of sending money out to Brent Jr. to supplement his bar earnings. *Where was he spending all his money, for Christ's sake?* thought Brent Wrigley, Sr.

Brent was getting ready for the Christmas Day crowd that would soon be coming off the slopes from their morning runs. He had a pretty good supply of coke left from his last purchase through Carlos and he wondered what had happened to the Latino. He had not heard a word from him since he had made the last buy. He remembered him leaving the night of the snowstorm with a huge pale guy who wore a dirty goatee. It was the guy's eyes though, that Brent would remember most, and he shivered. Just like those of some kind of reptile. Lifeless, yet alert.

"What's up, Jimmy?" Brent said to the young Asian as he saddled up to the bar. "You look pissed off at something."

"Yeah, I got let go last night. On Christmas Eve, by my own uncle, for shit's sake! Can you believe that?"

"That's too bad, dude." But he really didn't give a shit about this loser. "I thought you had something going there with the owner's niece?"

"That bitch! She's seeing some new guy who's playing in a band that just came in last week. In fact, I thought I saw them playing here one night the other week. There were only two of them at that time. They called themselves Fusion. From what I heard, they shoulda' called themselves *Confusion*. Get it? Ha! Ha! Ha!"

Idiot, thought Brent. The guy's obviously jealous of the dude who stole his lady. No matter, maybe he could move a gram or so of product here. "Need anything else?" He asked with a wink.

"Maybe tomorrow, man. I'm broke. Know where I can make a few bucks?"

"I'll see," said Brent. He was trying to remember something Carlos had mentioned to him. Something about the two guys Jimmy had just ranted on about. He was too busy at the moment to think about it. Oh well, customers were starting to arrive. Time to make a buck or two.

Chapter Forty-Four

Friday, December 30th
6:10 pm

THE NEW musicians at The Emerald Lounge were finishing their supper in the restaurant section of the club and they were reviewing their charts, comparing the song lists to ensure they had their notes synced correctly as to key notations, individual solo parts, any special line stops, pauses, or accents; the usual cheat notes that most bands used to help their shows go well.

The three former members were looking forward to working in a live session with Delbert. Their rehearsals had gone very well, and it was really cool to be able to just click with somebody who was totally new to them. The new genre they were attempting relied to a large degree on vocals and, so far, the old tunes were sounding good to Iggy's ear. Hopefully, the crowd here was going to agree.

The owner, Kenny Chou, approached their table and wished them well on their performance this evening. Suzie Lee was with Kenny, and Jake introduced her to Delbert. She promised to bring some of her friends with her tonight and they'd get the word out on the street. "So, you better be good, you Shuswap Doo Wops," she joked.

10:15 pm
The Shuswap Doo Wop Band had just finished their first set and from the crowd's reaction, things were going to be alright at The Emerald Lounge. The owner was pleased, and he was particularly happy the band had decided to take Delbert in as a fourth member. Kenny himself was only too familiar with racism in its ugly form and it was uplifting to see young men like the *Shuswap Doo Wop Band* unite as they did with Delbert.

The whole club was now in its busy season with Christmas having just passed and New Year's festivities just around the corner. Ordinarily, the restaurant section of the business had to be carried by both of the bars, the lounge and the karaoke section. But now, because many couples were eating out during the holiday season, the bar would have a bit of a cushion on which to work, even more so if the crowds continued to pour in to hear this new group.

11:45 pm
Well, how about this crowd, thought Iggy. They were into the tail end of their second set and the crowd kept growing. The interesting thing was that the average age here tonight was probably in the early fifties. He remembered what the owner had said about Doo Wop. How the "Older peoples like it very much." Well, that much was true. Iggy, however, still managed to stick to their plan of limiting the Doo Wop output to two or three songs a set. But the crowd didn't seem to mind, and they now got into "Up on The Roof" by The Drifters.

"Hey, this is a fun gig," Iggy said to the guys, and the others in the group apparently agreed. They were really getting into their sound and, man, Iggy was having a blast with the "older peoples." It was nice not to have to be concerned with some young kid overdosing in one of the washrooms, or some loudmouth ruining it for others. For a brief moment, Iggy's mind was at Sam's Bar in Whitefish, and the Big Bear Bar in Sunshine Village, and all the bad shit that had happened since then. Then he caught sight of Delbert giving him a quizzical look and so he snapped back into a happier state of mind. They closed the set with the Ben E. King 1961 classic "Stand by Me."

The crowd was applauding with enthusiasm and Kenny, along with Suzie, came over to the stage. Kenny was all smiles as he clapped hands for the band. "You Shuswap Doo Wop very good! You play here now steady, okay?"

"Yep," said Jake. "From now on we are your steady guys." The guys readily took the owner up on his offer and left for their room in the back of the bar.

Suzie caught up with them in the back hallway and made a point of pulling Jake aside. "So, it's going to be a steady thing, is it?" she said with that cute smile, her head tilted back at him. Jake caught the double entendre and replied in his best John Wayne drawl, "Well ma'am, there are some things a man just can't run away from." He looked at her with all the charm he could muster in his grin and gave her a big kiss before she had a chance to resist.

Yeah, they were going to have fun here.

What could possibly go wrong?

Chapter Forty-Five

New Year's Eve, 1971
4:15 pm

BRENT WRIGLEY Jr. was looking forward to tonight. New Year's in The Bear was always a great time and lots of his pals from university would definitely be here, ready to party. He was wondering who the bar had lined up for a band. That in turn brought his mind back to his conversation with Jimmy Chang on Christmas day. Jimmy had said the two musicians who had made a brief appearance here one night were now in Kelowna. As Brent recalled, the two guys came back to The Bear with a drummer after being introduced by The Jets, who went on tour from here.

The group that called themselves Fusion was also good, but now they were gone as well. Too bad, thought Brent. No matter, Dowl would no doubt have a good show for the crowd.

He was checking his stock of liquor and realized he was short on a few items. He was definitely going to need more rum and rye, say a couple of forties of The Captain dark and one Canadian Club. Also, a couple of two-fours of beer, make 'em Moosehead and Alpine for the Maritime jerks who would probably be here tonight. He left the bar after securing it and made his way to the basement where the club's liquor supplies were held. On the way he passed the front office and yelled out to Joan Wright, Dowl's assistant. "Hey, Joanie, I'll be right up, I'm just going down to the stock room for some booze."

Upon entering the hallway that would take him to the back of the basement, he thought he heard somebody coming behind him, and he checked to see if it might be Joan. She was the only other staff worker on duty this early as he recalled. And hey, he wouldn't mind running into her down here, he thought. Man, she was one fine looking lady. It was only last night that she had rubbed herself against him while they were behind the bar. And then she had the nerve to reach down the front of his pants just as a couple had come up to the counter for drinks. God...

Brent's fantasies of Joan were suddenly interrupted by a large hand that reached over his shoulder and covered his mouth while he felt a sharp pain on the side of his neck. He then heard a low voice with a strong Russian accent speak to him. "Not to say nothink, just go to the stockroom, Mr. Barman."

The guy's breath was horrible, but Brent had the feeling that would be the least of his problems as he was roughly pushed into the small area. He heard the door close behind him.

"Now we talk, barman," said the Russian. "You tell me where two musicians are that play here. What room they occupy, yes?" When Brent had turned around to face his antagonist, all his fears came crashing into his mind at once. It was the man he had seen leaving the bar with Carlos that night of the snowstorm, the week before Christmas. The guy with the reptile eyes. As he remembered these things, he realized his body was reacting strangely to something. The sting he had felt on his neck was surely a needle prick and he knew immediately he had been drugged. His mind wandered and he had trouble centering his thoughts on anything except an extreme fear of what might happen to him.

5:43 pm

Joan left Mr. Dowl's office and decided to check on Brent in the bar, maybe get a free pre-New Year's cocktail. When she got to the bar, she was surprised to see it was still locked and there was no sign of him. That's odd, she thought. It was over an hour ago when she heard him call out to her on his way to the stockroom. She decided to check it out and went down the stairs to the basement storage room. The light was off, which was also weird. Normally the staff left it on until the last hour before bar closing time. That made it easier to get around down here when you were in a hurry, which was usually the case. She carefully walked down the hall to the stock room and entered the darkened facility. "Hey Brent?" she half whispered. "Come on Brent, don't fool around. You're scaring me." She groped for the light switch inside the room. When she turned the light on, she saw Brent lying on the floor and she began screaming.

7:30 pm

Detectives Hansen and Riley were discussing the situation at the Big Bear Bar with Captain Miller and Sergeant White in John Dowl's office. The call had come into Hansen an hour ago from White who had in turn been advised of the incident by Constable Green of the Banff Town Police. They had spent the last half hour at the scene of the crime downstairs. At this time, there was no doubt in Hansen's mind that a crime had been committed, although the body of Brent Wrigley Jr. was set up in such a way as to suggest he had committed suicide. With everything else that had occurred surrounding the Big Bear Bar, this was simply too coincidental.

Interviews with the boy's father, along with Joan Wright who had first discovered the body, revealed the young man certainly exhibited none of the behavior normally associated with suicide. Additional meetings with other staff members and friends were expected to yield the same results. Also, Riley had detected an adhesive substance over the victim's mouth. They were sure this would test out as everyday duct tape residue. Finally, the detectives also noted a small needle opening, barely discernible on Wrigley's neck. No doubt a further examination of the body would reveal he had been drugged. Everything pointed to the fact that the bar manager had been subdued and questioned by somebody who was a professional at this type of work.

"Sergeant, we have reason to believe this is the work of the Russian, Grigori Ivanov, who is suspected as an accomplice in the attack on the two boys in Cochrane a while back along with the kidnapping and murder of the prison doctor last week. We understand the two boys are now in a group playing at The Emerald Lounge in your City."

"That is correct, Detective. Apparently, they have been talking with you, notwithstanding our advice to the contrary, in accordance with the intent of the CWPP."

This guy is a serious man, thought Hansen.

"Yes sir. Just so you know, Detective Riley and myself were initially instrumental in the placement of the boys in the Program, and we will not do anything to put them in jeopardy at this time. You should also know, however, that a young chap was recently fired from the bar where the boys are performing. It happened on Christmas Eve. His name is Jimmy Chang, and he was let go because he had been caught using drugs while at work. He apparently purchased cocaine at the Big Bear Bar here. You can verify this with his uncle, Kenny Chou, owner of The Emerald Lounge. We were getting around to talking to you about the incident just before this apparent homicide took place." Hansen looked guiltily at his boss when he said this.

"Captain, my bad on that and I apologize for not getting to Sergeant White earlier, but we've been running around trying to find the Russian through our network with the LAPD."

White was clearly a bit put out by this admission but decided to let it go.

"Gentlemen," said Captain Miller, "I don't think I need to stress the importance of keeping both of our departments in the loop on this investigation. Let's proceed." From the manner of his tone, the matter was finished in this setting, but Hansen knew he was on thin ice here and badly needed to make amends with his boss.

"Captain, Riley and I have developed a pretty good relationship with the musicians ever since last summer. I'd like to get Sergeant White's approval to continue our investigation with the boys directly in Kelowna."

"With your concurrence, that is," Riley quickly added.

The two superior officers agreed to the suggestion made by the detectives and at that point Riley and Hansen immediately made plans to fly to Kelowna and continue their work on the case. They would have preferred to take their vehicle to Kelowna and thereby be able to maintain more efficient and on-scene communications. Maybe Sergeant White could help them in that regard and Iggy would mention it to Captain Miller. Regardless, they should be in Kelowna sometime close to 10:00 pm. Their flight from Calgary was scheduled to depart at 9:50 pm but again, they gained an hour due to time zone changes.

Hansen told Riley to pack his suit, that they'd be going out to a New Year's dance at The Emerald Lounge.

"Jeez, Don, does this mean we're going on a date?"

~ * ~

Grigori drove at the posted speed of 65 mph along the Trans-Canada Highway West toward his destination of Kelowna. He was driving a rental Jeep Cherokee, the same vehicle they had when he and Carlos had attempted the hit in Cochrane on the two musicians. Too bad about Carlos, but that was the way it went in this game. The Russian was very pragmatic about what he did for a living. He had never exhibited any compassion for anyone else involved, whether the victim was on his side of the transaction or as his opponent. He simply did the job.

The "job" in the case of the young bartender back at the Big Bear Bar in Sunshine Village meant subduing the individual with a small shot of sodium pentothal, commonly known as truth serum. The drug in small doses acted as a barbiturate and a strong anesthetic. In larger measures it was used by the U.S. as one of the first lethal injection drugs during executions. For his subject, Grigori had used both drug dosages. Prompted through fear, young Wrigley gladly told Grigori what Jimmy Chang had passed on to him; he also gave the Russian a little book he carried on his person which contained the names and telephone numbers of people he had met since tying up with Carlos. He had the names of people who were buying product from him. He also gave him the name of the bar where Jimmy had worked prior to being fired. That was all he knew, but Grigori thought it would suffice.

So, another longer shot of the drug took him totally out. He checked the pockets of the bar manager and saw he was carrying a small amount of cocaine. This he dropped on the floor beside the body. He also left the syringe that he had used stuck in Wrigley's arm. While it would appear at first blush as a suicide, the Russian was under no illusions that it was only a matter of time before it was confirmed the young man had indeed been murdered. No matter, that's all he wanted at this point. Time. It was approximately a five-hour drive from Banff to Kelowna. That would get him there around nine forty-five tonight, and he would see if he might be able to find either the boy, Jimmy Chang, or maybe even the two musicians, his primary targets.

9:35 pm

The Shuswap Doo Wop Band had just started their first set. It was a packed crowd; everybody was decked out in formal wear for the New Year's party that was getting underway at a moderate pace. Young men in three-piece suits, women in long expensive gowns. At this stage everybody was still relatively sober, and Jake wondered how long that would last. At least this should be a civil affair, void of any ill will and animosity, given the time of year, the average age of the partygoers, and the traditional good cheer that went along with the festivity.

It was the band's game plan to keep their tunes to the easy listening genre for the first set; switch to some faster classic Rock tunes, radio top 40 and the like for the second set then go for the wilder stuff mixed with some good dance tunes for the last set. Mindful of a good segment of the over fifty crowd that would be coming, they would certainly have a minimum of three Doo Wop tunes per set, maybe even get some audience participation happening with the "older peoples."

Iggy had distributed two by four feet lay down charts to each of the four band members to use. The charts listed each song in order of presentation. Alongside each song there was a notation as to who was doing the lead vocal, what key the song was in, and any little side notes of significance. For example, the notation might show how the song was intro'd and outro'd. It was a good system and kept everyone informed. They were able to keep the ball rolling at a good pace and lend that much more professionalism to their craft.

Halfway through the number "Under the Boardwalk" by The Drifters, Jake looked up and saw a couple of familiar figures entering the lounge. Damn if it wasn't their two detective friends, Hansen and Riley. They sauntered over to the side of the room where they found an unoccupied table and surveyed the room as they got settled. A waitress came over and took drink orders from them, and soon thereafter they were joined at the table by the owner, Kenny Chou. Interesting, thought Jake. He wondered what had happened to bring the detectives directly to their venue. All in due course, as the ADA in Calgary had told them earlier. Whatever, he was heartened to know they were in safe hands with the cops here, and he continued with the first matter at hand which was entertaining the crowd.

Chapter Forty-Six

10:15 pm

JIMMY CHANG was alone in his apartment in downtown Kelowna watching the New Year's celebrations that had already happened in NYC. He'd change over to a local channel later to catch the scene in Vancouver. Now there's where he should be, he thought. Lots of ladies and lots of fun. Of course, he had no money, no job, and not even any prospects for work. To top it off, he was too proud to call his father and ask for help. Well, that wasn't really true. It wasn't that he was proud. It was just that he was sick of getting the lecture from his father. He might have to take some more of his shit, though, if he wanted to get out of here.

His telephone rang and brought him out of his reverie. At first, he thought it might be his father just calling to say hi or to ask him over. But he did not recognize the voice. In fact, it sounded like a foreign language, maybe East European or Russian?

"Need spik to Mr. Jimmy Chang, please," the voice said.

"This is Jimmy," he replied.

"Mr. Jimmy, I am friend of Mr. Brent at Big Bear. He want me to give you package...like a late Christmas gift. He say you need to help him sell some product though. That okay with you?"

Now, the average individual would see right through this as either a setup or at the very best some kind of scam whereby his "friend" Brent Wrigley would be coming out ahead of him. But right now, in Jimmy Chang's world, he was not seeing things from a clear perspective. He needed cash or drugs. He was being given an opportunity to have both.

"Yeah, sure man. Where can I meet you?"

"You give me address and I will be there as soon as I can. Need to go to party pretty soon, right?" By giving the request some urgency, he was not giving Jimmy any time to think about the unexpected offer that was suddenly falling into his lap. So, the Russian was given the address of the guy who could get him closer, if not actually in front of, the two who had ratted out his associates.

11:00 pm

The detectives and the band had arranged to have several tables brought together in the corner of the dance floor and they were all able to sit in one group setting. The owner sat with them, as did Suzie Lee and three of her girlfriends. Introductions were made all around and it looked like it was now possible that Hansen and Riley might even get to have a dance or two tonight. The Detectives though, were preoccupied with more serious thoughts and Hansen took Kenny Chou aside.

"Sir, I understand you are familiar with a young man by the name of Jimmy Chang. I believe it was necessary for you to let him go as he was using drugs here, despite previous warnings from you."

"That correct, detective. What he do now?"

"Oh, I would just like to talk to him about another matter. Do you know where I can find him?"

The owner gave Jimmy's address to Hansen and the two detectives took off for the downtown apartment in their unmarked RCMP vehicle that Sergeant White had been so kind to loan them. It was only a year old, a 1970 Ford Custom, black with no frills, but it had a 427 engine, and it would go like hell. Most importantly, it was outfitted with a full communications deck so they would be able to stay in touch with their people.

When they arrived at Chang's apartment, there was nobody answering the doorbell. Also, there was nothing to indicate where young Chang had gone, nor when he had left. The television was on, but that was it. The door had not even been locked. Weird. Hansen had a bad feeling about the situation but there wasn't much to do except go back to the dance at The Emerald Lounge.

11:30 pm

The party was in full swing when Hansen and Riley arrived back at the lounge, and they decided to relax and enjoy the show. The boys on the stage would soon be counting down the final seconds of 1971. Hansen didn't really like the whole New Year's party scene. Normally, he was on duty during the festivity and, as a result, his wife usually ended up getting pissed off because they weren't able to go out on a special "date." Truth be known, Don Hansen was just not a happy guy. He could be, but when he thought about it, he was usually most happy only when he was putting bad guys behind bars.

Maybe he shouldn't have married. Fifteen years now, no kids. His wife had her own little business as a hairdresser, and she liked to keep busy at that. It had been quite some time, probably six months or more since they had made love. As a couple they had drifted apart, and it scared him to realize that he should have been more concerned about the direction their marriage had taken.

His partner, Gerry Riley, on the other hand, was a different dude. He was a single guy, always looking for that perfect "one." Hansen had to keep reminding him there was no such thing. The way Gerry was now looking at Suzie's young girlfriend though, told Hansen he hadn't paid much heed to the advice he had given him.

Hansen was broken from his thoughts when he realized that it was getting very close to the end of 1971. Iggy had the mic, and he was shouting out the traditional countdown. "Ten, nine, eight..." Before he knew it, the girl beside him, another one of Suzie's friends, hauled him onto the dance floor. "Five, four, three, two, one...HAPPY NEW YEAR!"

And everybody around him was kissing the partner he or she was with. Hansen then found himself in the arms of a beautiful young girl who had maybe taken a drink or two too many and she was kissing him openly, letting him know it was okay for him to reciprocate. But he couldn't. *It just isn't right,* he thought. *What's the matter with me?* He walked back to their table, her following him closely.

The young girl smiled at him, more embarrassed at herself than anything, and Hansen started to try to explain his actions, but he found he was at a loss for words. "Look, I'm sorry, but I'm a lot older than you. You really want a guy like one of these Doo Whoppers," and he gestured at the band.

The girl, incredibly, only smiled more broadly and took his hand, guiding him back onto the floor. Before he knew it, they were waltzing to "Auld Lang Syne." "Let's start again," the girl said. "My name is Nancy. And you would be...?" she coaxed him, pressing her body hard against him, speaking intimately into his ear.

"Uh, Don, Don Hansen, pleased to meet you," he replied, finally getting into it. Hansen was suddenly happy. And it had absolutely nothing to do with putting somebody behind bars.

Chapter Forty-Seven

New Year's Day, 1972
1:33 am

DETECTIVES HANSEN and Riley drove back to their rooms at the Red Dragon Motel, only a block from the lounge. Riley was going into the room adjacent to Hansen's when he simply looked back and said to Hansen and the girl "Goodnight, guys, Happy New Year! See you for breakfast in the diner at 9:00, sound okay?"

Hansen nodded, and that was that. He had a number of feelings going through his mind, but he made a decision to just go with it. Deal with it tomorrow.

Meanwhile, in the parking lot of The Emerald Lounge, Grigori Ivanov was patiently waiting for Suzie Lee to climb into her late model Mustang. He assumed it was Suzie Lee, because that was her car, at least according to what Jimmy Chang had told him, and the Russian saw no reason to doubt what Jimmy had said.

When the young man had seen the point of the homemade shiv being held against his eye, he had been more than helpful, also providing the name of the owner of The Emerald Lounge where Suzie worked. The owner was another Asian, a Mr. Kenny Chou who was also an uncle to Suzie. It was all good information to have. If Suzie were unable to take him to the two musicians, certainly Mr. Chou could, being their direct employer. Jimmy unfortunately was of no further use. He would probably be found later today or tomorrow behind the alley where the Russian had left him. Just another OD. Such a waste.

A couple of minutes after Suzie had started the Mustang to warm it up, Ivanov watched as a young man got in the vehicle's passenger seat beside Suzie, glided over toward her, and gave her a kiss. *Sooo, this is the man that is stealink Suzie from Jimmy. Too bad Jimmy is no longer able to do anything about it*, he mused. The car with the two young lovers then made its way out of the parking lot.

He cautiously followed the Mustang to a modern apartment a couple of blocks away and parked out of sight as the young couple went in the front door of the building. A light came on from the first window to the right of the entranceway. It appeared to be a single story, four-unit building, and the Russian was pleased to see one of the front windows was within reach from the front lawn. He would wait for the right time to join them.

1:45 am

Iggy, Roger, and Delbert were beat. The four musicians were usually totally exhausted after any of their performances as the result of giving it all they had. It was also emotionally draining. When Iggy saw Jake leave with Suzie. He knew Jake's hormones were keeping his adrenaline higher than the rest of them. *Good for him*, Iggy thought. It was time his friend got some action. And he was pretty sure the two detectives were also going to get lucky as he watched them take two of Suzie's friends out through the lounge exit.

"Ain't love grand, gentlemen," he said to the remaining musicians. "Let's leave this stuff and go home. We can get it tomorrow. By the way, I was thinking of getting some skiing and ice fishing in for a change. There's a place called Idabel Lake that has rental gear just past Big White, which is only a half hour from here. I'm thinking we could ski and stay at Big White, then do some fishing at Idabel Lake. Sound like a plan?"

Delbert had never put on a pair of skis before, nor had he ever been ice fishing, but he was eager to try both. Roger had skied at a small hill in the Wentworth Valley near his hometown of Truro, but it was definitely nothing like the resorts here, so he was looking forward to the trip as well. They would pack their gear in the van and try to get away before noon tomorrow.

1:55 am

Jake and Suzie had gone directly to Suzie's bedroom. He felt he had to tell Suzie about his true feelings. He had reached a point in their relationship where he had to be totally open if it was going to be meaningful. And wasn't that where all this was heading? He couldn't get over how quickly he was getting so serious about her. He was hoping she felt the same about him and he decided to just dive into the conversation in that vein.

"Suzie, I need to tell you..." he started to say when they both heard a sound coming from the window next to the entry door. He immediately went into a defensive mode, thinking only of the peril they might be in. That night, last month in Cochrane, when they were attacked by the two assassins hired by the drug lords came flashing into his mind. Danger was again a reality.

Jake told Suzie to immediately dial 911 then lock herself in the bathroom while he stealthily moved along the wall of the hallway toward the front door. He was looking around for some kind of weapon and there in the foyer was a long-handled ice scraper for Suzie's car sitting in a large vase. It wasn't much, but it had a hard plastic head, and it was better than nothing. He grabbed the scraper and waited silently for the intruder to make his move. Then it happened.

The Russian never saw nor expected Jake, who was crouched beside the window when it was opened quietly in the pitch-black hallway. Grigori was coming through the open window headfirst, and he had only cleared his shoulders through the small frame when Jake swung the extended windshield ice scraper as hard as he could at the figure in front of him. With a loud roar the Russian fell back from the open window onto the snow-covered lawn and at that moment, a police siren could be heard approaching the apartment. Jake jumped up and saw the figure running around the corner of the apartment building, holding his head in obvious pain. He heard a car start up and roar away just as a Kelowna City Police cruiser arrived at Suzie's driveway.

Chapter Forty-Eight

Monday, January 2nd, 1972
10:04 am

THE GROUP sat around a table at the RCMP Detachment building on McIntyre Rd in Kelowna. Included at the table were the four members of the Shuswap Doo Wop Band, the two Calgary detectives, Sergeant White, club owner Kenny Chou, and his niece Suzie Lee. The meeting was called after the previous nights near disaster at Suzie's apartment. In addition, the body of Jimmy Chang had been found close to 6:00 am on New Year's Day in a downtown alleyway. There was no sign of any apparent foul play and it had initially been reported as a probable overdose.

Much of New Year's Day had been spent by the band at their home, reviewing the events of the previous night. In view of what had happened, Iggy had quickly put his planned ski trip to Big White on hold.

Jake, with the other three musicians, had earlier explained to Suzie a lot of the background behind the man who had assailed them at her place last night. The musicians also felt it was time to tell the story of their involvement in the witness protection program to both Suzie and Kenny. There was no longer any need to hide behind false identities since it was obvious to all that the Russian and probably any of his people were now on to them. Once these animals were captured, their lives could be returned to normal.

Earlier, on New Year's Day, the detectives had been directed by Captain Miller via a phone call initiated through Hansen's beeper to report to Sergeant White as soon as possible. Hansen had still been in the motel with Riley and the two friends of Suzie Lee when he had been paged. *Christ! How embarrassing?* Hansen had thought as he got up to leave the young lady *(Nancy. Her name was Nancy, dammit!)* in bed while he called White from his car phone.

Shortly after 6:30 am, when he had been told it appeared the young man found in the alley had committed suicide, Kenny Chou was sick with guilt over the death of his nephew, Jimmy Chang. Now, however, as they listened to Sergeant White, it was apparent Jimmy had been murdered. That realization remained unsaid at this time, and it was not likely to be discussed in the presence of Suzie and Kenny, but everyone else at the table had no doubt Ivanov was involved in the killing.

While the police continued their manhunt for the Russian, a patrol car had been stationed in front of the property as a deterrent for any further action Ivanov may have designed. Hansen and Riley were going to spend time with the forensics team at the scenes of both crimes, the back alley where Jimmy Chang was found and Suzie's apartment. When the meeting broke up, the boys went back to their bungalow and took Suzie with them, while Kenny went home.

Suzie sat with Jake in front of the living room fireplace while the other three went downstairs to shoot some eight ball. A fire burned warmly, and the only sound was the crackling of the seasoned oak logs as they stared at the flames, each with their own thoughts.

"I'm sorry you had to be a part of all this," said Jake. "And I'm sorry for what has happened to your friend, Jimmy" he added.

"Thank you, Jacob," She was now using his real name, and in fact Jake preferred the formal version of it as opposed to his nickname. Jake was taken by this small gesture and to him it made their relationship more intimate somehow.

"I should tell you more about myself, under the circumstances," Suzie continued. "I came to Canada from South Vietnam in 1964 as a student. It was necessary for me to have a sponsor and that was my Uncle Kenny.

"Kenny had left our former country in the mid Fifties, thank God! By the next decade things in my homeland had turned very unstable and only a select few were being granted permission to immigrate here, even as refugees. My parents had both been executed during the coup of President Ngo Diem. It was terrible. Another family, Jimmy Chang and both his parents, were also given refugee status by the Canadian government under

Uncle Kenny's sponsorship as well. So, we came to Canada.

"When we first landed here, it was not all fun. There were many who did not treat us as equals. At school, we were called names and subjected to racist bigotry and ill will. We have tried to lead productive lives here in Kelowna and, thanks to my uncle, we have made inroads in this regard. But I am sorry to say that some of us have taken the efforts of people like Uncle Kenny for granted. Jimmy had a falling out with his parents and unfortunately, he recently became involved with the wrong group of people. My uncle feels guilty over letting him go from his job, but he should not feel that way. Jimmy was not a good person in my mind, and it was only a matter of time before something like this had to happen."

Jake held both of Suzie's hands in his own as he looked at her.

"Suzie, I cannot imagine the hardships suffered by you and your family in your previous life. But you should know that you are now among people who love you and care for you very much. The police, along with my friends and I, will protect you now. The individual who tried to harm us last night will be arrested and our lives will go back to normal. That I promise. And another thing. I would very much like to be a part of your life."

Suzie then took Jake's hands in hers and kissed them. He held her close to him and they stared at the burning flames, feeling more secure in each other's arms. Iggy then appeared on the scene and apologized for interrupting their time alone.

"Okay, brother, what's up?" asked Jake.

"Well guys, we were thinking it would be nice to get away from here for a few days. Maybe do some skiing and other outdoor stuff at Big White. We definitely need a change of scenery. You up for it?"

"Hey, that sounds great. Whattya think, Suzie?"

"Sure, Jacob" she said. "Just let me call Uncle Kenny and let him know what we're doing."

Suzie had mixed feelings about Jacob. She was certainly physically attracted to the young man from the Maritimes. He was not the type to force his intentions upon her, always polite and considerate of her feelings. Actually, sometimes she thought he was being a little too considerate, she mused in a kind of naughty way. But to be fair, they were at the stage in their relationship where the physical act of lovemaking was only a heartbeat away. Had it not been for that awful incident on New Year's Eve, they would have definitely gone to bed together. So that wasn't really a problem.

She thought she might be in love with Jacob, but what about their mixed race and culture? They hadn't really talked about that side of things yet. For her, it really didn't matter what color a person's skin was. But she'd have to make sure Jacob's thoughts in that regard were similar to her own. She'd also talk to Uncle Kenny about her feelings and get his feedback. In fact, maybe he could come with the group on their ski trip to Big White. It had been a while since she was last there, and she was looking forward to the outing.

While the group at the bungalow were packing for the trip, Kenny Chou was entering his modest home in the northwest end of the city. It was now approaching noon. After leaving the meeting at the RCMP office, he decided to stop off at a nearby store and pick up a few groceries which he now placed on his kitchen table. As he walked down the hall toward his den, he heard what sounded like a conversation coming from that area. He was surprised when he walked into the room and there, crouched over his answering machine was a very large, pale man listening intently to a message that was playing. The man suddenly became aware of Kenny's presence and swiftly leaped toward him, brandishing what looked like a small knife.

Before Kenny could react, he felt a sharp pain in his chest and fell to the floor. He saw the man's legs running out of the room and he heard the door slam as the figure made his exit. It took all of Kenny's strength to crawl to the phone, and while he lay on the floor, he was barely able to dial 911 before passing out.

Chapter Forty-Nine

12:15 pm

JAKE WAS navigating as Iggy drove and he had a B.C. provincial map spread out over his lap in the front seat of their van. Suzie sat with Delbert and Roger in the body of the vehicle as the five of them left Kelowna heading south.

"Big White is a half hour from South Kelowna driving southeast on the Kelowna-Rock Creek Highway," said Jake. "Then take the Big White Road on your left. To get to Lake Idabel from Big White, you only have to drive back on the Big White Rd to the KRC Highway, then turn south and drive for five miles."

The five of them were looking forward to getting away from the events of New Year's Eve. It was a brand-new year, 1972. Surely the police would be successful in capturing the Russian. After all, a manhunt was now in full operation, and everybody was optimistic he would be found in the next few days. The van pulled into the lot of the Big White Ski Resort at 1:15 pm.

The group was admiring the powder that had fallen overnight and covered the slopes of the ski resort in a blanket of white. They were pleased to see there were not that many skiers out today, even though the weather was absolutely perfect for a day on the slopes...nothing but sun, and the temperature was around thirty-nine degrees.

Iggy noted there was a sign near the lodge entrance that made a point of noting metric conversions, no doubt for the benefit of its European tourists. Last night they received fifteen centimeters of fresh powder, it was supposed to remain at a high of five degrees Celsius for the next couple of days, and Big White was only eight-and one-half kilometers from Kelowna. *Gimme a break!* Thought Iggy. There was talk on the news that Trudeau would soon have the country converted over to metric by seventy-five. He couldn't imagine the Americans following suit.

They walked up to the registration desk and asked the smiling girl there if they might have suitable accommodations for a rowdy crew of Maritimers. Seeing the expression on the young lady's face begin to fade to a more serious tone, he changed his presentation. Taking the lady aside from his group, he now spoke in a collegiate manner to her.

"Actually, Miss, I was just kidding. We are here as a study group from UBCO on a group thesis program to examine the effect of urban sprawl on the confined wildlife struggling in areas such as Big White." He had no clue if the University of B.C. Okanagan had any such discipline. Whatever, the lady behind the counter was hot and he wanted to impress her.

"Gosh" she said, "we have tons of room available. What kinda setup do you need?"

"Well, for our married couple here," Iggy gestured to Jake and Suzie, "we'll need a private single. For the rest of us, maybe a large family type situation to accommodate five or six adults. We may have two or three more landing." He was thinking of Kenny and the two detectives. Suzie had mentioned she had invited her uncle in a message she had left on his machine. Iggy would make a point of calling Hansen later.

"Sure," she said. "My name's Heather and I'll be your contact person while you're here." She smiled at the others standing across the foyer from them. Then she looked back directly at Iggy and said, "You know, for whatever might come up." He held her eyes and gave her his signature grin.

"Well, Heather, you never know. Study groups can get boring after a while. Any good bands playing here this week that you could recommend?"

"Sure." again that come-on look. "If you like straight up rock there's a group just in from Banff. They're on tour, called The Jets."

Iggy couldn't believe it. Maybe it was an omen of good fortune coming their way? He might put this to the test later tonight at the bar if Heather was still around.

"Please book us in until Thursday, January 5th and hey, we'll see ya in a bit, Heather." They decided to take a quick run to the lake and check things out there while their rooms were being made up. Delbert and Roger just looked at Iggy with a huge grin on the way back to the lot. "So now we're a "study group," are we?" asked Delbert, giving his friend an elbow nudge. "Looks like you be studyin' the lady there, Iggy, not the wildlife." They all shared a laugh as they piled into the van again.

1:37 pm

The scene at Kenny's home in Kelowna was like a controlled beehive. It was busy with police collecting whatever evidence might be available from the violence that had recently occurred. Hansen and Riley were on the scene as the result of a call from Sergeant White. They had just left Suzie's apartment after spending a half hour at the alleyway downtown. Once again, an individual close to the musicians had been attacked and there was no doubt who was behind the attacks.

An ambulance had rushed the club owner to the Kelowna General Hospital following the 911 call Kenny had managed to make. He was currently undergoing surgery in an attempt to save his life and it was too soon to say at this time whether or not he would make it. Doctors at the hospital had told authorities they were giving him fifty-fifty odds at best.

And now at the scene of the attack they listened as Hansen was replaying the message that Suzie had left on Kenny's answering machine. The playback indicator showed the message as having been received.

"Hello, Uncle. It is Suzie and I wanted to ask you to join a group of us who are going to Big White Ski Resort for a few days to try and forget what happened recently. The boys would like you to join us for some fun if you can. We'll be leaving around noon today. If you come later, ask at the front registration desk for us. Love you."

"Let's go over to the hospital first, Gerry, and see if we can talk with Kenny," said Hansen. "He may be able to confirm that it was indeed the Russian who made this attack. If it was our guy, that maniac obviously now knows about the trip the group is making to Big White and is either there now or will be very soon. Sergeant, would you please call the lodge at Big White and try to reach the group...talk to either Iggy or Jake if possible and tell them to get in a room and lock all access avenues, the doors, windows, whatever. Tell 'em we're on our way."

~ * ~

186

Grigori was watching the lodge for any sign of the group. He was not aware of what vehicle they had driven here, nor was he even certain they had yet arrived. Moreover, he was reluctant to enter the lodge for fear someone might spot him. He would have preferred more people around him so he could try to blend in somehow or, as an alternative, even if he had some type of disguise. And more information on what the group had planned would be helpful. For the time being he decided to simply wait in an area away from incoming traffic and hope to spot the musicians coming or going.

Unknown to the Russian, he had missed the group by only ten minutes. Just before he had turned off the Kelowna-Rock Creek Highway and had driven onto the Big White Road, the group of five had already registered at the ski lodge and had then returned to the highway and turned south for Idabel Lake to do some ice fishing before going to the dance at the bar later tonight.

After another hour, the Russian had finally grown tired of waiting for the musicians to show up anywhere, so he decided to take a chance and he went into the lodge. He saw a beautiful young girl at the registration desk and walked over to her as the telephone on her desk began ringing.

Heather had just returned to her station at the front desk of the Big White Ski *Resort* when the telephone rang. Before picking up the phone, she acknowledged with a curt nod the huge man standing directly in front of her. The guy was really creepy with those weird eyes, and he certainly didn't look like he was here to enjoy the skiing.

The caller identified himself as Sergeant White with the RCMP in Kelowna and she automatically reached for her notepad and began taking notes by writing "RCMP" on the pad. He asked to speak with either a Mr. Miles or a Mr. England. "They should be there now," he said. "There was a group of five." he added.

Right away she remembered the older students that had landed around lunch time. "One moment, sir," she said, placing the call on hold. Let's see, she thought as she checked her index and found the group that had requested two separate rooms, one single for Mr. England and his wife and a large suite for the other three. The cute single guy was in that room, she remembered. When she tried calling his room, there was no answer, nor was there anyone in the smaller room.

She gave all this info to the sergeant, and he seemed quite concerned that they could not be reached. "Well, sir, I'll keep an eye out for them. They sounded like they were very interested in hearing a band that is scheduled to play here tonight."

"Is there anything else going on locally that might have attracted them for the afternoon?"

"I know they are here doing a study on urban sprawl and how it may be impacting the wildlife on the lake. Maybe they have gone to Idabel Lake?"

Now the Sergeant sounded more confused than alarmed.

"You're sure we have the right party?"

"Absolutely, sir. From UBCO. They're here working on a group thesis. Iggy is the cute guy with long blondish hair. And Jake is the one with the Asian wife."

"Ma'am, if you see these individuals, tell them it is imperative that they remain in a safe place until the authorities arrive to protect them. They are in extreme danger, do you understand?"

"Yes, sir."

Heather looked up from her notepad to see the man who had been watching her turn and make his way out the front entrance. She warily watched as he hurried over to the back side of the parking lot and entered a late model black Jeep Cherokee that had been parked behind another truck.

Chapter Fifty

THE THREE boys were really looking forward to seeing The Jets again. *Man, this was going to be a big surprise for their band buds from Whitefish*, thought Iggy.

"Jake, these guys from The Jets are gonna start to think we're stalking them," Iggy jokingly said. "Delbert, wait'll you hear these guys. Just a hard rock trio from Calgary but they really kick ass, right Jake?"

"They are awesome for sure. And three good dudes to boot. It's gonna be nice to see them again. Suzie, you are in for a treat. You'll be able to say, 'I knew them when...'" exclaimed Jake. The group was in a happy mood. Of course, they had not been made aware of the horror that had been visited upon Suzie's uncle nor of the precarious state his life was in at this time. They also had no idea that Ivanov was in their midst.

Idabel Lake appeared below them as they came over a rise on the Idabel Lake Rd. It was a beautiful scene. The lake was approximately two miles in length and narrowed in the centre to a couple of hundred yards. The boys read later from literature at the lodge that it was stocked with three to five thousand rainbow and brook trout. The average size of the species was twelve to fourteen inches, though much bigger fish were known to have been caught.

The lake had a mean average depth of six feet, although there were some holes of up to forty and fifty feet. For those winter days when the fishing was slow, there was plenty of entertainment in the form of ice hockey or skating on a section of the lake that was regularly cleared of snow by staff. As well, there were continuous sales of hot cider and chili, whatever you needed to keep warm.

They headed down to the lake to check out the action and they went to a series of huts where they found they were able to rent whatever they wanted. Jake and Suzie decided they'd like to do some skating, so they were fitted up with skates. Then a worker took them on a skidoo over to the skating rink. The other three were definitely into ice fishing and before long they each had short rods with full gear including reels, lures, and live bait. A young staff worker took them down to one of his favorite spots at the far end of the lake on a Skidoo that had a kind of sled attached to it for transporting more than two people.

When they reached the area where the kid had assured them of catching some good-sized rainbow, Iggy was given a gas-powered auger and quickly learned how to cut several holes in the ice. The kid left them at their pleasure and told them he would be back in about an hour.

The ice was about eight inches thick and apparently would remain safe enough to support the activity until mid-February. This little bit of information convinced Delbert that he was not going to suddenly break through the ice and drown.

It wasn't long after the three of them had started fishing. Iggy had to demonstrate to Delbert how to bait the hook and operate the spin reel and while he was doing this, Roger cried "I got one! I got one!" Sure enough, Iggy turned to see the drummer pull a twelve-inch rainbow out of the hole in the ice, the fish flopping all over the place, and Roger was beside himself laughing with pride at being the first to land one. The young staff worker was correct in his judgment about where to fish, thought Jake, as he soon landed what looked like a yellow perch, around eighteen inches. Not to be outdone, Delbert was soon yelling "Iggy! Iggy! Gimme a hand! I think I've hooked one!" as he pulled out a rainbow similar in size to the one caught by Roger.

This went on for another hour until the three had managed to take a total of ten fish from the lake. Perfect for supper, they figured. Soon thereafter, the kid arrived with his Skidoo and sled and brought them back to the other end of the lake to meet up with Jake and Suzie. The two lovebirds related to Iggy about how they had a great time skating, listening to old time waltzes coming from large outdoor speakers that had been mounted around the rink area.

While Iggy and Jake went to one of the fish huts to clean their catch, the other three had hot ciders and relaxed in one of the heated cabins which had been furnished with picnic tables, Coleman stoves, and a couple of cast iron frying pans.

Too cool, thought Delbert.

A small pantry provided them with other items to complete the meal such as tinned potatoes to fry, salt, pepper, bread and butter. Jake and Iggy arrived back in the cabin with two bottles of locally produced wine. It was an awesome afternoon.

Earlier; 3:45 pm

The detectives were in the waiting room of the Kelowna General Hospital hoping to hear good news from the operating surgeon who had attended to Kenny Chou. The doctors and nurses had been with him now for over two hours and the situation was looking grim. Finally, a door to the operating room swung open and a doctor approached them.

"He is a lucky man," said Dr. Brooks. "Another centimeter and he would not have made it. As it stands, he is very weak, having lost a lot of blood, but we think he'll pull through. He's obviously a man in good condition."

"Doctor, it's very important that you let us have a word with him. We believe there are several other people in the area at risk."

"Detectives, you can have two minutes, max. I mean it. His condition is still critical. Follow me." Dr Brooks led them down to the ICU where they saw the club owner lying on a bed with numerous tubes coming out of his body. He was barely conscious but appeared to recognize the detectives when they entered.

"Kenny, we are sorry this has happened to you. We only need a quick word with you. Do you know who did this to you? Was the man Russian?" asked Hansen.

Kenny seemed confused and only stared at the cops.

"It's important, Kenny. We think it was the same person who attacked Jake and Suzie on New Year's Eve, remember? Did you notice anything about the man?" prodded Riley.

The doctor started to lead the detectives out of the room when Hansen noticed Kenny raising his right arm. As he watched, Kenny slowly pointed to his own eyes and looked terrified at the cops. He then moved his hand down to his chin which he rubbed.

"Gotcha," exclaimed Hansen as he walked over to Kenny and squeezed his hand lightly.

"Get well, my friend. We'll make sure we get this psycho behind bars."

4:50 pm

"Man, that was the best fish I've eaten in quite a while," exclaimed Iggy. "Almost as good as Miramichi salmon," he said with a wink to Jake. Delbert and Suzie looked at him quizzically.

"I have a feeling you will get to sample that delicacy yourself pretty soon," Iggy said to Suzie. "Well guys, what say we move on back to the lodge, get cleaned up and check out the bar to see if The Jets are around?"

As they got on the road for the drive back, it began to snow again.

"Hey, looks like some more powder coming our way again. Tomorrow will definitely be our ski day," said Jake, as they all looked forward to tonight and another fun day tomorrow on the hill.

Chapter Fifty-One

5:00 pm

THE RUSSIAN had driven to Idabel Lake after he overheard the girl at the reception desk in the lodge speaking to who he was sure was a police officer. But after arriving at the lake, he learned that a group of five had left there only fifteen minutes earlier. *Shit!* He must have passed them on the highway on the way here.

The young kid he was now speaking with at the lake didn't know what kind of vehicle they were driving, only that they caught some fish, did some ice skating, ate their fish and left. The boy had cleaned up after them, and no, he didn't see their car. *God, this guy was pushy, and he was also very creepy!* thought the kid. He was glad to see the monster drive back toward the main highway.

What should he do? pondered Grigori. There was a good chance the police were on their way here now, so it would be dangerous for him to go back to the ski lodge. Yet the two young men he was here to assassinate might be staying for a while. He decided on a change of plans and drove back to Kelowna.

It was now 6:00 pm and Grigori had just left the Kelowna office of Best Deal Rentals, a branch of the same firm where he had picked up the Jeep in Banff. He traded the Jeep for a Ford Galaxie, "Something more comfortable," as he told the clerk behind the desk at the rental office. He had driven back to the city for that purpose, but he also wanted to find out more about the group's ski trip. So, he had called the lodge in Big White and pretended to be another party from UBCO who was going to be joining the group.

Grigori realized he was probably speaking with the same girl who he overheard speaking to some RCMP officer. He tried to change his accent to sound more like a westerner. "Yes ma'am, I'm hoping a group of people from the university are still there...I'm supposed to hook up with them."

Heather told the caller "Yes, sir. They mentioned there may be two or three more of you coming. They have room booked for you until Thursday, January 5th."

Excellent, thought Grigori. This was all good info he could use. He would drive back to the lodge, wait until Heather was off shift and then register with a new clerk who would not recognize him. He would be wary of any police around and he would also think about getting a cabin for more privacy. He had seen them adjacent to the lodge and assumed there would be vacancies, given the low number of vehicles around the area. But before going back to Big White, he had some other things to pick up and he went looking for a local sports store.

Chapter Fifty-Two

5:15 pm

HANSEN AND Riley rolled into the parking lot at the lounge in their unmarked RCMP loaner and proceeded to the check-in desk. Heather was on duty until six pm, so she warmly greeted the two men. "How can I help?"

Hansen replied "We're with the Kelowna RCMP office and we're looking for a group of young people, your age, five of them. They may have registered as UBCO students?" During his response to the girl, he remembered what Sergeant White had told him about his conversation with the lodge earlier.

"Oh yeah," said the girl. "I booked them in earlier today. I think they may have gone to Idabel Lake regarding their group thesis."

Hansen had no clue what she was referring to, but said, "Could you please call the lake there now, ma'am and see if they're still there?" Heather was dialing the number for the lake lodge when she looked behind the detectives and said "Hey, here they come now. Guys, over here, some RCMP people want to talk to you."

Iggy led the group over to the desk and seeing his friends, said "Glad you could make it guys. Hope you brought some ski wear, you're gonna look a bit silly in those outfits." Hansen asked Heather if he could borrow their office and very seriously told Iggy he had some more bad news for them.

"Oh, no. We've already got a large suite, Detective. Let's go there." He wearily led the way to their room as everybody followed. Heather saw her replacement coming over to the desk. The young girl noticed Heather was wearing a worried look and said, "Hey, Heather, what was that all about?"

"Gosh, I'm not too sure, Joanie. I'm gonna stick around for a while though and see what's going on. If a guy called Iggy comes down for me, tell him I'll be in the bar." She saw the concerned looks of each of the people on their way to the elevators. Somebody must be hurt, she was thinking.

When they were all seated in the suite, Hansen explained about the attack on Kenny at his house. After assuring his niece that he was going to be okay, he told them of how the Russian had no doubt learned of the group's intention of coming to Big White, having heard the message left by Suzie on Kenny's answering machine. When Suzie heard this, she started crying. "It's all my fault," she cried. "I should have known better than to have done that."

Jake had been sitting beside her and pulled her closer. "You can't blame yourself for this, Suzie. Any one of us would have done the same thing, right guys?"

"Jacob is correct," said Riley. "Look, we spoke with the doctor who looked after your uncle, and we were assured he was going to pull through. Right now, he needs rest, and we have a police guard watching his room in the hospital while he's there. So, there's nothing more to be done and you are certainly not to blame. We're gonna get this guy, believe me. In the meantime, he may suspect you guys are here, but he doesn't know what you're driving so just stay out of sight while we check out the lodge." The two detectives went back downstairs, Jake and Suzie went to their room, and Roger asked if anyone wanted to play cards.

"Fuck this!" said Iggy. He was irate. "This Russian asshole is NOT going to keep me holed up like some goddamn animal in a cage. I'm going to the bar for a drink. You guys stay here and lock the doors...keep your ears open in case you hear Jake or Suzie yelling out for help."

Iggy left the suite and went to the front desk, thinking he might see Heather again. Instead, a new girl was on duty, and she told Iggy when he asked for her, that Heather was expecting him in the bar. *Expecting him. Now those were words to warm the heart,* he thought as he made his way into the bar. He spotted Heather sitting over by the stage and quietly walked up behind her.

"Hey girl, what have you ordered for me?" he said. Heather jumped, startled but obviously glad to see him.

"Nothing yet. I'm waiting to see whether or not you're a criminal, maybe some escaped convict, you know? I try not to drink with felons."

"Well, I might have to take you hostage, but I'll be gentle about it, okay?" said Iggy with that big smile, his trademark grin.

"Sit yourself down then, stranger, and tell this little girl all about it."

And for the next hour he did. They ordered a couple of glasses of wine and some munchies. When Iggy finished telling Heather the story of their trip from New Brunswick, the loss of their friend, Bug Canning, the hook up with the detectives, the undercover work in Whitefish and B.C., the formation and evolution of Fusion to the Shuswap Doo Wop Band, and finally their enrolment in the CWPP, he felt exhausted. It really was incredible.

Heather, he found, was a great listener. He then sat back and listened to her. After prodding from Iggy, she told him something about her own life. "Nothing so exotic and exciting as yours," she said. "I moved to Kelowna from Hope, B.C., mainly for work. Plus, I came here for a weekend with a friend and fell in love with the mountains and lakes, the serenity of it all. Oh, I've spent time in the big cities; Vancouver, Calgary, Montreal. But it wasn't working for me, you know? I come from a large family, they're all at home. Four older brothers who are loggers and a younger sister still in school. My mom is at home with them. I lost my dad in a logging accident last year."

She looked pensive at the table and Iggy lightly brushed the side of her hand.

"I'm sorry," he said. "Why don't we go up to the room and meet the rest of the gang. I think we all need some cheering up, okay? Hey, didn't you say there was a band called The Jets supposed to be playing here tonight?"

"Yes sir." Her mood brightened. "Feel up to hearing them?"

"Willlld horses...couldn't keep me away," he sang the refrain from one of The Stones' tunes off their last album, *Sticky Fingers*. She looked at Iggy admiringly as they left for his suite.

~ * ~

The detectives checked with the front desk to make sure they did not have any new clients that may have checked into the lodge in the past day or two and once satisfied that the Russian was not here, they went back to the suite to meet up with the group. A very small error on the part of Joanie, the night receptionist, would prove costly, since she didn't think to check the new registrations for the cabins. That entry book was kept separately in a different drawer under the desk.

Chapter Fifty-Three

7:36 pm

THE RUSSIAN laid back on a sofa in his small cabin that was situated about a quarter of a mile from the main lodge. From his back deck he could see much of the activity around the main gondola lift that took skiers to the summit, making several stops along the way for some of the easier runs on the front side of the mountain. He had purchased a set of Nikon night vision binoculars, which he was able to use during daylight hours if he so desired. He tested the binos now and found they worked perfectly. He could see a pair of young people walking hand in hand in the light snow that was falling, apparently lovers. Look at them, such fools, these Westerners. He was anxious to get this assignment over with and go back to Russia. He would not be able to expect any more work from his former boss, Dino Martini. The old Italian mobster was likely going to die in prison along with his boss, Vinnie Fellino.

He turned on the television and decided to watch some porn movies. Twenty minutes of trying various channels proved unsuccessful and he was forced to watch an episode of The Mod Squad. *Idiots!* He finally gave up and went to bed, confident he would finish his assignment in the morning. He would wait here with his binos and see if he could spot them when they went skiing.

9:15 pm

They all went down to the bar after playing several matches of backgammon, a board game which was popular in the mid-sixties. Somebody had been kind enough to leave the game behind and it was a good way to get away from all the bad things that were happening. The bar was starting to fill up with a young crowd, thirsty for rock and roll. The party of eight broke into two groups: Jake and Iggy with Suzie and Heather; the two detectives with Roger and Delbert.

As the detectives walked toward the front of the bar to order drinks, they told Roger to get a table for four and they'd be back after checking out the scene. Actually, they wanted one more look to assure themselves the Russian was not there.

Iggy and Jake had a great view of the stage from their table where they were seated with their dates. At nine thirty, the crowd warmly welcomed The Jets and the two Maritimers hid their faces when their friends came on the stage and were in full view, only ten feet away from them. They wanted to surprise them, and they were playing it by ear, waiting for a good opportunity to arise. They certainly weren't there to take play time away from The Jets, so they thought it would be best to simply enjoy the group's talent for the first two sets and maybe hit them with the surprise play in the last set.

And man, could these guys rock or what, thought Jake. He was taking his turn for picking up drinks at the bar and decided to check out Roger and Delbert to see what they thought of the band so far. He spotted them sitting alone and dropped over. "Hey boys, where are the cops?" he asked.

"They went to check out the rooms, making sure the Russian's not around I guess," said Roger.

"So, whattya think of the band, Del?"

"These guys are so good," said Delbert.

"Man, and you guys got to play with them, huh?" added Roger.

"Yup. Had a great time and never thought we'd run into them again. Small world. See y'all in a bit."

Towards the end of the last set, The Jets were still not aware that their friends from Whitefish were in the bar. They were thanking the crowd for coming out, encouraging them to take in their shows for the rest of the week, and to stay safe. Just as they were about to announce the last song of the set, Iggy yelled out, "Play something by CCR." Donnie looked around the room for the heckler who was rudely yelling out, and not seeing anyone, they started to intro a slow tune by Bread.

"No! No! We want CCR!" shouted Iggy again, this time standing in front of the stage with that huge grin. Donnie saw him at the same time as Brad and Jared. The three of them fell down on the stage laughing so hard they thought they might piss themselves.

"You two! Get your Maritime arses up here," Donnie yelled into the mic. "Folks, we have a treat for y'all." he continued talking to the crowd as Jake and Iggy made their way onto the stage. "We met these dudes in Whitefish, then again in Sunshine Village," said Donnie. Then he spoke to the two, "Now what? Y'all can't get work? Tryin' to follow us around for some practice? Come on."

Cool, pretending to be mad at the boys, The Jets were into it. But the crowd was really into it, knowing they were about to be further entertained. Iggy looked over at their table and gave a huge grin to Heather as he and Jake got into the role and took the instruments offered up by Donnie and Jared. They did the same CCR medley they had performed in Whitefish. While the full house sat and enjoyed the performance, Suzie and Heather immediately got up and began dancing together. This got the rest of the room in action, including Roger, Delbert, Hansen and Riley; all coming on to the dance area and getting down with the girls. It was a great way to end the show.

Tuesday, January 3rd
12:45 am
Iggy said to Donnie, "Man, this is the last time we'll break up your set, I promise."

"Well, only if you don't happen to run across us again, which will probably be a given," said Donnie. "Seriously, you guys know y'all are welcome to join us on stage whenever you want. We mean that, right?"

"Thanks man, means a lot. We gotta run, so be safe guys." and the group retired for the evening.

As they all got in the elevator, things became a little awkward. Iggy was clearly becoming comfortable with Heather, but he had already set the suite up for himself and the other four guys. Heather then unexpectedly came to the rescue when she suggested Iggy walk her to her room which was on the third floor, one above the rooms that had been set up for the group as a whole. So, Suzie and Jake got off the elevator as did Hansen,

Riley, Delbert, and Roger. Jake and Suzie went to their assigned room, the four guys stayed in the suite where they decided to have a nightcap, and Heather took Iggy up another floor to her room.

This turned out to be a staff suite furnished with a sitting room, a bedroom which held two cots, a bathroom, and a small kitchenette. It was often used by lodge staff during snowstorms, emergencies, and the odd tryst. It was the responsibility of the occupants to ensure it was left in a clean condition.

"Well, well," said Iggy. "This is nice."

"I hope you are not getting the wrong idea about me," said Heather. "There are several of these suites available for staff to use in emergency situations. And wouldn't you agree this was an emergency?"

"Clearly," Iggy agreed. "One thing. You mentioned earlier you came here for a weekend with a friend. Is he, ah, still around?"

"*She* is still here, works on the front desk with me and her name is Joan."

"Ahhh, I see," he said. He moved closer to her, toe to toe. "Say, can I kiss you?"

"I would be disappointed if you didn't," she smiled, her face upturned to his. And he did. It was wonderful, nice and easy, no anxious breathing, just as if they had known each other for a lifetime.

Now they were getting into it, and they moved toward the bedroom. He saw the two cots and looked at her, his eyebrows raised. She said they could use them both and they quickly pulled the cots together to form one large bed. Perfect.

They made love, and it was good. Better than he was expecting. Sometime during the night, he woke with her face beside his and saw her looking at him, a soft smile there. He reached for her and again they made love. And it was even better than the first time.

7:45 am

By the time Iggy and Heather showered, they were starving. Iggy called Jake on the room connector phone and had him arrange with the others for all of them to meet in the dining hall for breakfast at 8:30. He was looking forward to getting in a good day's skiing. It was a beautiful day;

another five inches of powder had fallen overnight, and he was eager to try out the pair of 190 cm Head skis with Tyrolia bindings that he had purchased last week as a Christmas gift for himself.

Iggy was particularly glad Heather and Suzie seemed to be hitting it off. It was ironic to think only last week he was chiding Jake for falling head over heels for Suzie. Now, he examined his own feelings, and it frightened him to think he might be headed the same way! *Well, let it be*, he thought. It was time he got serious about his life, and he suddenly knew he definitely did not want to end up being a loner.

Everybody met in the diner, and they dug into a buffet style breakfast. Pancakes, bacon, scrambled eggs, sausages, Belgian waffles, fruit, mounds of toast. It was a feast. And then they indulged themselves with OJ and champagne.

Detectives Hansen and Ryan wanted to meander around the grounds outside and keep an eye out for the Russian, although it appeared by now that he had simply gone with the wind. Who knew, maybe he had left for Los Angeles. Delbert and Roger, who were not keen on breaking any bones, opted out on the ski adventure. They thought they might work out at the gym, then maybe check out the bar for some ski bunnies. Roger said there was supposed to be a karaoke party happening later in the afternoon and maybe they'd take that in.

Consequently, Iggy and Jake left with Suzie and Heather to go upstairs and suit up for the slopes. It was almost noon by the time they left the dressing area where most skiers put on their boots. Here, they made last minute adjustments to goggles and checked their bindings. As they climbed aboard a gondola with five other skiers, a light snow had begun to fall.

Same Day
Earlier 11:15 am
The Russian looked out the back window of his cabin and watched through his Nikon binos as skiers started to form a line leading to the gondola gate. They appeared to be coming from a large building which he assumed contained areas for the sale of day passes, rental gear, rest rooms, plus a room for people to get their ski gear in order. He was certain this building would be his best chance of finding the musicians and he

immediately left for it. He had an idea.

12:45 pm

The gondola was designed to carry a total of ten adults and as such, they were tightly grouped in the transport vehicle. All skiers wore full suits of various styles and colors. Some, like Iggy and his three friends, wore toboggan toques with ski goggles strapped over their heads. Several of the passengers were wearing protective helmets which included a full-frontal Plexiglas face mask in lieu of goggles. The front masks were tinted, and it was impossible to see a face behind them.

As the gondola made its way up the slopes toward the summit, Iggy attempted to make conversation with the other skiers.

"Great day for skiing, eh, folks?"

"You bet," replied one of the young men. "You guys from the area?"

"Nope. Came here from back East. The hills here are a tad bigger than we're used to, right?" said Jake. The lift slowed down for the next exit which was designated a "Green" run and two of the five unknown people got off. As they continued upward, Iggy asked the big man who was wearing a one piece plain white suit with the full helmet face mask, "So where's home for you, my friend?"

The giant just shrugged his shoulders and moved his arms around in a circle to indicate "everywhere."

Weird, thought Iggy. He was about to ask the man another question when the gondola again slowed for another transfer gate. Iggy checked the area map he had brought with him from the lodge. According to the layout, this should be the last stop before the summit. The huge man in the white suit rose to leave the lift at this stop and it was necessary for Iggy to move aside to allow his exit. As the man was passing Iggy, the man turned his face mask in his direction. It was impossible for Iggy to know whether or not the guy was staring at him, but he stood that way for several beats and Iggy was certain the guy was silently laughing at him. The man got off the lift and skied away. Iggy automatically felt a sudden chill that had nothing to do with the weather. He instinctively felt behind himself for his backpack and the comfort of the outline of his .45 semi-automatic.

The Russian studied his map of the various runs that he had picked up as well. From what he could tell, he was on a run called Easy Rider, an intermediate red rectangle-designated run which was the only route available before Widow Maker, the trail that the two musicians and their girlfriends were going to take. Grigori could see where the upper, more difficult run hooked up with the one he was on. Easy Rider followed a relatively straight track for about a quarter of a mile until it veered sharply left to avoid a steep drop off of some fifty feet. *Excellent.* He came up with a plan to at least eliminate one of the musicians.

Iggy and Heather stuck to the right side of Widow Maker and maintained the lead ahead of Jake and Suzie by about a hundred yards. The snow was beautiful, with powder totally unfamiliar to the Maritimer. He found he had to lean a little more aggressively toward the fall line compared to riding the boards on the harder packed snow back East. *Keep your tips up,* he had to constantly remind himself and moved his feet more to accomplish this. He also found he had better stability by making wider "C" turns.

He glanced over at Heather who was staying with him turn for turn. She was an excellent skier, and it was obvious her upbringing here in the mountains had engrained this talent in her.

A sign posted on the side of the trail warned them they were approaching an adjoining run, Easy Rider, and Iggy recalled from reading the map that it was a nice flat-out run for about a mile with only one major turn on it. As they entered the new trail a huge man in a white suit rudely came from nowhere across their path.

Shit, it is the same weird guy in the gondola that rode up the slope with us. What the hell's he up to? thought Iggy. The guy continued to keep pace with him as they raced down the hill and he was now between Iggy and Heather. Before Iggy had a chance to slow down, he could see where the trail ahead was going to veer suddenly left, but the huge guy continued straight, thereby forcing Iggy to do the same.

All at once Iggy felt his body go over the edge of the trail and he was airborne. He literally sailed over the tops of pine trees and his heart hammered as he saw the most amazing view...the lodge far below him, the highway that they took to get here, a stream that came out of some lake. He crashed into a tree and suddenly the ground slammed up against his body.

Then everything went black.

Chapter Fifty-Four

Kelowna General Hospital
Wednesday January 5th, 1972
11:00 am

IGGY AWOKE to the smells of antiseptics and beeping sounds of monitors hooked to his body as he lay on a hospital bed with tubes connected to an IV that hung overhead. He was in a lot of pain, and he almost lost consciousness when he tried to get up. At that point a nurse came running into the room and she immediately lowered him back onto the bed.

"You must lay down and rest," she said. "The doctor has been made aware you are awake and will be here any minute."

Iggy tried to remember what had happened. The last he could recall was flying through the air after some idiot in a white ski suit had forced him off the trail. Then everything came back to him, and he suddenly realized it was the Russian. And Heather?

"Nurse, can you tell me if my friend Heather is okay?"

"Heather is fine! My name is Nancy and I'm a friend of Suzie's. I was with her at The Emerald Lounge for the New Year's dance where you and your friends performed. Heather came here with Jacob and Suzie and the two other band members yesterday afternoon. You are not in very good shape, but the doctor will explain everything in detail, okay?"

Doctor Brooks then entered the room and looked appraisingly at Iggy.

"Mr. Miles, we've gotta stop meeting like this," said the doctor.

"Yeah, this is not proper. How bad is it, Doc?"

"You were lucky to fall through a spruce tree prior to hitting the ground," he said. "But even with that, you managed to crack several ribs, sprain your ankle, and rupture your spleen. The latter is the most serious and will require strict bed rest for the next two days, minimum. Your immune system is at risk while the spleen is recovering. So, there you have it."

"Am I allowed visitors?"

"They're outside waiting, and I can authorize a few at a time for now. It's close to 11:30 so how about seeing two groups before lunch, then some rest?" Receiving a nod from Iggy, he spoke to the nurse, "Nancy, send in the first group please."

Iggy thought the doctor sounded like some game show host, for Christ's sake.

"Hey, how's Jungle Jim Hunter doin' today?" said Jake as he came through the door, referencing the Crazy Canuck downhill racer.

"Doin' good. Fill me in brother, what happened?"

"Well, from what we saw, some big guy cut in front of you and you were forced off the run. You fell fifty feet and fortunately went through a couple of trees which softened the landing. I was able to get the EMTs on an emergency phone just a bit further down the run and they brought you out on a sled. An ambulance was waiting for you at the lodge. Suzie, Heather and I have been hanging around here this morning. Roger, Delbert and the two detectives are out there waiting to see you too. You were lucky, dude"

Heather came over to his bedside and took his hand.

"We were all so worried you might have been killed," she said.

"Naahh...I might be a bit run down for a few days, but otherwise okay. Look, why don't you let me say hi to Roger and Delbert then the two cops. After that, the doc wants me to rest, but I want to see you later if you can make it, Heather," he said as he gave her hand a light squeeze.

After assuring the other two band members he was going to be okay, he got to speak with Hansen and Riley.

"Well, guys, it looks like our friend is still around. That giant in the white ski suit, full frontal tinted face mask. Man, he was in the gondola with us on the way up to the summit. Incredible. I really wanna get this asshole."

"Take it easy, Iggy. Let us do our job. I know it's difficult to have confidence in us after what's been happening, but we've got you covered, man. There'll be an armed cop outside for the next couple of days and we're checking the local hotels, motels, any places of accommodation. Car rental firms, airports, whatever. We'll find him."

"What about the rest of my group? Won't he be after them as well? How can you protect everybody?"

"We've thought of that. Actually, the best place is probably your bungalow which we can modify a bit to accommodate everyone. This guy is not a ghost. His size alone is going to make it difficult for him to hide from us. The important thing right now is for you to get rested up and back on your feet. That will make our job that much easier, right?"

Doctor Brooks came in at that time and advised the detectives that the patient was now going to have lunch and bed rest thereafter. He'd be able to see his girlfriend after that for a short visit, but right now, rest was the order of the day.

"Oh, and by the way," the doctor said to Iggy, "Kenny Chou is being released tomorrow. He may be around this afternoon or this evening to see you for a brief visit."

~ * ~

Big Al Gabrazzi was not a happy man. He had just got off the phone after talking with the Russian guy that was supposed to have looked after the matter of eliminating the two jerkoffs who had betrayed them last summer. Apparently, he was still not successful in his attempts to make them disappear.

"These guys, they are like the cat with nine lifes," the Russian had said.

Christ, thought the capo, *what was the matter with this ass-wipe?*

"Dennis, c'mere!" he shouted into the next room. Dennis was his "go to guy" for any difficult wet work that came up. It looked like it was going to be necessary to send him up north to get the job done. Jesus, good help was hard to find these days.

"Yeah, boss?" asked Dennis as he came into Al's suite. Al was watching a boxing match on the TV. He looked up and saw the stocky forty-year-old hood standing beside him. Never even heard him come in. Jesus, the guy was scary. Dennis had his greasy hair pulled back in a ponytail that fell over a simple black shirt with a black tie. Over this he wore a black polyester suit. *The guy was not going to win any Best Dressed Man of the Year awards,* thought Al.

"Remember the two schmucks that took advantage of us in Canada last summer? Was supposed to be working for Dino, then pulled the scam so's Vinnie and him are in stir up there, probably gonna die in Spy Hill on accounta them rats."

He was really pissed off, Dennis could tell.

"I wanted them dead! Not living!" He smashed his huge fist down onto the coffee table. Big Al realized how worked up he was getting and tried to calm down a bit.

"The Russian, Dino's man, was gonna make 'em go away, but apparently he needs help." He placed his hands on Dennis's shoulders. "The two are still alive. So, Dennis, be so kind as to get in touch with the Russki and make it happen. *Capische?"*

He gave Dennis some paper with information on it where Grigori could be contacted. "And Dennis? I really want this matter finished up, like, yesterday, right? And if the Russian gets in your way, you know what to do."

Dennis obediently left the suite, then headed for LAX.

Thursday, January 6th

Grigori slammed the phone down on its hook. He was furious. How dare this Italian gangster talk to him like a *peon?* After speaking with Gabrazzi, he was sorry he had bothered to call him. His loyalty was still with Mr. Martini, and only for that reason did he agree to put up with the bullshit from this *goombah* in Los Angeles. And, okay, there was the matter of the money that was still owed to him for his work to date. When this job was settled, he had a good mind to pay a visit to Mr. Gabrazzi and see how much of a man he was.

He remembered Dennis, the guy with the ponytail, from the cutting farm. He was not that impressed with the short, stocky man. Whatever, he could work with him, so long as he did not get in his way. He might even be able to use him somehow. He'd see. In the meantime, there wasn't much else he could do but stay holed up in this cabin in the middle of nowhere. He felt safe where he was, in some little town called Salmon Arm, north of Kelowna off the Trans-Canada Highway. He had stolen a set of plates off another vehicle and put them on the Ford Galaxie, so he should be okay. Also, the cabin was not on the mainstream motel/hotel listings. He doubted very much if the police would be checking here for him.

Dennis was expected in by 9:00 pm, so again he was a hostage to the idiot box and the Western drivel that went with it. At the moment he was stuck with watching another episode of "The Mod Squad." Something about three hippie cops who worked undercover for the LAPD. He was amused, though, that their stupid clothes and haircuts allowed them to infiltrate the drug culture in the U.S.

How ridiculous, thought the Russian.

Dennis "the Asp" Mancini drove along the Trans-Canada Highway after having just left the Lear jet that had arrived from LAX at Abbotsford International Airport on time at 3:10 pm. The drive to Salmon Arm, B.C. would take approximately four and a half hours. He was driving in comfort in a rented Lincoln Mark V, and he listened to Pavarotti performing "O Sole Mio" through the sound-surround system in the Mark V. *Beautiful.*

His thoughts took him back to his hometown of Palermo where he had lived until the age of thirty. He had worked as an assistant baker at his father's pizzeria until it was destroyed in a firebombing by a gang headed up under the notorious Don Stefano Bontade gang. His father had simply refused to pay "insurance" to Don, The Falcon, Bontade for his shop, and so ended up paying the ultimate price. By a stroke of good fortune, the young Mancini, who was twenty-five at the time, had been dating a young lady the night of the bombing and was spared the fate of his father. Dennis knew, however, that his father was being coerced by the Bontade family for some time. At that point he sought the assistance of Bontade's opponent for revenge. Enter Big Al Gabrazzi, who quickly took to the young ex-baker and refined his talents over the next five years to suit his needs. Because of the silent way in which he approached the type of work he was now assigned, he became known in the trade as The Asp.

As it turned out, Gabrazzi had been requested to move his operations to the U.S. by his partner Fellino. Big Al had insisted The Asp join his U.S. team and he had been living in LA since 1965. Ironically, Dennis had read yesterday where The Falcon had been arrested this week by the Sicilian Government in the recent Anti Mafiosa Wars. He smiled to himself at the thought and enjoyed the talents of Pavarotti along with the beauty of the Okanagan Valley.

Four hours later, Dennis found himself in the small city of Salmon Arm which lies at the southern inlet or "arm" of Shuswap Lake. The city has a population of approximately fifteen thousand and relies heavily on tourism where people enjoy the beautiful scenery of the lake and participate in boating, swimming, hiking, and fishing. The winter months provide travelers with ice skating on the lake, cross country skiing, and snowshoe trails. The cabin where Dennis was now headed was a mile outside of town in a secluded copse of spruce trees, far from any prying eyes. It should work for the plan that he and the Russian had developed over the telephone yesterday.

Chapter Fifty-Five

8:25 pm

"DO YOU have all the necessary equipment?" asked Dennis, after they rehashed the purpose of the meeting and talked briefly of the current condition of the two Mafiosi now in prison, as best as Grigori could relate.

"I believe you will find all to be in order, Dennis. Let me say, I am most anxious to accomplish this assignment. The two in question so far have been very fortunate indeed."

"Grigori, I have every faith in your ability. We shall succeed this time, no worries." *So long as you stay out of my way.* Dennis said to himself. The plan was basic. Abduct this girl, Heather, while she was driving to work in Big White, bring her to the cabin. At the same time, abduct the girl, Suzie, while she was going to The Emerald Lounge, bring her to the cabin as well. Drugs would assist in the kidnappings. Contact the boys and have them come to get the girls, no police. Eliminate all four. Easy, peasy.

Normally, Dennis was not in favor of disposing of people who were not a direct part of the aggravation that precipitated the action. In this case, as far as he knew, it was only the two musicians who were the parties involved in the betrayal. The Russian, on the other hand, had no problems with doing away with the ladies. Dennis tried not to think about this aspect of the plan, and he reluctantly accepted it as presented.

While Dennis and the Russian were going through their plan to kidnap the girls, Iggy was talking with his visitor, Kenny Chou, at Kelowna General. Kenny was in his wheelchair, and he was feeling much better. The entrepreneur was asking Iggy many details about his ongoing feud with this gangster who seemed to be plaguing the area, and by extension he was of course concerned with the safety of his niece. Iggy again apologized for the whole mess and sometimes wondered if it might be better for all concerned

212

if he and Jake were to simply take off. Let everyone here get back to their normal lives. But somehow, he felt the Russian was not going to give up that easy. He was like a dog with a bone and until he was behind bars, they would have to be on their guard. There simply was no place they could go and not have to worry about the madman one day finding them.

"Kenny, I know you are worried about Suzie. But believe me, Jake is in love with her, and he will do everything in his power to see she is kept out of harm's way in all of this. The detectives have given us their assurance that we'll be safe. So, let's get some rest my friend, okay?"

Kenny wheeled out of the room and left Iggy with his own thoughts regarding the safety of everyone. He was expecting a call from Jake to let him know the latest plans being developed by Hansen and Riley.

Heather lived in her own apartment in Kelowna, but at the suggestion of Detective Hansen, she was now staying at the boys' residence and was actually in Iggy's room. Likewise, Suzie was staying with Jake at the bungalow rather than going to her own apartment. Delbert and Roger were there as well, so at least everyone, for the moment, was under the protection of the police in one unit, save for Iggy and Kenny who were safe at the General Hospital.

While everyone in the residence was playing a game of Hearts at the kitchen table, Hansen and Riley were making rounds in the unmarked RCMP vehicle, keeping an eye out for any suspicious-looking individuals. They had checked with FBOs at the airports and were assured no incoming passengers had entered Canada from LAX in the last three days. That was the first of two errors committed by the police. Had they checked further into this, they would have determined that one Dennis Mancini had arrived in Abbotsford International from Portland, Oregon. A quick stopover as a ruse had paid off for the Sicilian.

The second error was the fact that they had misread the audacity of the two assassins. Never for a minute did they expect them to boldly kidnap the girls. It was against the code of the Mafiosa to involve innocent civilians.

Dennis and Grigori figured the two girls would probably be leaving for work in the morning. It meant they would have to grab them one at a time. Since they knew where both girls were employed, they thought the best way to accomplish this was to first capture Heather as she left her job at Big White, then get Suzie on her way home from The Emerald Lounge later in the day.

Friday, January 7th
4:30 pm

It was cold and snowing as Heather walked across the main lodge parking lot of the Big White Ski Resort. In view of the pending storm, she thought it best to get on the road early. Besides, Iggy was expected home this afternoon from the hospital, in fact he may already be there. She was anxious to see him again. The short time they were apart helped to convince her that this was the guy she wanted to marry. Wow! She could admit this to herself, she thought, as she climbed into her two-year-old VW Beetle. She failed to see the black Ford Galaxie containing the two men as it pulled out behind her onto the Big White Road.

Her windshield wipers were having trouble keeping the Volkswagen's window clear of the rapidly accumulating snow as she made her way along the Kelowna-Rock Creek Highway, and it was quickly getting dark.

Suddenly out of nowhere, a large black vehicle pulled up beside her and she was forced to pull to the side of the road. Two men jumped out and roughly pulled her from her vehicle. She screamed as the larger of the two brandished a syringe which he jabbed in her neck area. The last thing she saw was the face of the man with those awful reptilian eyes, then she was unconscious.

Grigori placed her in the back seat of the Galaxie while Dennis got into the VW, and they drove northwest to Kelowna.

It was about an hour's drive and by the time they reached the lounge it was just after 5:30 pm. Fortunately, Grigori spotted Suzie's Mustang in the parking lot, and he drove by it, at the same time pointing it out to Dennis who was following behind him. The Russian kept driving and parked at the opposite end of the lot while Dennis parked behind Suzie's car, got out and in no time, he was crouched in the back seat of the Mustang. At 5:45 pm Suzie came out of the front door of the lounge and carefully walked toward her vehicle. She had entered the car and she was turning the ignition key when she felt a sharp jab in the back of her neck. Her first thought was that it was some form of insect, maybe a wasp? But that was crazy, it was winter! Then she blacked out.

The Ford Galaxie, followed by the Mustang, slowly left the parking lot of The Emerald Lounge, each with their precious cargo, as they made their way to the Okanagan Highway. This would take them to their destination in Salmon Arm, about one and a half hours away. The two could then relax and make further plans.

Earlier at 4:45 pm

Iggy arrived in the driveway of their residence late in the afternoon, but still earlier than Doctor Brooks had initially estimated. He was a bit weak from his ordeal, but was recovering at a good rate, and he felt he would be back to normal by the morning. Kenny had also been released and was resting at his home.

"Hey, everyone, I'm home," Iggy shouted.

Jake was the first to greet him and give him a big hug. "Good to have you back, bro'," he said." We'll lay off the brewskies for a bit, get you in shape, eh?"

"Where is everyone?" Iggy asked, looking around.

"Delbert and Roger are shooting pool downstairs and the girls should be home within the hour from work. I've been listening to some tunes. Not a great day out there, man, looks like a storm coming in."

Iggy decided to put a spaghetti dinner together while they awaited the arrival of the girls.

6:00 pm

It was now dark, and Jake and Iggy were concerned. No sign of their girlfriends and the storm was getting worse. Certainly, Suzie should have been home by now. Jake picked up the phone and called the lounge. Iggy watched as a worried look came across Jake's face. When he replaced the phone, he said to Iggy, "This is not good. She left her office at five thirty according to the barman. I had him check the lot and the only car there is a Volkswagen Beetle."

"What?" said Iggy. "That's strange, Heather owns a Beetle. Do you think maybe she decided to meet Suzie at work, and they may have gone somewhere?"

"Maybe, let's check out the lot." They quickly dressed for the storm that was intensifying. They drove to the parking lot and, as expected, the Beetle was the only car they could see. Iggy opened the door and he suddenly felt sick to his stomach. The keys were still in the VW's ignition and there was a woman's purse on the front seat. He looked in the purse and inspected several documents in a wallet he found there as well. He was not at all surprised to find Heather's driver's license.

Back at the house the boys were in a panic. They called Hansen and explained their findings to the detective. Hansen told them he was sending a forensic team from the Kelowna PD to the vehicle in the hopes they might find some evidence; something to give them a clue as to where they may have taken the girls. He and Riley would be over to meet with the boys in ten minutes.

6:30 pm

Heather was the first to regain consciousness, probably because she was the first to be drugged. She looked around and realized she was chained by her left wrist to a ring bolted into the bare wooden floor on which she lay. Suzie, who was also chained in a similar way, was lying beside her. The room that held them was small. It appeared to be a secondary bedroom, no windows and only one light from the ceiling. There were no pictures, the walls were gypsum board, painted a pale yellow. There was one bed and a single bathroom attached. The chain length just barely allowed them access through the bathroom door. While Heather took in her surroundings, Suzie roused with a groan. Whatever drug had been used on them, it certainly left them with searing headaches.

"HELP! HELP US!!" they began to yell. The sound of a lock being turned was heard, and the single door to the room opened. Standing before them was a giant of a man. He had a scruffy goatee and the most evil looking eyes either of them had ever seen. The man studied both of them like they were some interesting bug species.

"Good evenink," he said. "Welcome to our cabin. We shall brink you somesink to eat in a moment. You must not be yellink, or we will be gaggink you, okay?" It was a polite request, but the way it was delivered, the message was clear. This man and whoever else was with him were not concerned with their well-being. Furthermore, the scariest thing was that the giant didn't even bother to hide his face from them. That spoke volumes to the girls. The door was closed, and the girls could hear a muffled conversation coming from behind the door.

"Call the Asian as planned," said Dennis. Already he was getting tired of this guy's theatrics. He was anxious to get the show on the road. The Russian just looked at Dennis, lids half closed and almost smirked at him. He went to the phone, consulted a piece of paper that he took from his pocket, and dialed a number.

"Yes, Mr. Kenny," he said. "Please know we have your niece. We want one thing from you, and she may live...the number for either of the two musicians you hired recently."

Unknown to the Russian, the police had already been speaking with Kenny about everything that had happened, and he was half expecting the call when it came from Ivanov.

"Sir, I implore your decency," he replied. "Please do not harm her," and he quoted the number the police had given to him for this purpose. When the Russian called that number, it rang three times before being picked up by Iggy.

"Yes, hello," he said.

"Mr. Dave?"

"Ah, my Russian friend," said Iggy. "How can I help you?"

"Actually, you can help your girlfriend."

"So, you have her? Where are you?"

"Not so fast, Mr. Dave. I very much want to meet with you, but you would probably bring police and that would be a big mistake. Your girlfriend would not enjoy it, I am afraid."

"Oooooh. Big bad Russian man, I am so afraid. Listen, you asshole, I will tear your fucking head off if you hurt either of those girls. So, I want to see you, too, scumbag. But not tonight. In case you haven't noticed, the roads are all closed now, we'd never be able to make it wherever you are. But give us until tomorrow and my partner and I will gladly meet up with you. Just name the time and place." Iggy was acting as a tough guy, trying to bait the Russian into a *mano a mano* confrontation.

"You know where they skate at the outdoor rink in Salmon Arm? Over by the wharf? You come across the frozen ice on lake so we can see you. No police, only you two. We let girls go when we see you cominic. You come no later than 1:00 pm. Roads should be all cleared by then." The line then went dead.

7:15 pm
"So, there we have it," said Iggy.

As much as Iggy and Jake were against immediately racing to the area described by the Russian, they both knew the girls would have to put up with their plight for the rest of the night. Hopefully, they would be spared any harm, now that the two musicians had agreed to meet with them. Iggy now believed there were at least two abductors. Ivanov had mistakenly used the pronoun "we" in their conversation, indicating the Russian now had at least one accomplice with him. That made sense, since it would have been extremely difficult for a single person to kidnap both girls using only one vehicle.

"Okay folks, here's the plan," said Hansen. The group of six men, which included Roger, Delbert, Iggy, Jake, and the two detectives, hunched around the kitchen table at the safe home and discussed their moves. Outside, the storm continued unabated. So far, a total of eight inches of snow had fallen and with the wind, there were drifts one and a half feet in places.

When Detective Hansen finished with his instructions to the civilians, he got on the phone to Captain Miller, followed by a call to Sergeant White of the RCMP.

Chapter Fifty-Six

Saturday, January 8th,
8:15 am

THE GIRLS had been awake for two hours, and according to the radio clock on the small table in their locked room, it was now after eight. They were exhausted, not having been able to sleep much last night. The fear of what was probably going to happen to them was overwhelming. After the huge man left them supper, they again heard sounds coming from the living room. It sounded like an argument of sorts; they were not sure.

And now they heard the familiar sound of the lock opening. Again, it was the man with the snake-like eyes. He brought them what turned out to be cereal. It looked like corn flakes, also two bowls on a platter with toast, butter, milk, and two glasses of OJ. This time there was no conversation, simply the offer of breakfast, and the girls ate quickly.

"You gave them the correct doses of the sodium pentothal?" Dennis asked the Russian. Grigori simply looked at Dennis. Didn't say shit, just the look with the deadpan eyes.

This guy, thought Dennis. *I so wanna whack him.*

Then the Russian surprised Dennis.

"Tell me, Dennis, how much are you being paid to help me with the assignment?" and he scowled at Dennis as he queried him.

Dennis thought he'd play the jerk along, maybe get in his head a bit. "Not nearly enough, since I have to put up with all your bullshit," he said. "Only ten grand, for Chrissakes. You?" He knew from Al that the deal was for Ivanov to get five, and he was getting the same. Now he saw the look in the eyes of the Russian pop out and he knew he hit a sore spot with him.

"The same," the Russian spat out. "But just so you know, I have been doing most of work and will want more when we are finished here."

"That's between you and Mr. Gabrazzi. Let's get our gear together and rehearse our plan."

Cool. Let's see where this goes, Dennis mused.

They checked with the girls and found they were still zonked. The pentothal in the OJ worked fine. The Russian then shot them again with sufficient doses to keep them docile until the job at the lake was done.

They got their gear together and set out. Grigori wore the same white ski suit he had worn in Big White when he forced the young man off the run. Dennis had a long black leather coat, denim jeans, a black toque and leather Wellingtons boots. *Christ,* thought Grigori. He always has to act the hoodlum.

With them they brought a duffle bag which contained a power saw, handguns, a high-powered hunting rifle with a scope, and a pair of binos.

Then the Russian went into the room where the girls were. They were conscious, but only barely. He threw their outer clothes at them, told them to get dressed, they were going to meet their boyfriends. Big smile not reaching the evil eyes.

The storm from last night had stopped, however the wind that swept fiercely across Shuswap Lake from the Northwest caused the drifting snow on the open area to reduce visibility considerably. The wind created a mournful sound as it swirled around the two figures that lay prone on the ice facing the southern end of the arm.

"What the hell are they doing?" Iggy asked Jake. The two of them had left Kelowna earlier at around nine am and had set up their blind about five hundred yards from the wharf. They were established behind a large mound of snow they had fashioned to make it appear as if it had been formed by the wind. They both wore white ski suits similar to Grigori's. Iggy had his backpack on, and they both came equipped with cross country skis, poles, and binoculars.

"Looks like they're cutting a large hole in the ice, probably pretending to be ice fishing." said Jake as he trained his own binoculars on the two hoods. The snow had resumed lightly, and visibility was now even worse.

"Ready when you are," Iggy said, and they started skiing toward the wharf. When they judged themselves to be halfway there, they stopped and lay down on the ice surface. Parts of the frozen lake were perfectly clear, and Jake could see the clear water beneath him, reeds flowing back and forth from whatever current flowed into the lake. He looked across the surface of the lake for some sign of the girls but saw nothing. They had decided to stay put at this point until the assassins provided proof of life for the girls. Jake again thought of the hole in the ice that these animals had fashioned. He would not allow his mind to think further about the intent of the hole. He looked around the lake and realized they were the only people out here.

"Now what?" asked the Russian. They were hidden behind two of the hundreds of large pillars that sustained diagonal struts. The struts in turn supported the four-hundred-foot pier that reached out over the lake. He was looking at the boys through his binos. "They have stopped. They must want to see the girls. You take them out halfway," he growled at Dennis.

Dennis was about to shoot the guy until he remembered he made a promise to Al regarding the job at hand. No biggie, he'd get the Russian later.

Grigori watched as Dennis led the girls staggering ahead of him toward the pair who were lying on the ice. He was thinking of this Italiano getting paid twice the amount that he was, and he was livid with rage. *That would not happen,* he promised himself. *Shoot them all, cut them up with the power saw and throw the body parts in the lake.* It would be a lot of work, but he could do it. There was nobody around to know what would have taken place.

He took the Remington 700 high powered rifle from the duffle bag and checked for ammo. There were six .300 Magnum cartridges in the chamber. One of these alone would do the job, and he jacked a cartridge into the barrel. The rifle had been outfitted with a scope which he now trained on the two men lying prone on the ice about 250 yards away. Okay, there they are. Now, lay the scope on Dennis. There he is. Walking slowly across the lake in his Wellington boots and his black leather gangster outfit, pushing the two girls ahead of him, but what the hell? There was another man there now. Hey, it was the guy called Joe, the one who graded the cocaine for his boss.

He looked back at the two laying on the ice and dialed the scope's power up two digits. *Shit.* The boys weren't there after all, just their empty ski suits filled with snow to make it look like them. He now brought the scope back to Dennis, the girls, and Joe.

Jake walked up to Dennis who stood ten feet away from him. This was the moment of truth. Dennis held Suzie and Heather by a chain which had been linked to their two wrists. It was obvious they had been drugged and they were shivering as they stood in front of him. They looked at Jake forlornly, silently pleading with him to somehow do something to save them. Jake caught Suzie's eye, gave her a smile and a wink.

"Hey, Dennis. Didn't think I'd see you here today. What's going on?"

"There is a matter of an old family tradition that has been entrusted to me and the Russian. Much as I detest working with that animal."

"I understand. Unfortunately, what happened with your family was of their own making. We have also been seeking revenge for an innocent victim who became caught up in this affair."

"You know then why I'm here."

"Well, I suspect it's not because you want to do some ice fishing."

At that point Jake looked over to where he had last seen Grigori. He was wondering where Iggy was, since the plan they had drawn up earlier called for Iggy to sneak up behind the Russian and surprise him. Hopefully, at that point the detectives would reveal themselves, and the accomplice, who he now realized was Dennis, would surrender to the authorities.

He would never forget what happened next. It was so goddamn fast, First, he saw a flash of light coming from something the Russian was holding toward them. He then heard a loud CRACK and felt at the same time a PUSH of air passing in front of his face. This was followed by the sound of a SPLAT and he turned to see Dennis's neck explode. He immediately dove into the girls and brought them down on the ice with him.

The Salmon Arm Wharf is billed as "The Longest Wooden Wharf in North America" and stretches 442 feet into the southern arm of the Shuswap Lake. It is like a small version of a train trestle with all of the wooden supports holding up the massive structure. When Iggy and Jake left their suits on the ice, they each went in opposite directions: Jake toward Dennis and the girls, and Iggy toward the Russian. But Iggy kept more to the far side and crouched low against the ice as he glided on his skis. He managed to make it unseen to the bridge supports behind Grigori, just left of him. The Russian was standing in front of a large rectangular area he had cut out of the ice. Iggy watched in horror as he fired a high-powered rifle at the group of people where Jake was standing.

"NOOOO!" Iggy screamed, as the Russian pivoted and racked the bolt on his rifle, pointing it at him.

Before he could shoot, a voice shouted "POLICE! DROP IT!" and Hansen moved from behind one of the pilings underneath the wharf, aiming his .38 in both hands at Ivanov. When Grigori heard Hansen, he spun toward him, giving Iggy the chance he needed. In his earlier years Iggy had never really liked track and field as a sport. In fact, he had never held a spear or javelin before. But he threw the long cross-country ski pole he had been holding as if he had practiced the sport for years.

The pole flew at the Russian like a javelin and lodged itself deep in the back of his massive head. Grigori Ivanovich fell backward into the hole he had created earlier, and slowly sank under the far edge of the ice, his arms outstretched. Iggy was mesmerized by the look in the eyes of the Russian as the current took him under the ice and into the weeds. It was no longer one of evil, but rather one of pure surprise.

Detective Hansen came over to Iggy.

"Jesus!" he exclaimed as he watched the Russian sinking, the ski pole dragging into the water with the Russian's body. "There's something you don't see every day."

Iggy just stood in place staring blankly, shivering and shaking, clearly in shock.

The sound of police sirens filled the air as numerous vehicles filled the park area surrounding the wharf. Jake and the girls came over to the scene at the wharf and Heather, now lucid by the time they got there, ran to Iggy and wrapped her arms around him. Riley was next to arrive with the other two boys, Delbert and Roger. Out on the lake a group of policemen had arrived on snowmobiles and placed the body of Dennis Mancini in an ambulance that had backed onto the frozen lake. The park would remain closed to the public for the rest of the day. Hansen had earlier arranged with the local authorities to have the main highways and all access to the park closed. They now had to recover the body of the Russian and a group of forensics would scour the area for any further evidence that may have been left behind.

The group of musicians, the girls, and the two detectives all left in two vehicles, the van and the RCMP unmarked car, and headed for a meeting with Captain Miller and Sergeant White in Kelowna.

It was finally over.

Epilogue

Five Years Later
June 15, 1977
5:45 pm

"Don, come on, we're running late. What are you doing anyway?" she asked, going into their den where he was sitting at his desk with a scrapbook that had been opened to the first page. He was gazing at a newspaper clipping he had pasted in the book over five years ago.

MAY 18, 1972, SALMON ARM
The Guardian
GRISLY DISCOVERY YESTERDAY IN SALMON ARM

Two teenage boys made a grim discovery yesterday at 3:30 pm while fishing off the south end of the Salmon Arm Wharf. Twelve-year-old Darryl Lang said he had made his "best cast of the day" toward the deep end of that part of the arm when his weighted lure got caught on something.

When he was finally able to bring his gear to the surface, both boys were amazed to see what at first appeared to be Shuswaggi, the fabled monster of the lake!

In reality, the young man had snared the body of a white male, aged somewhere in his mid-forties. The badly decomposed body of the individual was taken to the Kelowna Medical Examiner's Office. Neither the Kelowna Police Department nor the Kelowna RCMP Detachment could provide any further information at this time.

A witness to the recovery of the body, who wishes to remain unidentified at this time, told The Guardian, he was certain he saw what looked like a ski pole attached to the back of a man's head.

Don Hansen looked up at his wife Nancy and smiled. "I'll be right with you, hon, just reminiscing a bit," he said. He laid the book on the table, and it fell open at another page, obviously one that had seen frequent visits. He could not help looking again at the clipping from the Calgary Herald...

OCTOBER 9,1974
CALGARY
The Calgary Herald
FORMER MAFIA DRUG BOSS MURDERED

Mr. Baxter Johnson, Warden at the Calgary Spy Hill Corrections Facility, has today announced that former drug lord Don Vincento "Vinnie" Fellino was found dead early this morning in the prison laundry area. Johnson added that it appears a form of Mafia revenge has been exacted on Don Fellino.

The discovery of the infamous inmate's body has sent rumors of fear among the City's underworld as to who may be next in this clandestine world of treachery, betrayal, and swift mob "justice." According to Johnson, his throat had been cut in the signatory Mafioso style, leaving no doubt as to the intent of the message being sent to other associates of the victim. Fellino was scheduled to appear before a Committee on Organized Crime in federal court next Tuesday to give testimony surrounding the illegal activities of his former partner, Don Alberto "Big Al" Gabrazzi. It has been rumored that Fellino has been ailing of late. He no doubt had been hoping to have his sentence shortened which might have been possible by giving state's evidence as leverage. In the meantime, Gabrazzi is currently residing in Los Angeles and was not available for comment.

Another mobster, Mr. Giovanni "Dino" Martini, a subordinate of Fellino's, was incarcerated with his boss, Fellino, in 1971 along with a Russian associate, one Grigori Ivanovich. Martini, himself in failing health, was also not available for comment.

Ivanovich escaped from the facility shortly after his arraignment in 1971 to allegedly wreak havoc from Banff through the Okanagan area as far as Salmon Arm. His whereabouts are unknown.

Don went into the kitchen, helped his wife on with her light jacket and guided her out the door. "You feeling okay?" he asked.

"Your boy has only kicked me five times in the last half hour so, yeah, I'm good," she replied.

"We won't stay long, promise."

"That's what you always say." But she was smiling. She was looking forward to the evening, actually. Nancy was five months pregnant with their first child and Don was as proud as a peacock. He drove their new Chevy Impala to The Emerald Lounge where a special event was being held this evening. Kenny Chou had suggested the event when he heard about Don Hansen's upcoming retirement. Initially, Hansen was reluctant to go along with any kind of ceremony, but Nancy would have nothing to do with his arguments against the event. Also, Gerry Riley was a big help in getting things organized and he was here tonight. And with another new girlfriend, Nancy pointed out to Hansen. "That's our boy," he said.

Upon entering the hall, they were not surprised to see a large crowd of policemen on hand for the celebration. Nancy noted to her husband that there were also many police*women* on the force now. Times were changing.

Don and Nancy grabbed a table near the stage, but they were immediately moved by Detective Gerry Riley to the middle chair at a table that had been hastily set up, right on the stage itself. More chairs were brought in, and they were all set on the stage, so they were facing the floor and Hansen was becoming more embarrassed by the minute.

What the hell? Hansen groused to himself. He was afraid of this. Now Captain Miller and Sergeant White took seats on his left while the Captain and Chief of the Kelowna Police Department sat to Nancy's right. *Wow! All the heavy hitters are here.* thought Hansen.

When everyone was seated and their drinks had arrived, the lights in the lounge were dimmed. Kenny Chou came on stage and introduced Detective Gerry Riley as the MC for the evening. Gerry then came on and warmed up the audience with a roast to his good buddy Hansen, regaling everyone with anecdotes from their many years of experience.

This went on for a good half hour until he handed the mic back to Kenny. Then Kenny, in his amiable way, said to the audience, "Ladies and

gentlemen. Everybody here, and especially all you older peoples."
Everybody laughed. "I know you here for good time. Pretty soon we have
plenty good music with your favorite group, The Shuswap Doo Wop Band."
He waited for the large round of applause to settle, then said "But first, only
few words from Police Chief William Butler. Chief Butler?"

Chief Butler came over to the mic from the table and said to the
crowd "Thank you, Kenny. Fellow officers, ladies and gentleman. I told
Kenny I'd be brief. So let me just introduce to you a couple of people that
really need no introduction at all. They came to us over five years ago and
they have been working very hard ever since arriving in Kelowna. I know
you will want to give them a big hand on... RECENTLY RECEIVING
PROMOTIONS! Folks, meet DETECTIVES NAT MILES and JACOB
ENGLAND." Iggy and Jake then came on the stage from behind a partition
in the back curtain to a huge round of applause. They had their wives,
Heather and Suzie with them and amid loud shouts of congratulations and
more applause, they waved to the audience.

The two transplanted Maritimers were beaming, proud of this city
that had accepted them and had provided them with all they wanted. The
boys had sold their ranch house in Cochrane and moved permanently to
Kelowna. Hansen had arranged for the transfer of Jake's Beaumont to the
city as well, where, in fact, Jake was currently having it restored to its
original state.

The Canada Witness Protection Program had terminated their
involvement in the program once everything had been settled with the
incident in Salmon Arm. It was at that time that Iggy and Jake decided to
take Detective Hansen's advice and enter the Kelowna Police Academy.
Since then, they had both married and purchased their own homes. The band
with Delbert and Roger was retained and they played regularly at The
Emerald Lounge, albeit the passion for their craft that had at one time taken
hold of Iggy and Jake had faded a bit over the past five years. Careers,
building families, and community work now took up most of their time.

The Chief passed the mic to Iggy who threw his free arm around
Jake's shoulders, saying "Folks, this is the best day of our lives. Thank you
so much for making it all possible."

Then Jake took the mic and added "We never, ever, thought things could work out so great for a couple of young musicians. We love you guys."

Again Iggy had the mic and he said "But ya know what, Kenny, now that we're able to go back to our own actual names, we decided to change the name of the band back to its former title. So, from now on we simply want to be called...Fusion."

And here the curtain fully opened, exposing Roger behind his full Ludwig drum kit and Delbert on his Yamaha keyboard. Heather handed Iggy his newly purchased Fender Stratocaster guitar, and Suzie carried Jake's Precision bass, which was almost as big as she was, over to him. Roger gave a four count, and he immediately started the congo solo intro to their cover of "Your Love Keeps Lifting Me Higher" by Jackie Wilson. At this point, Don and his entourage on stage all took their chairs to the floor and started dancing with their wives.

Jake then came in on bass, then Delbert on keys using the organ mode with his newly purchased Leslie speakers, and finally Iggy began striking his high D major 9th bar chord.

The room was rocking, and Fusion was back in business.

About the Author
jardinetom53@gmail.com

Mr. Jardine is retired from the Canadian financial service industry. He is a part-time musician and lives with his wife, Alexandra, and Clancy, their three-year-old Biewer Yorky, in the beautiful Annapolis Valley of Nova Scotia where he is working on his fourth novel.

VISIT OUR WEBSITE
FOR THE FULL INVENTORY
OF QUALITY BOOKS:
http://www.roguephoenixpress.com

Rogue Phoenix Press

Representing Excellence in Publishing

Quality trade paperbacks and downloads

in multiple formats,

in genres ranging from historical to contemporary romance, mystery and science fiction.

Visit the website then bookmark it.

We add new titles each month!